CHAOS FALLS

CHAOS RISES #3

PIPPA DACOSTA

'Chaos Falls'

#3 Chaos Rises

Pippa DaCosta

Urban Fantasy & Science Fiction Author

Subscribe to her mailing list at pippadacosta.com & get free ebooks.

Print ISBN-13: 978-1979614795

Print ISBN-10: 1979614792

www.pippadacosta.com

PROLOGUE

For two hundred thousand years, hominids have walked this earth. *Humans.* Two hundred thousand years of fine-tuned evolution lifting them out of the dirt, straightening their backs, honing their language. From beasts able to create fire to beings on the cusp of deep space travel.

Two hundred thousand years and they are still critically flawed.

Unlike me.

Perfect from the moment demons split from humans. Perfect and unchanging. A predator. A being of divinity. A god among mortals. I look upon these creatures as they were: animals clawing in the dirt for beetles to feast on and killing each other for territory.

I am above them.

I am the epitome of perfection.

I am Pride.

Or, I was. Until the day the veil fell, and I fell with it.

CHAPTER 1

"*S*top. Don't make me shoot you."

It wasn't the officer's words that brought my train of thought to a jolting halt, nor was it her tone—designed to control and contain—more the position she had found me in.

Parts of the mass of meat I was crouched over glistened on the road yards away. The body could have been male or female. The tattered clothing confirmed the victim was human. And here I was, hunched over the carcass like the lesser demon the trigger-happy human probably believed me to be.

I lifted my hands and stretched the tips of my black feathered wings. "Stop what, exactly? Stop looking at the body, stop being so devilishly handsome, or stop breathing, perhaps? You'll have to be more specific."

The weight of her gaze warmed my back. "Stop talking. Stand up. And step back."

I started straightening.

"Move slow, demon."

Her radio crackled, but she hadn't reached for it to call

for backup. Foolish human. I could have killed her the moment she opened her mouth to demand I stop. Could kill her now with little more effort than a thought. Clearly, she had no idea who she was pointing her useless gun at.

Slowly, as she had ordered, I stepped away from the body and lifted one wing back, to unveil the little police officer at the corner of the sidewalk. It was a wonder she had survived the Fall if this was how she approached demons. Perhaps other instincts kept her alive, because had she been smarter, she would already be running. Little thing with dark skin— not as dark or smooth as mine. Blue eyes from rogue genes, eyes that were trying to drill through my chest. Her pert lips held a snarl just for me.

Still behaving, I turned some more and spread my wings until their tips stretched the full width of the street, ignoring twinges of pain. The glossy black feathers had frayed over the past few weeks, but under the pale hue of the street lighting, all she saw was their magnificence. Her eyes widened, lashes fluttering, and fear hid behind her police training. All humans reacted the same, eventually. Fear, admiration, attraction. They loved me, wanted me, wanted to *be* me. Men and women both. It was impossible to look upon my glory and not feel—

The gun fired and the little bullet punched into my chest, through a lung, and blasted out my back, taking fragments of rib with it.

I shook off the pain and stretched a shoulder, to help the fizzing wound edges stitch back together. "That was uncalled for."

She blinked, swallowed hard, and steadied her stance. "I said don't move or I'll shoot." Her voice trembled as she realized how unprepared she'd been to encounter me.

"You also said to step away from the body. I doubt you know what you want from me, officer." I started forward, one slow, deliberately placed step at a time. There was no use in terrifying her. "Or perhaps you do."

Her aim wobbled. She lifted her chin, determination holding her rigid.

"You have to admit," I purred. "I am entrancing. Have you ever seen such a fine demon specimen as I?"

"What?"

I gestured at myself and wiped the dribble of blood from my sculpted chest, the bullet wound fully healed. "Your little human mind can barely comprehend what it means to be in my presence."

She stepped back, realized she had given me a small victory, and lifted her gun again, peering down its sights. "Stay back, *demon*."

"Or you'll shoot me again? Please do. It tickles."

"I've killed hundreds of your kind."

"Oh, little lady, there are no other demons like me." Before the last word had crossed my lips, I'd come undone, collapsing my perfect self into my element—air. A flittering mist had gathered where I'd been standing moments before. She thought me gone. *"I didn't kill your victim."* My words— whispered against her neck—instantly scattered tiny goose bumps in their wake. Such a delight to see them there. She shivered and spun, aiming wildly. I wound myself around her —ghostly, barely there at all, just enough for her to know she wasn't alone. *"But whoever or whatever did will kill again."*

Fear permeated the air like the smell of hot copper. I didn't want her afraid. Humans easily lost their meager minds, and there was something about this woman that intrigued me. Releasing her, I sailed upward onto the edge of a nearby roof and drifted there, unseen.

After spinning on the spot and breathing out a sigh, the officer holstered her gun. She stood, perfectly still, listening. I listened too. The thudding of her heart, the race of her breaths, and finally the background din of the city. There was no sign of anything or anyone who might have caused our dead body. Whatever had killed the victim was long gone. From my kind, at least, she was safe. Realizing the same, she plucked her radio from her belt. "This is Officer Ramírez, badge number seven-six-eight-nine, division six-L. Code two-Charles-one-eight-seven."

Backup arrived fifteen minutes later and sealed off the street. Over the next few hours, panel vans and more vehicles with flashing lights arrived. Ramírez stayed, and when homicide sidelined her, she lingered until the sun had risen over LA's jagged skyline. Tiredness showed around her eyes. She left only when a senior officer ordered her off the scene, but not before casting a glance up at the roof and spearing her glare through me.

Part mist, part air, and virtually invisible, I studied her, knowing she couldn't see me. It took great courage to look fear in the eye and stand your ground. I admired that.

With Ramírez gone, I returned to the rooftop of my restaurant building and lifted my face to the morning sun. It would be another glorious day in the City of Angels. The city that had survived the Fall and driven back the demons. And tomorrow, another shredded body would feed the flies. Today's body was the fifth in five days. Each was a warning. A message. I wasn't the only predator left in LA.

CHAPTER 2

*P*ain.

    It wasn't something I feared. For countless centuries, I had been untouchable. A Prince of Hell. Pain had been no more than an irritating distraction, much like the demons I had ruled over in the netherworld beyond the veil or the inconsequential pain of the officer's bullet passing through my chest.

But as I looked in the wall of mirrors in my apartment bedroom, I knew real pain. I had known it for every month, day, and hour since the veil fell and I became a shadow of my former self. The unending, radiating ache of loss. It beat inside my bones and throbbed in time with my heart. The loss of power, the loss of everything I had been, the loss of my home. My wings burned—not visually, though I vividly recalled the time they had been burned to cinders. They burned with the memory of having my title stripped. *Pride* was my weakness, my name. With the demon Court sealed away in the netherworld, on the other side of the veil, I was a prince of nothing, and my power faded with each passing day. Agony throbbed through my wings, reminding me over and over of how far I had fallen.

I spread my wings, feeling every strained muscle grind, every seized tendon pop. The pain throbbed hotter, sinking its fingers down my back. I stretched farther, reaching silvery feather tips toward the walls of the vast bedroom, reaching as far as they would stretch. Pain pushed at my thoughts and blurred my vision. I gritted my teeth and bore the weight of it. And there, in my reflection, a single black feather broke free and spiraled toward the polished marble floor where it settled, barbs curled in, edges brittle.

I let my wings fall and, with a gasp, turned them to mist. In the mirrors, I was just a man once more—an astonishingly handsome man, a god among men, but no longer obviously demon. Crouching, I picked up the feather and held it up to the sunlight streaming through the windows. My feathers had once been flawless. Black as night, so black they absorbed color, and edged in silken silver. A single feather was more than it appeared. They were promises, they were tokens, they were each a part of me. The one I held had dulled and contracted. Its vanes had split, rendering it useless for flight. I ran my fingers down its edges, feeling the velvet break and crumble.

Somewhere inside my apartment, a phone rang. I ignored it and walked to the bed. From underneath, I dragged out a wooden chest, used air to push at the lock, and opened the lid. Forty-three feathers were nestled inside. Some larger than others. Some primaries from my wings' leading edges, and some secondaries that made up the bulk of my winged expanse.

I set the latest feather inside and gently closed the lid. More would follow. By the end of the year, my wings would be bare, the pain would be constant, and in my reflection, a monster would be looking back. I had been magnificence given flesh and spirit before time began. And now, with each fallen feather, I was a shade.

The elevator chimed. "The restaurant opens in fifteen minutes," Noah, my restaurant manager, informed me through the intercom. "You have an appointment with that TV streaming executive in an hour, and there's a cop downstairs. She looks pretty comfortable, like she isn't going anywhere until she speaks with you."

I dressed with a flick of my hand, building on the already perfect male body by wrapping it in a purple shirt and black pants and jacket. I made Target clothing look like the height of fashion. Perfection was my church. I preached from its altar daily.

The elevator door whispered open, revealing Noah with his long-lashed eyes trained on his cell phone's screen. Dusky-haired with a few haphazard curls that naturally fell over his eyes, he often caught the eyes of the staff and customers. But Noah drew a line, keeping his work time professional. Those were the lines I blew away.

"You should have led with the police officer," I told him, adding a smile. "Female?"

He nodded. "Not your type."

I stepped into the elevator beside him and hit the button to the restaurant. "I wasn't aware I had a type."

"Oh, you have a type, all right." He chuckled, locking his phone and jabbing it into his back pocket. "They line up in pairs outside every night. There's an online group that trades tips on how to catch your attention. Apparently, you're fond of dark chocolate and strawberries."

True. "Sounds delightful."

An online group dedicated to the Church of Li'cl? Wonderful.

"Invite only," Noah added. His smirk often won him a week's worth of wages in bar tips a night.

I arched a brow. He sounded familiar with this group. "You're suggesting my type is any woman?"

He snorted a laugh. "You said it, not me."

I straightened my jacket and cuffs. "You're wrong. Why limit oneself to a single gender?"

A glitter of mischief flashed in his hazel eyes. "You're such an attention whore."

I grinned, and my reflection in the mirrored walls grinned back. If perfection were a crime, I would be serving a life sentence. "Most definitely." The almost invisible scar on my chin only added to my impeccable image. "If my type is all women, then what is the police officer waiting for me if not a woman?"

His smile slipped. "Trouble."

Trouble. I liked the sound of trouble. A challenge was difficult to find these days. I didn't need to ask Noah for the officer's name. If Ramírez was good at her job, she would have recognized me—even with the wings. I never had been one to drift in the shadows like some of my kin. I much preferred the spotlight. It wouldn't take anyone long to mark me as the owner of several LA nightclubs and restaurants. Someone like Ramírez would have made the connection almost immediately.

The elevator pinged and opened onto the restaurant floor. The first-shift restaurant staff prepared to open for lunch, and the female officer sat at the bar. *Not* Ramírez.

How disappointing.

She turned to face Noah and me. Her tight-fitting pantsuit cut away all her natural curves, and pumps declared you would have no trouble running down her perps. No jewelry, no earrings, and only a touch of makeup. Her middle-aged years had benefitted from her neither smiling too much nor frowning. I could make even the iciest person smile. It was one of my many talents.

Noah cut me a "told you so" look. Challenge accepted.

He veered off to prepare the bar while I approached the police officer and offered my hand. Without hesitation, she shook my hand. Her grip could crack nuts. Her look left me in no doubt that she would like to crack mine—with her knee.

"Mister Leel Shahar, my name is Catherine Styles. I'm a detective with Hollywood homicide."

"*Li'el* Shahar," I corrected.

"Lee-all?"

"Lee-elle."

"Unusual."

"European with a little Hebrew spice."

Her flinty eyes gave nothing away. "I'm sure."

"Catherine is French."

"Is it?" she asked, utterly disinterested.

"Would you like to know what it means?"

"No, I'd like you to tell me what *this* means." She produced a cell phone from inside her jacket and handed it over. Among reports of flash flooding in Inglewood and the latest celebrity gossip, one headline on the *LA Post* website read: DEMONS RETURN? A grainy color photo below showed a winged demon striding down an alley. The victim had been cropped out of the image, probably because publishing photos of mauled bodies would be in bad taste. I knew the body was there because the demon captured in motion was me. The image was blurred enough to make identifying my facial features difficult, but nobody else had such fabulous bone structure or wings that size. "A handsome devil."

She looked me in the eye. "A killer."

My smile was a careful one, but also confident. All demons were killers. All demons were monsters. That had been true until recently. Everyone who had survived the Fall knew it was fact. They had seen partners, families, and friends slain. They had fought for their lives and for their homes. Only now, almost a year later, were they recovering.

I waved Noah over. He sloshed bourbon into a tumbler and offered it to the detective. Catherine declined, but she watched me lift my drink to my lips and taste it. She watched me roll it around my tongue, her analytical mind working. She wasn't here to talk about headlines, so she must have known I was connected to demons. My restaurant had seen a few demon attacks and I was rumored … to have been involved in a few demon incidents, but that was in the past. People had moved on. The demons were gone. As far as my public profile confirmed, I was a businessman and nothing else.

I set my drink down and handed the phone back. "Ask your questions, detective."

"Do you know anything about this demon?"

"Why would I?"

"That photo was taken near here."

"Was it?"

"And emailed to us and the press shortly after we discovered a young man apparently killed by demons."

"Terrible. I thought all the demons were gone."

"The email contained this image and the name of this restaurant, *Decadent-I Taverna*." She paused, either waiting for me to talk my way into being guilty or considering how far she could push without giving away how much she thought she knew.

"I see. That must have taken some stellar detecting to arrive on my doorstep."

She ignored my dry tone. "You run an upstanding business here."

"Thank you."

Her lips twisted around a sour taste. "And you said you're from Europe?"

"No." My smile grew. "My name is. I'm from somewhere much hotter." Europe. Netherworld. Hell. All of the above.

"It's strange. A socialite of your reputation leaves quite a paper trail, and you have, but there's nothing from you directly until a few months ago. Before that, you could have been a ghost. No photos. No social network presence. Nothing."

"I was on a journey. Call it a sabbatical…" Before a few months ago, I'd been *resting* in a cage, guarded by an ambitious demon who thought he could create a new demon Court, and before that, I'd been a prince among the Dark Court of the Eleven Princes of Hell. Catherine didn't want the truth because, once she had it, the genie would be out of the bottle, and it wouldn't go back in without a fight. I had earned my right to live in LA. I'd fought demons just as she had. It didn't matter that I *was* one. This city was as much my home as hers. LA had been my territory long before the veil fell, before the settlers arrived in their wagons to stake their claims.

"No photos of this journey?"

"I'm camera shy."

She smiled a smooth, slippery smile. "You're something, Mister Leel, but shy isn't it."

This time, I didn't bother to correct her on my name.

She placed her card on the bar. "In case you remember something."

Then she left through the open front doors. I was beginning to think, as strange as the thought was, that Catherine Styles didn't like me much.

I SPENT the rest of the day and into the early evening fulfilling business obligations and fielding various invites to make sure I was seen in public doing all the things expected of a human male of my social standing. Los Angeles and its cliques weren't my first foray into pretending to be human. I'd perfected the act over the centuries. Admittedly, in the beginning, I may have pushed too hard and asked too much of humans. They had worshipped me as their god, and why not? Had I been clever, I would have kept my presence in the human world subtle. But subtle wasn't me. My exploits hadn't gone unnoticed by the other princes. When Mammon, the Prince of Greed, saw what I'd created in this realm, in this world, he'd wanted it all for himself.

Greed.

The demon prince had barred me from this realm, burned my wings, and scarred my chin. He'd had no right to take from me. No right to stop my escapades—

But I'd been... different then. I was not the same demon people had once called Lightbringer and the religious had named the devil. Recent events had me questioning whether I was demon at all.

The restaurant was in full swing when I returned. I slipped into my role of successful charmer. The music beat hard enough to drown out my unending ache of loss, and the people who found my bed, men and women, helped distract my thoughts. I pleasured many in my bed, and they pleasured me. But lately, pleasure wasn't enough. I had seen the veil fall, and I'd waited, biding my time and rebuilding my strength, for the right moment to break out and create a new Court. But something had changed in me during those months locked away from the world, severed from my pride. An icy half-blood girl had reminded me that life on this side of the veil wasn't like the one I'd left behind in the netherworld. I didn't have to be demon here. There was another way.

If only it were that simple.

In the early hours, just past three a.m. when the air was

14

cooler and LA pretended to sleep, I peeled myself from the tangle of warm, satisfied human bodies and took to the roof of my building. My human vessel and all its earthly illusion fell away, and I became my element, air. I drifted far, stretched wide, splintered into countless tendrils and reached through the city's veins—the streets, the wide alleys, the almost-empty parking lots, the beaches. I listened to whispers, to the couple pressed against a wall, to a father comforting his daughter, to someone crying alone and others cheering together. I absorbed the quiet nightlife of my city and touched the lives of those I passed.

"I am air and everywhere."

Some were afraid. Some were joyful. All were a wonder.

I found the newest victim by the void her cooling body left behind in a beachside parking lot. A living, breathing person should have been occupying the air around the parked Jeep, but the remains were too still, the warmth leaving the skin, the presence already fading.

In moments, I was solid again and a few strides from the Jeep. The streetlight above the vehicle was out—an unlikely coincidence. Just a few cars occupied sand-covered spaces. Tire tracks left zip-like marks in fresh sand. The woman's footprints scuffed the sand around the Jeep's front tires. Smaller circular depressions also dotted the area—claws. Demon.

I turned away from the body and scanned the parking lot and the street beyond. Palm trees gently swayed, and air hissed through their fronds. I reached out with my element and became that air. With it, I could feel the space every item in the area occupied. There, hunched behind a dumpster, was a pulsing taint. The stench of hot rubber permeated the air around it.

"Get down on the ground!"

"Get down now!"

Two cops. They charged in from behind the Jeep, and behind them, the demon emerged from the shadows. I ignored the human police, reached out a hand, and yanked the air from the demon's lungs. It wasn't as easy here as in the netherworld. The air in this world was thinner, weaker, but demons still needed to breathe to live. The demon clawed at its throat, trying to open its airways. It would do it no good.

"Get down, now!"

Ramírez. It was no coincidence she and her partner had arrived seconds after me. I would have to deal with those implications later.

"Get down or we open fire!"

Their little bullets couldn't do much damage, but the demon at their backs would tear into them if left unchecked.

I had it in my grip. It writhed and bucked against the invisible hold choking the life from its body. In seconds, it would be dead.

"Don't move!" Ramírez ordered.

This again? *Get down. Don't move.* She needed to work on her orders. "If you would just wait—"

One of them fired. The round bore down on me, cutting through the air, charged with anti-elemental markings. *Demon-killing bullets.* The LAPD had upgraded. The bullet grazed my side and would have hit home had I not twisted away.

I might have laughed if my grip on the lesser hadn't slipped. Like an enraged animal, it sprang out from behind the dumpster and galloped across the parking lot. Ramírez's partner had the misfortune of standing in its way. The lesser vaulted over the hood of a car and launched itself onto the officer's back. Claws raked deep into the officer's chest. Blood arced across the asphalt.

I collapsed into air, crossed the distance in a second, and

tore the demon off the teetering male. Ramírez's scream accompanied the beast's grunt as I slammed it into the ground. The skull caved in under my fist, in a satisfyingly gory pop.

Ramírez fired again, and this time the bullet punched into my back. Agony blasted up my spine. My wings sprang free, both for protection and as a reflex. The little cop let out a cry somewhere between shock and awe. She and I would have words once I'd saved her partner's life. I scooped up the fallen male to a hail of more gunfire—*Don't these fools recognize when they're being saved?*—and beat my wings, taking to the air. The ER was only a few blocks away. The officer in my arms would die if left on the street, waiting for backup to arrive.

With every beat of my wings, fiery agony flooded my veins. Just pain. I knew it well.

I gained enough altitude to soar over the squat building and dive toward the hospital. I came in hot and landed in a run that almost sent me sprawling through the glass doors. Screams erupted around me. People lifted their phones, cameras flashing. The old me, the part that would have seen these fools on their knees, sent an internal snarl their way, but I kept it off my face and delivered the officer through the hospital doors and onto an empty gurney.

He caught my arm as I pulled away. "Thank... you," he wheezed. Pain tightened his eyes, but didn't mask his compassion. Compassion... for me?

I nodded and lifted my gaze. Doctors, patients, and EMTs had gathered around. They saw my wings and my ghostly outline.

"Someone shoot it—"

"—help that man."

"Call the Institute!"

"Kill it!"

I turned away and shoved through the people who didn't scurry away quick enough. Once through the doors, I became air, vanishing from their sights and their hissed accusations. Their hatred burned as much as the gunshot wound.

CHAPTER 3

"*E*veryone out."

I leaned against the bar in my apartment living room, fighting the shudders trying to undo me. In my absence, an all-night party had moved upstairs to my place, as it often did, and stretched on into the morning, but I was in no mood to entertain.

"Out!"

My "guests" scurried out, some half-dressed, some high or drunk or both. I only recognized a handful of them. Several steered my way but quickly reconsidered when they caught my expression.

The elevator doors had barely closed when I fell against the bar, using it to prop myself up.

"Damned Institute bullets."

Simply turning my clothes to air would expend too much energy, so I carefully eased the jacket off, letting it fall where I stood. The shirt went next, dripping blood. The bullet had sailed through cleanly. The exit wound low on my back throbbed, and the entry wound tingled above my hip. I'd heal, but it would take energy I sorely lacked.

I called Noah, told him I wasn't to be disturbed, and sought refuge in the wet room. Standing under the shower's hot jets, I pulled my focus in and concentrated on rebuilding my vessel. Muscle, bone, veins, skin—I stitched it all back together and smoothed it over, almost to perfection. A stubborn dimple remained. Some wounds never healed, like the scar on my chin. It would have to stay. I didn't have the energy to banish it.

I freed my wings and hugged them close against my back. Water pattered against my face and chest. Turning, I dropped to my knees, bowing my wings over me, and let the water pound against the feathers. Heat against heat helped.

"Kill it."

"Shoot it."

I couldn't blame humans for their disgust, but that didn't make it hurt any less. I was meant to be admired and loved. Their hatred would stalk my dreams.

Black feathers circled the drain.

Shutting off the water, I scraped the feathers off the shower floor and gathered them into my arms.

So many...

My flight had cost me. Too much? No, the male officer was alive. A life was worth a handful of feathers, wasn't it?

Yes, I had done the right thing. Human life was precious, just like my feathers. Helping them was better than the alternative. Helping them was good. Even if they despised me.

I sat back, drew a knee up, and pulled the feathers close. I was a good demon. The first. That meant something, no matter the cost. Didn't it?

～

LATER THAT DAY, rested and healed, I stepped out of the elevator, eyebrow raised. The restaurant's thirty staff members were gathered with Noah at their head. This would be interesting.

They looked at one another, waiting for someone brave enough to speak up.

"We can't open today," Noah said.

"And why is that?" I headed behind the bar, grabbed a glass and a bottle of bourbon, and poured myself a drink. A chill skittered across my skin. "Is it cold?"

Nobody replied.

Outside, sunlight flooded the streets, slicing through sections of the drawn blinds.

Noah leaned against the bar and murmured, "It would be dangerous to open."

"Dangerous?" I laughed, picked up my drink, and downed it. The warmth soothed the strange disconnected feeling left over from the night's events. Dangerous was facing a demon horde. Dangerous was dancing with the Princes of Hell. Dangerous was me on a red carpet during opening night.

"You need to see something," he added.

Clearly, this *something* had unnerved the staff, but I wasn't sure I could rouse the energy to care. Noah's determined glare wouldn't go away until I saw whatever he seemed so desperate for me to witness.

"All right." After refilling my glass, I followed Noah through the back doors and kitchen, and out the rear exit onto the street. Walking to the front of the restaurant, traffic buzz filled the air around us. Cars rumbled by. A few early bus tours rumbled down the boulevard toward the part of Hollywood where you couldn't move for tripping over Elvis clones.

I sipped my bourbon and rolled some liquid around my tongue as Noah revealed the artwork plastered across the front of *Decadent-1* in fat red letters.

DEMON GO HOME

Noah sighed and looked at me. "Some of the staff are talking."

"Naturally."

His lips ticked at the corners. "Not in a good way. Rosa said you weren't here last night, and then there's this…" He dug out his cell phone and handed it to me.

Among reports of the small tremors and unseasonable rain, there was a photo of me carrying the bleeding police officer into the hospital. Instead of the headline reading, "Handsome Demon Saves Cop," it read, "Killer Demon Strikes Again." The picture was as crisp as daylight. I couldn't deny the winged Adonis was me, and why should I have to?

I handed the phone back and took a drink, squinting at the graffiti. Noah had worked in my restaurant for years, longer than I had been on site. Back when, I was merely a name on the accounting statements. He'd joined the staff right out of college as a bartender and worked his way into management. When I'd returned from my "extended sabbatical" away from human life, he had brought me up to date on how things worked in Hollywood. I could have slipped back into the role I'd left decades before without him, but it would have taken longer and more effort. He knew how my life worked. He knew how I got around without the use of a car or public transport. He knew I kept unusual hours and had interesting associates, like the icy half-blood girl. Noah was no fool.

"Who takes portrait shots in that light?" I scoffed.

He smiled. It was a good sign. "I figured you were different." The shrug sealed it. "I get it, man. But some of the others, they don't know you like I do. They see demon, and they just see the bad stuff."

"As long as their opinions don't interfere with their work, it doesn't matter." Echoes of last night muscled their way back into my thoughts. *Kill it!* "This…" I gestured at the paint job. "Get this cleaned up and the restaurant open for business. It will take more than some paint and poorly framed shots to ruffle my feathers."

"I just…" Noah ran his fingers through his hair. "All the demons, I mean. Those that weren't killed, they left. They're all supposed to be gone. Why did you stay?"

Where would I go? "LA is my home. It has been for a very, very long time."

He nodded and offered an understanding smile, but a touch of fear dampened its edges. It was one thing to suspect your employer was a demon, but quite another to have it confirmed.

I smiled and lifted my glass. "I have everything under control."

CHAPTER 4

*O*fficer Ramírez's little bungalow was tucked in among its neighbors along the Venice canals. A small dog yapped somewhere, and a TV chatted from across the narrow waterway, but most homes were empty. Rentals. LA's tourism industry had a long way to go before they recovered from the Fall.

I knocked on Ramírez's door and waited. The calming energies of the home kept me from forcing my element inside. Homes were one of the only safe-havens humans had from higher demons. Homes tended to be "controlled and calm" spaces. Being a creature of chaos at my roots, I couldn't breach her walls unless invited.

The seconds ticked by, turning into minutes. The door swung open. Ramírez held a can of pepper spray angled at my face. "How did you find me?"

"I am air and everywhere."

"I'm not inviting you in. That means you can't come in." Her tone held the hint of doubt. She had likely learned these facts in various Demon 101 classes. I briefly wondered if I was mentioned in those classes.

PIPPA DACOSTA

"Correct. I may only enter public spaces uninvited. But your doorstep is as good a place as any for me to be right now."

She lowered the can, more confident behind her threshold. "If you threaten me in any way—"

"I have no intention of hurting you or anyone. I came to talk."

"Talk?" She swallowed and hooked the pepper spray onto the waistband of her leggings. A pink and gray sports top snugly embraced her breasts, leaving little to the imagination. Earbuds hung from their cord around her neck. I had seen Ramírez twice before, but each time she had been on duty, wearing the black and white law enforcement uniform like armor. Out of uniform, she was all feminine curves, but in a way that proclaimed strength, unlike the lightweight ultra-thin examples often found crowding red carpets.

"Talk, then," she prompted after I'd spent too much time admiring her physique.

"How is your partner?"

"Alive." She crossed her arms and pressed her lips into a sharp line. "If you hadn't been there, that thing would have killed us both."

Another question disguised as a statement. "Probably, although you were equipped with specialized bullets, I noticed."

"With demons, we're taught to shoot first."

I had noticed that too. "You were facing two dangerous creatures. Once they were done fighting, the winner would have likely attacked you. You fired to protect yourself and your partner. I understand. No apology necessary."

"I wasn't apologizing." She hesitated, mulling over my words. "The rounds didn't work."

Her attention dropped to where her bullet had punched through. I wasn't about to tell her that her shot had found its

26

mark, rendering my evening into a spectacular disappointment. Besides, she could have filled the awkward silence with a thank you, considering what rescuing her partner had cost me. That apology would surely happen any time now.

"Did you see the pictures of my gallant rescue in the press?" I asked.

"No... I... Hold on." She disappeared inside her house. Through the gap in the doorway, I spotted a cluttered kitchen counter, a handbag, two used coffee cups, fresh-cut flowers, and a bundle of mail. She didn't wear a ring, as was the human custom when two people were in a relationship, but some chose not to. Did she live alone? Where was her family? Did she often have friends around?

"I see..." She reappeared, phone clutched at her side. "That's not fair—what it says online. That's not how it happened."

"But it makes for a good story." Was she troubled by the lies on my behalf or something else?

Opening the door wider, she leaned against its edge and asked, "Why were you there?"

"The same reason as you. To find out who is killing people."

"Who? Not *what?*"

"I'm sure you've noticed the bodies were all left within a block of my building?"

She nodded. "That's how I got there so fast. I've been patrolling the area, looking for demon activity."

"Lessers can't plan their attacks or, for that matter, take photographs. After the Santa Monica event, they're also exceedingly rare."

"Lessers...? Like the thing in the parking lot that got Jimmy?"

"Yes. They're tools, little more than wild animals.

27

Dangerous when provoked, but otherwise incapable of premeditated murder."

"Unlike you."

"I am more than capable, but I'm not your killer. If I was going to kill, I certainly wouldn't leave the remains out in the open. There's an art to everything I do."

"An art in killing?" she asked, eyes hardening. "You crushed that demon's skull. I spent time with the remains while I waited for backup to arrive. Was that your so-called art?" Her tone held an odd edge.

"What would you have had me do? Let it eat your partner?"

She studied my face, searching for something. A lie, perhaps, or the truth. Had I been lying, she wouldn't find any trace of it. I doubted Officer Ramírez fully understood what was standing on her doorstep. She attempted to use her training to read my expression and my body language, analyzing the way I leaned a shoulder against her doorframe as though we were just two people discussing trivial things. But while she examined me, I admired the proud tilt of her head and the fierce strength in her stance. She was not a woman easily manipulated. Nor was she like those who waited in line every evening hoping to catch my eye. Physical attraction was simple to pin down, but I wanted to go deeper, to know her sharp mind, to know her.

She pulled back, realizing how close we were standing. "Did you save Jimmy to make me think good of you?"

"No. I saved him because it was the right thing to do."

"You must think I'm some naive cop you can twist around your demon finger?"

"Not at all—"

"Your kind nearly decimated the LAPD when the veil fell. Most of this city is still uninhabitable. Hundreds of thousands of people died. I found you in that alley, hunched over a body." I considered telling her I didn't *hunch*, but her glare made it clear that while she spoke I was to listen. "I didn't know what you are, but the wings... and then, last night, there you were again. The bodies were shredded. Clearly demons killed them. And there you are." She tossed a disgusted gesture at me. "Clearly demon. I shouldn't even be talking to you."

"You believe I had nothing to do with those killings." Not a question. I knew her thoughts better than she did. "That's why you're talking with me."

"You saved Jimmy. I was right there. I saw it. Saw you..." She wet her lips and failed to find the right words to describe me. "Our training says not to trust higher demons, that everything you do is a game to manipulate those around you. What you did, killing that demon and saving Jimmy, was that a game, Mister Li'el Shahar?"

"No." She knew my name. That hadn't been in the news article. Ramírez had looked me up. "Lives aren't games to me, Officer Ramírez."

Her training was right. Everything about me was designed to manipulate her. I crafted myself that way on purpose and had for millennia. I could lie effortlessly and seduce just as easily. If I wanted, I could charm her into inviting me in. Not so long ago, I would have. Manipulation was a difficult habit to break. Her heart rate hadn't increased by chance. She stood inches from a Prince of Hell. Her mind didn't know exactly what I was, but her body did. Increased heart rate, flushed skin, dilated pupils, a shot of adrenaline to the veins. Fight or flight, or something else entirely. She had seen all of me last night. She would remember the wings above everything else. Humans always did. If her upbringing had included religion, those wings might have told her another tale, the tale of the angel who had saved her partner. There were no angels. Only demons. But I could be her angel. I could show her what it meant to be in my presence. Yes, this was a dangerous game, and I could feel myself falling into its dance with her.

But these games never ended well.

"I'll let you return to your run." I turned away and walked a ways down the path.

She called out, "You're the department's prime suspect, yah know. They just don't know how to handle you."

I paused and turned. She was leaning beyond the safety of her doorway but had one hand on the frame, ready to duck back inside.

"The lead detectives called in the Institute to consult on the case."

Of course they had. The Institute was supposedly a highly trained group of demon specialists, but in my experience, they had more questionable morals than most demons.

"Are you concerned for my safety, officer?"

"I believe in justice."

"Even for demons?"

With an uncertain glance, she stepped back inside her bungalow.

～

WHEN I RETURNED TO *DECADENT-I*, the line outside reached all the way down to the first star in the Walk of Fame. Music spilled from inside, into the street, washing over the glitzy crowd. Considering my recent notoriety, I'd expected a cooler turnout.

"Li'el!"

"Li'el, c'mon man, can you get me inside?"

"We've been in line for hours!"

I plucked a few people I recognized from the line and, to the dejected groans of those left behind, had the bouncer lift the rope for us. The man and woman I'd let in were quick to sample my hospitality. The crowd soon swallowed us as I cruised through the number. *Decadent-1* hadn't been this busy in weeks. Seeing the smiling, joyful people warmed the part of me I had yet to fully understand. What did it matter that these people were happy? It shouldn't, but it did.

A drink already awaited me at the bar. I settled into the role I knew so well of the charming, smooth-talking Hollywood elite everyone wanted to be seen with. Whispers spilled into my ear, and promises were made. Fingers trailed over my shoulders and down my arms with the thrill and desire to touch.

"Is it true?"

"You're demon?"

I neither confirmed nor denied it, but it didn't matter. The mystique was real, and I played it effortlessly to my advantage. There had been another time when my people had admired and worshipped me. This time would be different. The veil was sealed and all the demons but me were gone. I could have the pleasures of human company again. Why should I hide my nature? Why should I pretend to be something I was not?

The elevator delivered me to my apartment, and a party ignited in my wake, but this was different. These people suspected I was demon. I didn't need to hide my gloriousness like I had before.

"Show me your wings."

"Let me touch you."

They begged.

I unfurled my wings, revealing half of my wonder while containing enough of me not to terrify my rapt crowd. A woman fell to her knees and sobbed. Another laughed in wonder. I embraced them, held them close, let their hands touch and their mouths caress. And I pleasured them in

31

return. Men and women. Beautiful. Adoring. I had forgotten what it meant to be Pride, but I remembered it now. Why had I concealed the wonder of me?

With my crowd spent, I left them sprawled in my bed, grossly satisfied, and returned to the restaurant in search of more to join me. And they came, one by one by one. So eager. So willing.

I was about to steer my new admirers to the elevator, when I recognized the bouncing blond hair and brilliant smile of *Hollywood Now* magazine's lead reporter cutting through the crowd.

"Li'el, how does it feel to be outed as demon?" she squawked, blocking my path. "It hasn't affected your business." She grinned her dazzling, shallow smile. This woman and I had past grievances. She had tried, on more than one occasion, to get into my infamous after-parties. My refusals often resulted in negative articles.

The crowd around me gave a collective chuckle at the reporter's gall.

"Jenny... It is, Jenny?" I asked, pouring liquid seduction into my voice.

Her smile faltered. "Jacqueline."

I extricated myself from a few arms and met her in the center of our rapidly growing circle. If only her desperation hadn't shown, I might have invited her along.

"If I were demon," I began, loud enough for all to hear, "do you think I would waste a second of my very long life caring about what you or your small readership think of me?"

She stepped in closer, and her smile fell away like discarded paper. A blankness passed over her expression and hollowed her gaze as though someone had flicked a switch, turning her off from the inside.

She lifted a gun—people squealed—pressed the barrel to her temple, giggled, and pulled the trigger. The entire left side of her face blasted over the people unfortunate enough to be standing in the wrong place. Blood and brain matter painted the rack of bottles behind the bar.

Screams erupted. The crowd boiled and heaved, dashing for the doors. Jacqueline's body collapsed at my feet.

A second, that's all it had taken. A blink, then a gunshot. Gone.

I... hadn't expected it.

It didn't make sense. *Why?*

The screams dulled behind my racing thoughts. Soon, there would be sirens and questions.

I scanned the fleeing crowd for anything out of place, for any human or demon not running for the door. Camera flashes from outside the windows scorched my eyes.

I looked down and saw Jacqueline's fingers twitching beside the fallen gun. This changed everything.

CHAPTER 5

A police officer stood guard at the one door in and out of the interview room, thumbs tucked into his gun belt. Buckles and buttons gleamed against the black of his uniform. The lines around his eyes told me he'd seen things, some of them likely bad, many of them probably in the last year, and a few of those probably demon-related. A snarl threatened. Months had passed since the Fall, since he'd defended his species, his country, his city, his home. I wondered how many demons he'd killed.

Leaning back in the plastic chair, I stretched out a leg beneath the table. The officer's right hand shifted toward his holstered gun.

The Institute could have equipped the LAPD with etched bullets, but I doubted it. They kept demon-killing ammunition for themselves. Still, Officer Twitchy couldn't wait to turn my handsome self into a pepper mill.

"Can I get a glass of water?" I wasn't thirsty, but I was interminably bored.

He jerked his chin toward the water cooler in the corner.

I showed him the cuffs locked around my wrists.

He shrugged.

If I moved, he'd go for his gun, claiming self-defense.

The camera's red eye winked in a corner. The only reason he and I hadn't already gotten personal.

Ramírez entered the room. "What is this? Is Shahar under arrest?"

The uniformed cop shrugged. "Above my pay grade."

She was shorter than her colleague, but her tone commanded more authority. She glanced at me, saw my cuffed wrists resting on the table, scowled like it was all my fault, and left the room. I smiled at Twitchy.

Ramírez returned moments later. "Uncuff him," she barked.

Twitchy—back straight, face blank—approached. He plucked a set of keys from his belt and tossed them onto the table, making sure I had to reach to collect them.

"Get out," Ramírez snapped, "before I tell the sergeant what happened here."

With a grunt, Twitchy left the room. Ramírez scooped up the keys and perched on the side of the table. She leaned over and slipped the key into the cuffs. They fell away with metallic clunks.

I rubbed my wrists. "A black man in cuffs. What could possibly go wrong?"

She bristled, either pissed at me or pissed at Twitchy. "It's not that you're black…"

"Ah, demon, then."

Her braided hair slipped over her shoulder. She flicked it back angrily and tucked a few loose strands of her dark hair behind her ear. "You're not under arrest, but Styles wants to ask you some questions. I suggest you cooperate. They're looking for any excuse to put those cuffs back on."

After that, it would be a private firing squad out back. Ramírez didn't say it, but she didn't have to. The injustice of it blazed in her eyes. She wasn't the best at hiding her thoughts.

"If I didn't want to be here, I wouldn't be."

"I'm not worried." Her gaze bounced around the room, looking anywhere but at me, and she pushed off the table. "We have a dozen witness statements confirming Jacqueline died by suicide. We also have footage from your security cameras. This interview is just routine. You're not under arrest, and they haven't charged you with anything."

What had happened wasn't routine. I'd seen death, seen fields of rotting carcasses stretching to the horizon. I'd killed countless people and demons. But I'd always had a reason. For power or to bargain, manipulate, threaten, or inspire fear. The reporter's death had been different. She hadn't visited my restaurant intending to commit suicide. She had been there for the story like everyone else in my restaurant. The exposé on Li'el. Something else had triggered her devastating last moments.

"Did you know her well?" Ramírez asked, her voice softer. She had mistaken my silence for grief.

"No. A little. Was the gun hers?"

"Registered to her, yes—"

Catherine Styles breezed into the room in a storm of beige and cream work attire with a file tucked under her arm. "That will be all, Officer." She set a small recording device on the table and pulled out her chair. "Interview with Mister Leel Shahar. Present are Detective Styles and Officer Ramírez." She rattled off the date and time. "I apologize for making you wait, Mister Shahar."

I smiled at her insincerity.

"What did Jacqueline Evans say before she took her own life?"

"She asked me what it was like to be outed as demon."

One of the detective's eyebrows arched high. "Are you demon?"

"Is that relevant?"

Unfazed, Styles continued. "How did her question make you feel?"

I rested an arm on the table and drew in a long breath. "I felt nothing."

"Angry? Frustrated? Miss Evans interrupting your evening must have been inconvenient?"

I waved a hand and relaxed back in the chair. "I'm used to the attention."

The detective opened her file and flicked through the pages. "Your restaurant was the scene of a fatal demon attack several months ago…"

"Regrettably."

She didn't look up and seemed more engrossed in her paperwork than our discussion.

Ramírez watched the exchange near the water cooler. She caught my eye but didn't glance away as I'd expected. She held my gaze for a few heartbeats, trying again to read me. I could have let her admire me all day.

"There was a string of gruesome murders close to your business. We presume the attacks were the work of a rogue demon. Demon activity is unusually high around you. Does that concern you, Mister Shahar?"

"No." *Because I am the apex predator, and everything exists to serve me.* I smiled again, and eased some of the predator through my act. The stillness came first, a prelude to an attack. I wouldn't go that far, but the detective could use a lesson in respect.

"You don't worry about it affecting your business, considering there are few demons left in LA and you appear to be one of them?"

My smile grew lighter. Without moving or changing my

expression, I eased some of my elemental control into the room. It wasn't visible, bur rather a feeling that the room had shrunk around us or that the air had thinned. "It'll take more than a few rogue demons and a detective looking for a new demon-notch in her belt to worry me." I tightened the air and watched Catherine's throat bob as she swallowed. The pulse beneath the thin skin of her neck fluttered. So easy to cut there or kiss. "Is that all, Ms. Styles?"

The detective loosened the top button of her blouse. "What were you doing in the hour leading up to Miss Evans's death?"

"Three men and four women, most explicitly."

She opened her mouth, I assumed to ask me to explain, and then fell silent when her mind put the pieces together. "Did Miss Evans say anything else to you?"

"Nothing." I skipped a glance at Ramírez. She blinked back at me, unmoved. A steely professional all the way.

"She didn't say anything at all right before she put a gun to her head?"

I let my smile die and got to my feet. "Why are we continuing this charade when you clearly don't believe a word I've said? I'm demon, so I must be a liar and a killer? I convinced a reporter to shoot herself in the middle of my restaurant, packed with witnesses. Let me ask you a question, detective. Why? Even as demon, why would I do that?"

Catherine slapped her file closed. "There are scientists paid a lot more than me working on why demons do anything."

"But you're the detective, so what's your theory?"

She held my glare. "Because you thrive on attention. Because you were bored. Because that poor woman was in your way. Because she said something to damage your *pride*. Because you're not just any demon, are you, Leel?"

Detective Catherine Styles knew who I was. I wouldn't

win this argument, and really, did I need to? This wasn't about the suicide. This was about her getting the last demon off her streets. She wouldn't look for the killer because she believed she'd already found him.

"Unless I'm under arrest, we're done here."

Catherine bowed her head and smiled. "I think we are."

I had done my part. I'd answered their questions, for all the good it would do me. There were future victims out there, and something had them in their sights.

LA was my city, my home, my territory, and if the human authorities wouldn't police it, I damn well would.

AFTER THE LITTLE icy half-blood girl and I thwarted a higher demon's ambition to create a new Court, the Institute killed most of the remaining demons. But not all the lessers had been wiped out. It was those leftovers I sought out now. Lesser demons had mauled all the human victims. If I eradicated the lessers, I'd greatly reduce the pool of suspects. I knew I wasn't responsible for the killings, and I also knew I wasn't the last demon despite the press painting me as such.

Many of the stray lessers had found their way back to Santa Monica, drawn by the residue of chaos energies. The famous pier was long gone, as was much of the beach and a large chunk of the cliff, behind which the Fairhaven Hotel had once stood. A demon-controlled tsunami had reshaped the coastline and killed most of the demons.

I stood on the sand, watching the Pacific surf gnaw on the beach, and I remembered the demon who had summoned the ocean to do his bidding. Torrent. The power required to pull on the ocean and control it, so it destroyed the demons and spared half of LA would have been immense. Torrent had likely perished, despite early reports of a demon matching his description being seen along the coastline. I had looked, for Gem's sake, but found nothing.

Torrent had been different.

"A prince in all but name."

"Torrent" was a new name for the immortal higher demon Kar'ak, Prince Leviathan's firstborn son. His father had possessed the ability to control human minds. He'd twisted mortals into puppets and made them into slaves for his amusement.

Leviathan had been killed before the veil fell.

But could his son Kar'ak have lived on?

The reporter's eyes had glazed over the moment before she'd pressed the gun to her temple. I had seen that look before.

I scanned the dark fringes of the beach.

Movement caught my eye. A lesser, not much larger than a Doberman, rooted around in the sand. I reached out with my element, wrapped air around its thin body, and plucked it off the sand. The lesser howled—I pulled the air from its lungs and wrapped a tendril of power around its neck. It thrashed three feet off the sand before slowing and finally dying in my grip.

I dropped the body and reeled in my element. The beach returned to its abandoned stillness.

Torrent was gone, wasn't he? "The City of Angels is my city," I said, raising my voice over the sound of the waves. Dropping the appearance of my vessel in a swirl of dark smoke, I revealed my true form, part demon, part mist and air and nothing at all. I arched my wings back, and pain throbbed both hot and cold. I ignored it. Quieter, I added, "If you are out there, Torrent, do not provoke me."

I turned, collapsed my wings into mist, and walked back up the beach, hoping I was wrong.

CHAPTER 6

*R*amírez was sitting alone at the bar, fingers resting on the side of her untouched drink. Noah had called, alerting me to her arrival with a "definitely not your type," but considering her sophisticated layered blouse and simple black pants, she wasn't on duty. A personal visit. Color me intrigued.

It was still early. A handful of customers occupied the tables near the front of the restaurant, and the lighting was too bright to be intimate.

"Miss Ramírez." I leaned against the bar beside her. "It's a pleasure to see you."

Her lips warmed to a smile. "You live above?"

"I do. I'd invite you up, but I doubt you would agree, and my fragile ego couldn't take the rejection."

She snorted a delightfully throaty laugh and nodded at Noah drying glasses while chatting with a waiter at the other end of the bar. "Your spy told you I was here?"

"Little happens in this restaurant without Noah noticing."

"You're very good at answering questions without actually answering." She turned back to me, and I caught the glimmer of a small golden cross on a chain.

"I'm very good at many things."

She laughed a real chuckle that dimpled her cheeks and brightened her eyes. "I bet you are. Your reputation is… quite infamous." She lifted the glass to her lips, hiding part of her smile. "There's an online group. A few actually."

"Ah. You've been checking up on me?"

"Just asking around…"

"Are you a member?"

"Ha, no."

I waited as she observed the staff working around us. Light music played from the restaurant speakers. Chatter rose and fell. She seemed in no hurry to address the reason she was here, but she had come for a reason. The small talk, as nice as it was, was menial.

"There was a girl," she began, shifting in her chair to face me, leaving no room for me to maneuver away from her glare. "Her name was Gemma. She asked me to help her find her brother. They were both half demon. She worked here for a while."

"She did."

"Do you know where she is?"

"She's safe in Boston, staying with friends."

"Demons?"

"Half."

Ramírez nodded. "Did she find her brother?"

"Yes." *Found him. Killed him.*

I waved Noah over, giving myself time and space to break away from Ramírez's gaze. Noah poured a drink and returned to his bubbly conversation. Ramírez continued to wait for more information on Gamma and her brother. As much as I liked Ramírez, Gem's life was not up for discussion.

"For someone who doesn't care about demons, you're very interested in our activities."

"Curious..." she corrected. "After the Fall, the world got crazy for a while. Some of it is still hard to believe. I'm trying to understand it."

"Understand demons?"

"Yes, I think that's it. Gemma was different. I didn't even know there were half demons until I met her. I can't imagine what that's like..." She frowned.

"So, now you're here to figure me out?"

"No. Well, yes. I wanted to know about the girl, if she's okay, and I wanted to apologize. The way they treated you at the station was unacceptable."

"It's nothing."

"My job... my life... I like to think I protect people who can't protect themselves. If someone is wronged, I do everything I can to right it. My papa says I'm too much of an idealist. I... well... He died. During the Fall."

"My condolences."

"My sister too." Her smile hardened, and her drink trembled in her hand. "They were driving back from hockey practice when the veil fell. Demons ambushed their car." Ramírez threw back her glass and downed the remains of her rum in one. "It was quick." She winced at the burn of the alcohol or the memories. "At least, that's what the coroner said when their bodies were finally identified." She touched her necklace and teased her cross between her finger and thumb. "I miss them."

Oftentimes, words were not enough. I leaned over the bar and grabbed a rum bottle. After twisting off the top, I refilling both our glasses.

"Styles told me who they think you are. One of the higher ones." An odd expression arrested her face between anger and regret, making her difficult to read. "I figured you'd have answers if I asked the right questions."

"Not all of them."

"Why?" she asked.

"Why what?"

"Why did you come here? Why did you kill so many of us?"

You as in all the demons. Of course she would group the lessers and me together. Most humans did. Demons were demons. There was no gray area. "It's in our nature to kill. In the netherworld, our society is built on survival of the fittest. We're terrible at negotiation. We take what we want, and what we can't take, we kill. It's a predatory world. If you're not at the top, you're food for something else."

"And you wanted our world?" She kept her expression blank, hiding her true thoughts.

"Taking yours was almost too easy to resist." I hadn't wanted to take anything. When humans had worshipped me, they had freely given their devotion. But my demon kin were different.

She took the words in and considered them. "Did *you* come through and kill people like the others?"

"No." I hadn't cared enough then to concern myself with the lives of hundreds of thousands. "I was too focused on revenge to consider what my kin were doing. Regret… that came later." Pain washed down my back at the memories. I shifted against the bar and pushed the past away. I was not the same demon as I was a year ago.

"Are you lying to me?" she asked. She touched my chin, skipping across the scar and delivering a small shock. I let her turn my face toward her. "Are you?"

Slowly, I closed my hand around hers, intending to push her away, but that didn't happen. Her touch was soft, gentle, with no trace of fear. "I rarely lie. There's no point to it."

"But you manipulate? You're good at using people to get what you want." She searched my eyes, needing answers.

"Until recently, yes."

"What changed?"

"I did."

"How?"

I considered telling her about my burned wings and the months I'd spent recuperating in a cage, but that wasn't the real reason. "The little half-blood girl you mentioned, Gem. She is something special. I wanted to protect her. Not for me, but because she deserved to have a life. She has so much potential hidden inside her human heart. Once I realized how much difference one girl could make, I wondered about all the other people and what they could do if given the chance. I found I wanted to protect that too. I always had. Your lives are so fragile, but also so limitless. You're all flawed. It's really quite lovely."

Ramírez's lips parted as though I'd said something surprising. She plucked her hand from mine and looked down into her refilled glass. "I er... I should be going. I have a shift in..." She glanced at her watch. "Soon." She scooted off the bar stool. "Er, thank you, for the drinks... I should..." She dug into her pocket for cash.

"Please, don't offend me by paying. You're welcome."

I watched her head for the door. I hadn't meant to shake her, but something I'd said had unsettled the determined cop.

"Losing your touch, oh mighty one?" Noah grinned.

With a laugh, I left the bar and headed for the elevator. It would be dark soon, and the killer was still out there. Whatever Ramírez thought of me, I'd told her the truth. What she did with that was entirely up to her.

≈

AFTER A NIGHT OF FRUITLESS HUNTING, I rematerialized on the roof of my building. Blue lights throbbed outside *Decadent-I,* washing the street in cool pulses. Panic tainted the air, as did a mixture of fear and anger. Something was wrong inside my building.

Noah met me in my apartment, his face pale. "It's Rosa. There's..." Trembling, he bit his lip. "The police are here. They're looking for you." He followed me into the elevator. "I said you were out, that you weren't even here when it happened, but they have a warrant. I slipped away and came up here to see if you were... back."

An attack. In my restaurant. The smell of blood clung to Noah's clothes, mixed with odors of food, cologne, and alcohol.

"Li'el..."

The elevator slowed.

Noah touched my arm, drawing my attention to him. The worry in his eyes wasn't for him or what he'd seen. "It's a witch hunt," he whispered. "Don't go out there."

The elevator chimed.

"It always is," I told him.

The doors opened. I managed three steps before a line of police in riot gear charged in. It didn't matter that I was unarmed or that I'd lifted my hands. Lights sparked against my sensitive sight. I instinctively stepped in front of Noah. The butt of a gun cracked across my jaw, and something knocked my leg out, dropping me onto my hands and knees. Something vicious dug into my side and delivered a jolt of electricity. Inside, my interminable patience fractured.

I could have turned to air and revealed all of me. I could have banished all the air from the room and rendered every single assailant unconscious in seconds. I did none of those things, which would have been used as evidence against me.

Nothing they did to me would be permanent.

"Li'el!" Noah cried out. I twisted in time to see him swing at a riot police before another plowed in and clocked him with an elbow to the jaw.

A snarl crawled across my lips.

They jabbed the prod into my side again, electricity jolting me. I snatched it out of the armored cop's hands, saw his eyes widen through his helmet visor, spun it in my hand, and jabbed it into the gap between armored plates around his knee. *See how you like it.* He howled and dropped. The line of officers reared back, expecting me to launch a full assault. I tossed the cattle prod instead. It bounced off a shield and clattered to the restaurant floor.

"You people have no idea what you're dealing with." They wanted demon. I'd give them demon.

"I do," a male voice growled close to my ear. I didn't recognize it, and as I turned to face him, sharp pain stabbed into my shoulder. I glimpsed the clear liquid inside an injector's vial as a plunger drove the substance into my veins. *Institute.* It didn't matter. They didn't have anything powerful enough to drop me.

My wings reflexively sprang outward, throwing half the armored troop back, driving others against the bar and toppling tables. I tried to pull on my element and turn myself into mist. I reached for it, but the response was too slow.

I got to my knees, wings stretched at awkward angles. The drug plucked on my control and undermined my strength. It unraveled my thoughts so I couldn't think to get a grip on my element and wield it against them. Another cattle prod jabbed me in the back where my wing muscles strained. Hot, vicious pain slammed me back down to my knees. This was wrong. This shouldn't be happening. I was stronger than this. I'd always been stronger than them, than anything.

"Stay down, demon," the male with the injector ordered. So calm. So calculated.

I searched for the source of that voice, but the room tilted and the walls moved.

I heard, rather than felt, my wings brushing against the floor, heard the feathers swish and flutter, trying to push me upright. Loose feathers spiraled in the air. My feathers... Where was my strength? Where was my damn pride?

Human eyes watched me flounder. People I knew. People who thought they knew me, Li'el... their charming employer. The man they loved, the man they admired, the man they wanted to be. But what they saw was not a man. Just a demon. A thing, a monster. And among them, I saw Ramírez's blue eyes looking triumphant. A demon had killed her father and her sister. She had probably witnessed demons kill hundreds. Of course she'd consider my downfall a victory.

But I'd thought she might have been different.

What a fool I'd been to think humans could see me as anything other than demon. And, really, it was no more than I deserved. What was a few months doing good against tens of thousands of years of being everything they feared?

I dropped my wings and lay panting. The Institute's cool drug crackled through my veins, coiling its invisible chains tighter.

A figure sauntered into my line of sight, dressed in black, his blond hair bright in contrast. He crouched to look me in the eye. He would see only the swirl of air in my eyes.

"You, my demon friend, are the last of your kind." The blond man smiled. "And now you are mine."

His hand draped over his knee, and on the back, two entwined scorpions blackened his skin. *Institute.* The sight of the branding followed me into unconsciousness.

CHAPTER 7

I had never been caged unwillingly. By choice, yes. But captured? Never.

The plastic cube I woke inside had one clear wall. The floor and ceiling were smooth, white, and molded so the seams were almost invisible. An anti-elemental barrier of glyphs pushed in from all sides, trying to crush me into something smaller and lesser. It restricted my element, making it and me virtually useless. I stood in the center of the box, wings opened as far as the walls allowed, and stared into the empty room beyond the transparent plastic window.

This was part of the Institute, but it wasn't possible. After failing to stop the Fall, the Institute lost their funding and their numbers were reduced to a handful. How had they gotten the resources for my current residence? How had they produced a drug powerful enough to render me unconscious? In Boston, they perhaps still had the resources to execute such a feat, but in LA? I knew everything that happened in my city. Had the Institute been developing new drugs and new "cages," I would have known.

I am air and everywhere. How could I have missed this?

A dull thud traveled through my plastic room, and a man strode into sight. The same man who had captured me in *Decadent-I*. He stopped a few inches from the glass and folded his arms across his chest, the black Institute branding stark against the back of the hand clutching his bicep. After a few moments, his lips lifted at the corners.

Young and lean from physical training, he had all the confidence of an immortal. A soldier, I assumed by the way he had handled my capture. An enforcer—one of the Institute's elite demon hunters. The name stitched into his overalls read "C. Burnstein." He assessed every inch of me like a hunter admiring a rack of antlers displayed on a wall. Fury burned in my chest. I welcomed it, let it simmer, stoked it higher.

"I would have preferred to kill you." He strode to the left and stopped, measuring his words. "All past encounters with Class A demons such as you have resulted in failure. For safety reasons, we should put you down like the stray dog you are." There was no spite or anger in his words. He believed them. In his mind, his words were facts.

"And knowing what I do about you, *Pride*, you'll wish I had." He unfolded his arms and tucked his hands into his pants pockets. "Perhaps that day will come."

He waited for me to contribute to this monologue. He'd be waiting a long time. One of us *was* immortal. The other just a cocky demon assassin. I'd known many like him. So eager to ride into battle and be the right arm of good. Fortunately, heroes were often the first to die. His pride would be his undoing.

My lips twitched.

He noticed. "You should have left LA when you had the chance. If you had gone into hiding, maybe disappeared in the hills or the desert, you could have been spared the humiliation of what's to come. But you couldn't, could you? Your pride wouldn't let you. That's the problem with all you Class A demons—you so-called princes—you're all so predictable."

I approached the transparent wall. This man was nothing compared to me, physically or mentally, yet he lifted his chin and looked into my eyes without a shred of fear. Was he a fool? Or did he truly believe this would end well for him?

"My employers will run tests on you," he said. "But that won't be the worst of it. Not for you—"

"What's your name?" I interrupted. He enjoyed the sound of his own voice, whereas I did not.

"Christian."

"Interesting. Are you a religious man, Christian?"

"You mean, do I believe in god and the devil?" His edged smile sharpened. "I have one standing right in front of me. I believe in what I can track and kill. But the myths and legends around you and your name? No. To me, you're a disease humans discarded thousands of years ago. And now we have destroyed you again. London, Tokyo, Dubai, Sydney. They all report that the demons are gone. You're an endangered species, but nobody will put you on a list and save you. Rest assured, when the time comes, I will be the one to kill you."

I pressed my hand against the clear plastic and leaned in as close as the wall allowed. "You should pray that when I escape, you are very, very far away, Christian."

"Not this time, *Pride*. You see…" He tossed a gesture at the sparse room around him. "This is not the Institute. Oh, I used to work for them, but the Institute failed the second the veil fell. I'm from a department you won't find on any government accounting sheet. You haven't heard of us, and if we do our job right, you and the people we keep safe outside these walls never will."

"Military."

He didn't confirm it. Didn't need to. "When we're done

extracting everything we need from your body, this box"—he rapped his knuckles on the plastic window—"will be placed inside a secure facility, somewhere obvious, somewhere with excellent infrastructure that'll allow the thousands of tourists to park right by your new home and pay thirty bucks a pop to come see you in all your glory. The Demon Freak Show. There was talk of sitting you beside the natural history museum. Folks will drag their kids from all over the United States to see the demon in its cage. The last one of its kind. They'll all come to see the spectacle, to see how you are nothing to fear. You're going to be LA's next big tourist attraction. Ironic, isn't it, *Pride?*"

A stream of thousands of admirers. That didn't sound too bad. "You have me all wrong if you think I won't enjoy humans admiring me."

He chuckled and stepped back from the glass. From his pocket, he produced a feather. One of mine. A ripple of pain traveled through my wings. "It won't be admiration, prince." He dropped the feather, let it see-saw through the air, and when it settled on the floor, he twisted the heel of his boot over it, grinding the feather to dust.

A snarl bubbled free, my rage heating. I slammed my hand against the plastic wall. "This plastic box cannot hold me."

"You are not the demon you once were. I think the box will work just fine." He laughed and walked out of sight. A dull thud signaled a door had closed.

Make a mockery of me? No, it would never happen. It was impossible. I was Pride. They couldn't reduce me to an attraction in a box. It wouldn't happen. It couldn't happen. Yes, I was weak, but I was still stronger than any human, stronger than Christian and the military outfit he worked for.

"I am Pride..." I snarled, hearing my words fill the space around me and travel no farther.

They would have to enter this room to begin their tests. I could wait for the right opportunity. I had all the time in the world to wait.

~

I WAITED for the people to come and the tests to begin. They didn't. I waited for voices to crackle through a speaker, but all I heard was my own rustling feathers. Under the constant glare of white light, time became meaningless.

Why hadn't they come?

They had a prime demon specimen in their grasp, so why weren't they exploiting the opportunity? Where were the scientists? Where were the people? Why weren't they falling over themselves to study me?

I didn't need to eat to survive. They brought me nothing. I didn't need to relieve myself. I did none of those human things, so nothing about me or my cage changed. But there was one way in all this nothingness with only myself for company that I could track the passage of time.

My feathers fell.

One after another after another, they fell. I gathered up the first ones and placed them gently in the corner of my white box. But more fell, and soon they carpeted the floor. My box was six strides by six strides. I paced. One, two, three, four, five, six. Turn. Back again. One, two, three, four, five, six. Turn.

Why weren't people coming to admire me?

My wings ached. Burdens on my back. I couldn't stretch them, so they had seized half-open, feathers thinning with every turn.

One, two, three... Humans had always admired me...

four, five six. Turn. What was I if nobody looked upon me? One, two… I had been a shadow before. Now, I was a ghost. Three, four, five, six. A ghost in a white box. Turn. Would they forget me? What a terrible thing for people to no longer see me, remember me, love me.

How long had it been? Weeks. Months. At the rate my feathers were falling, it could have been longer.

I thought of the time I had risen as a god among mortals, of the years humans had worshipped and loved and admired me. I thought of Ramírez and the satisfied expression on her face as I was brought to my knees. She had every reason to hate demons. They all did. But I was different. I hadn't fought them, though I could have. I'd exercised restraint. I'd saved people. I was *good*. Didn't that count for anything in this post-Fall world?

"Look, Mommy, a demon."

I lifted my head and looked in the little girl's eyes. A tiny thing, no taller than her mom's waist. Perhaps it was her sparkling eyes, but something about her seemed familiar.

She pressed her small hand against the plastic window and spread her fingers. "He looks sad."

I didn't remember them arriving… No, I did, but I didn't *want* to remember. The people had started coming long ago. Streams of them stood, pointing and staring. They whispered things. Some prayed. Others cursed and ranted and blamed me for the crimes of my kin. So many anonymous faces peering inside my cage. Did they see a prince or a monster? Some time ago, I'd stopped seeing them, stopped caring, stopped listening.

Around me, feathers had fallen and shriveled like dead leaves. I picked one up—the smoothest and cleanest I could reach—and got to my feet. The ache wasn't physical. It gnawed on my mind, dulling the edges. I hadn't moved in a long, long while.

Everyone but the mom and her little girl pulled back from the window. The latter looked up, lips parting.

My wings burned hot and sharp. I didn't need to look to know only shredded flesh and naked bone remained. It hurt to move, but the pain was good. If it hurt, it meant I was still here. Not a ghost. Not vanished and forgotten.

I crouched close to the window and lifted the feather.

The girl's soft, plump lips stretched into a wide grin. "A feather, Mommy. Can I have the feather? Please, Mommy. Can I?"

"No, dear." She pulled her daughter away. "Remember what Daddy said. It's a trick."

"But Mommy..."

Her little hand vanished, leaving a small, already fading outline on the plastic.

"You must never trust a demon." The mom gripped her daughter's hand and fixed her stare on me before hurrying away.

The girl looked over her shoulder and smiled a goodbye. Too soon, the crowd closed in and pressed against the glass, pointing camera phones and waving selfie sticks. What a game it was to see the demon in a box.

The little handprint had all but vanished. Strange how I wanted it to stay so I wouldn't be alone when the people left.

I straightened and turned to gasps, not of admiration, but of horror. The sound only made my wings ache more.

The girl had seen what the others could not. She would have treasured my feather. Perhaps one day, when she was older, she would remember the demon in his plastic box and how he had offered her the last gift he could give.

∼

"MY SUPERIOR ASKED me what would be the best way to

break you." Christian's voice roused me from my numbed state. He stood at the window, alone, and took a bite out of the apple he was holding. The flow of people had left. I measured time by their comings and goings like the ocean tides.

"I told them pride is his strength and his weakness." He waved the apple as he spoke. "Take it away, and he has nothing."

Looking at the feathers surrounding me, it would be hard to argue that I was not broken, just… conserving energy for a chance to escape. There would be one. There always was. They still wanted to run their tests. They couldn't resist such a wonderful specimen as I.

"This isn't personal," he continued. "It's just how the world works now."

"You said there would be tests." I didn't sound broken, did I?

The question lit his dark eyes with amusement. "Ah, were you waiting for those? They …decided against it. Any inter-action might pander to your sense of pride. You're not wanted, my demon friend. The only reason you're still alive is the increase in tourism you bring in to the city. In the last six months, you've brought in an estimated six hundred thousand dollars. You're good for the morale of the local population too. It does wonders letting people see how you're nothing to fear. You're the perfect exhibit. Low over-head, maximum profit. You'll soon have your own merchan-dise and profits will increase tenfold."

They had held me captive for six months. It felt like longer. I had lost too many feathers. What else would I lose in this box? My mind? "I have lived for thousands of years and seen civilizations rise and fall. I ruled in the netherworld as one of the Seven. And this box is the best you could come up with?"

He shrugged. "Sometimes the best solutions are the simplest. Why complicate things?"

"There are things I know. Things I have seen. I have witnessed history unfolding. Keeping me here, like this, is a waste."

Christian finished the last bite of his apple and chewed slowly, dragging out his reply. "You're not grasping the situation. You are obsolete. Demons are extinct. Nobody cares what you know or what you've seen. When the veil fell and the demons came, we learned from you. You slaughtered so many that we had to find new ways to fight you. That's the marvelous thing about humans: we learn, we change, and we get better at what we do—"

"Don't preach to me of humans," I snarled. "I have known more of you over time than the number of those alive today."

"We studied your ways, and then we evolved, just like you. Your time has ended, and so you'll stay in this box for as long as you continue to make my employers money. The second you become a burden, I'll execute you."

"Evolved how?"

His smile widened. "Before your arrival, we didn't even know the veil existed. Now we know exactly what and where it is."

Dread shivered down my back. "The balance of the veil and its energies are not to be upset."

"Upset?" He chuckled. "So like your ancient kin. So rooted in the past you can't see the potential for the future."

I approached the window. "What do you intend to do with the veil?"

"Do with it? Nothing. From what I've heard it looks as though the veil could be the clean energy source we've been looking for. Ironic that the most devastating war known to human-kind might provide its salvation."

Somehow tap into the veil? "You can't draw energy from

the veil. Only higher demons and half-bloods can do that. The Institute's half-blood experiment was terminated, and all the higher demons are gone."

His eyes sparkled. "We've come a long way since your kind tried to take our world. Now be a good demon and perform for the masses. Maybe I'll come by in a few months to let you know how things are going."

Christian left, and after a few hours, the ebb and flow of people continued.

Day after day they filled the room outside my window, and night after night I stared into the empty room they left behind, their handprints smudging the plastic window. I had already tried breaking the seals around the door, but without my element, and with my strength waning, my efforts did more to occupy my mind than get me closer to freedom, but I tried again as part of my routine. Pace and try the door seals. Pace and try the window seals. One, two, three, four, five, six. Turn. The door. Turn. Pace. The window. Turn.

Drawing power from the veil? Princes at the height of their power could draw energy from the veil's chaos energies to bolster their own. The Institute's half-bloods, as rare as they were, could draw power from both sides of the veil, making them extremely powerful. I knew of only three half-bloods—Muse, Stefan, and Gem. They were all in Boston and none of them would ever let a military entity use them. They knew the dangers that came with manipulating the veil. They wouldn't risk it. How then were Christian's employers considering tapping into it? The veil *was* the elements. It couldn't be tamed or farmed or harnessed. Could it?

Humans and their ingenuity. Manipulating the veil would get them killed or open the door to the netherworld all over again, but humans and their adventurous spirit... They couldn't help themselves. Fools. Dreamers. There wasn't much difference between a pioneer and the hundreds who had failed before him or her. Perhaps they *could* harness the veil's energies. Perhaps I was wrong to doubt them. Time and time again humans had picked themselves up from the mud and powered through adversity. Why should now be any different?

What would my princely brethren think? That thought alone brought something of a smile to my lips. Humans tapping into the veil would rile the princes up. I had once enjoyed seeing my kin bicker and squabble like vultures over scraps of meat. But it would be different beyond the veil now. Many of the princes were dead. The others were trapped there in a dying world, the King of Hell somehow keeping them all in line with his Queen of Chaos subdued beside him.

A shudder shook my naked wings. There were worse places to be than inside a plastic box.

CHAPTER 8

*C*hristian returned roughly a month later, more subdued than the last time he had sauntered into sight. He brought a chair and sat in front of the window.

"Did you have…" He struggled to find the right word. "Did you have offspring?"

"Many." I was sitting in the center of my box, the only place where my wings didn't brush against the edges of the room. The arches still pushed against the ceiling, but in this position, they didn't hurt as much as when they touched the walls. "At one time, I copulated profusely with mortals."

He scowled, and I smiled back, knowing perfectly well how my past grated on him.

"Producing half-bloods?" he asked, grimacing.

"Yes. Most died during childbirth. Those who survived their first few hours were later slaughtered." Burned alive, most of them. I touched the scar on my chin, and then I withdrew my hand and curled my fingers in. It had been a long time ago. The memories were old and fragmented.

"Who killed them?"

"Why are you so interested, Christian?"

He waved my query away. "Who killed them?"

"Another prince." My wings throbbed. I would never escape the memory of fire licking over their expanse. "Do you have offspring?"

"Me?" He huffed a laugh. "I wouldn't tell you if I did."

"Should I escape, I might seek you out, hunt them down, and torture them while forcing you to watch?" I nodded. "If I were a demon cliché, I most certainly would do those things."

"You're never getting out of this box." He leaned back in the chair and stretched out his legs, getting comfortable on his side of my window.

I studied him. Worn trainers, untucked shirt over black jeans. Fingernails chewed down to the quick and a shadow of a beard across his chin. He had aged since caging me. Brought on by what, I wondered.

"What do you see?" He jerked his chin, daring me to answer.

I folded my arms. "What use is a demon hunter once the last demon is caught?"

He didn't react, meaning he was hiding any expression that might give him away. I suspected my demon hunter had fallen on hard times. A world without demons didn't need hunters.

"Did you come to remind yourself of your finest moment?" I asked. "To remind yourself that you're not a failure? That you once had a purpose?"

He stood, shoved the chair to the back of the room, and left.

The grin on my lips felt good. He would be back.

~

THE PEOPLE HADN'T ARRIVED. They should have been streaming through to point and remark hours ago, but the quiet had lingered longer this time. With no more feathers left to fall, I relied on the tourists to count the days, and when the door didn't open, I paced. Six steps. No more. No less. Check the window. Turn. Six steps.

A ground tremor rumbled in the distance like a far-off train but soon shuddered closer. I'd heard it before. Most Los Angeles residents had. Earthquake.

The floor shifted an inch sideways. I spread my weight, staying balanced as the floor shifted one way then back. A crack darted up the plastic window. Chips splintered off, falling among my feathers.

The earthquake rumbled off, and silence returned. It had left me a gift. I pressed both hands on either side of the jagged crack and tried to summon enough of my element to ease it through, but the glyphs were still intact. Curling my hand into a fist, I punched the plastic. It didn't crack. I punched it again. Nothing. It had to be at least four inches thick and reinforced. But a crack was good, a crack was a weakness I could exploit. I switched my attention to the door and ran my fingers around the seal. If I could just—

"Is today the day I kill you, demon?"

Christian.

I ignored him and stretched high to run my hands over the top of the door.

"I've been meaning to ask," he began. "The day I brought you down, why didn't you fight? You could have. PC-Eighty takes around three seconds to kick in and roughly ten seconds to render a higher demon unconscious. You could have suffocated a handful of my men in that time."

"I could have." There, a small misalignment. A bump in the seal, really, but it was enough for me to work on. There were no cameras in my box. Once Christian was gone, I would work on my box's new weaknesses.

"So, why didn't you?"

"Why do you think I didn't?" I replied, turning to face the demon hunter through the window. He'd moved his chair close again, and he sat there now with his rifle resting on his lap. The shadow of a beard was as thick as the dark circles under his eyes.

"You were keeping up the charade that you're a good demon. You thought you'd escape later when there weren't as many witnesses."

"Sure, that's exactly it."

He scratched the whiskers on his chin and frowned. "That's not it, though."

"What do you want me to say?"

"The truth."

"The truth?" I laughed, surprising us both. I hadn't laughed in… When was the last time? With Noah at my restaurant, perhaps. "Just because I can kill, it doesn't mean I want to. You were a soldier before the Institute trained you as an enforcer?"

"Marines." Pride sparkled in his eyes.

"Did you kill at every opportunity?"

His glare narrowed. "Is that what you see yourself as? A soldier?"

"I am demon, I am Pride, I am One of the Seven. I am an angel and a devil. I am a great many things to many people. But I am not the people's enemy."

"So, if I let you out, you wouldn't kill me?"

"Oh, it's definitely on the list."

His dry laugh held no humor. "You saved a cop. Why did you do that?"

"He was dying, I was there, and I could help him. It's quite simple."

"For a man, yes. But for you? What does his life mean to you? Do you plan to use him later? Use his gratitude to get closer to the police and the cop who visited you?"

He knew of Ramírez? I swallowed the question burning on my tongue. *Was she safe?* "No. Human lives are short. His death would have been a waste."

Christian chuckled, implying my words were insincere. "You're good, you know. So convincing. Class A's are always so damn persuasive, right before they turn around and rip your spine out."

"That seems like an inefficient way of killing someone." Although quite tempting in his case.

"You'd know."

"Yes, I would. I also know how to kill demons, how to pull the perfect pint of Guinness, and how to pleasure at least four people at once, men and women. Ask me what I know about you."

He leaned forward, grinning like a confident fool. "All right, I'll play. What do you know about me?"

"I know you were married, but you're now separated. I also know you were recently dismissed from the military or sidelined. You have a daughter, around six years old—"

He shot to his feet. "How!?" Rage twisted his mouth and curled his hands into fists.

So easy to read. Would he open the door to my box to sate that anger?

"I know you come here seeking redemption I can't give you. You're a killer, Christian, just like me. You enjoyed your time as a marine, and you enjoyed killing demons because it gave you an excuse to kill and be a hero. You like the spotlight. You want people to see you, just like me. We are not so different, you and I. Each time you visit, I wonder which of us is truly caged. I will outlive your human years, and when your bones are dust, I will still be here, very much alive. But time will forget you."

"Son of a bitch!" He punched the window and then withdrew, realizing his mistake. The plastic didn't give, but it could have. That knowledge turned his eyes cold. "Manipulating me, huh? You think you can make me break you out?"

"It might have crossed my mind." I smirked.

"You can't know these things. Someone told you all this."

I slammed both hands into the window, jolting the hunter back. "You took my element from me and you crippled my wings, but you cannot blunt my mind, demon hunter. I will escape. And the day is coming when we will meet without this barrier between us. That day we will learn who deserves to live."

He snarled and shook a finger my way. "Any time, demon. Any fucking time."

CHAPTER 9

The door seal wasn't giving, and neither was the plastic window. Nobody had tried to stop me from working at both weaknesses, betraying their belief that the seal would not fail. I hadn't seen anyone since I'd revealed to Christian how easy he was to read. Without the flow of tourists and with no feathers left to fall, time blurred.

Weeks passed like hours, or was it the reverse? Hours like weeks. Days like seconds. I couldn't tell. There had been times in my past when I'd lost myself to time, fallen into its trap. Sometimes, years would pass in a blink. The years I'd spent reveling with humans had passed like that. I had once spent a netherworld decade roaming the broken continents as air. But that had been different.

This nothingness was not of my choosing, and I could do nothing to break free of it.

If Christian doesn't come, I have nothing left.

One, two, three, four, five, six paces. Turn.

If something catastrophic happened outside, would anyone think to release me? What if they had forgotten me?

LA was prone to seismic activity, more so after the last

69

demon-triggered earthquake that had helped Torrent pull a tsunami out of the ocean. Aftershocks had been plaguing the city for weeks, but the recent tremor had been substantial enough to crack my reinforced window. Had it been demon related?

Earth elementals could trigger earthquakes. But there were no demons left. A few lessers, but nothing princely. Just me...

Pace, turn, pace, turn.

What if humans had tapped into the veil? What if they had upset the balance of the chaos elements, collapsing the veil? What if the veil had fallen while I'd been pacing inside my box?

I would have known if the veil had fallen, I would have felt it.

Turn.

No, inside my glyph-protected box, I wouldn't have felt a thing. Inside my box, I was hidden as well as caged.

I stopped at the windows and spread my hands over the thin cracks.

What if the tourists had stopped coming because there were no people left to come?

~

THE LIGHTS HAD FLICKERED and died days ago.

I paced in perfect darkness. *One, two, three, four, five, six. Turn.*

I should have killed Christian's soldiers when I'd had the chance. If I'd reacted like a demon, I would be free to help others. But I had chosen not to kill, and here I was, as useless as an apex predator in a zoo.

How long had it been?

I didn't know. I couldn't grasp time and wrangle it back under my control.

I had been forgotten, of that I was certain. Unless this was Christian's way of punishing me, but I doubted the man had either the imagination or the motivation. My capture had been a job to him, nothing more and nothing less. He would have come if he could. He couldn't resist gloating over his prize. So why hadn't he come?

"Li'el?"

A flashlight beam washed over my face, flooding my sight. The sudden invasion of a familiar voice set my heart racing. But I could have been imagining her. I had long ago given up hope of seeing her face in the stream of tourists.

Ramírez pointed her flashlight at the floor. I blinked to adjust my focus. Her face was thinner, eyes colder and crowded with fine lines. The rifle hitched over her shoulder looked similar to the one Christian had brought with him on his last visit. Was she here to finish what he couldn't? No, there was no sign of triumph on her face now. Like the weathering on her face, wrinkles and tears aged her clothing.

"A deal?" She approached the window. "You sometimes like to bargain, right? I'll let you out if you'll help us."

She could have released me out of the kindness of her heart and asked nicely and gotten the same result, but Ramírez had a ways to go before she trusted me. "Agreed."

Some of the light had vanished from her eyes, replaced by shrewd intensity. It had always been there, but now it was all I saw. "If I let you out," she repeated, "you'll help us?"

In my weakened state, one Institute bullet to the head would leave me vulnerable, but why bargain at all if all she planned to do was render me useless? "You have my word."

She lifted the flashlight, pointing with it to the corner of my box. The beam skimmed my wing, or what was left of it.

She stilled, and I saw the Ramírez I'd met in the alleyway. Uncertain but determined. Fearful but strong.

"Move to the back." She dumped a rucksack on the floor, dug out a small box the size of her hand, and fixed it over the cracks in the window. "You should shield yourself."

I retreated into the dark at the back of my box. The device exploded a moment later, peppering me with debris. Dust swirled in the torchlight. Blood wept from dozens of cuts, but the pain was inconsequential. The window had shattered.

Ramírez offered me her hand. I accepted it and climbed through, awkwardly pulling my wings behind me. Her hand lingered around mine a moment too long, and her gaze lingered on my wings until she noticed I had seen. She let go, adjusted her rifle on her shoulder, scooped up her rucksack, and approached the figure standing in the open doorway.

Christian. He lifted his rifle, aiming between my eyes. "You agreed to help us."

The glyphs still pushed in on me. I didn't have my element and had no interest in killing him—yet. I straightened and approached the hunter. His finger flexed around the trigger. If he moved, his rifle wouldn't save him.

"Step aside," I said. I *needed* to get outside—to feel the air on my face, to open my wings, to see what held these two in the grips of fear—and this hunter wouldn't stop me.

"Your word," he snarled.

"I agreed to help you. I keep my word." My agreement was so ridiculously open to interpretation that I could have knocked the gun out of his hands and killed him where he stood and claimed I was helping him, but in the spirit of the agreement, I let him believe he had me on a short leash. "Now get out of my way."

"Christian," Ramírez snapped. "Move."

He stepped aside.

Outside, the pressure of the glyphs I had become so accustomed to peeled away, and my element tentatively stirred awake. I could think of nothing else but the air and how it wrapped around me and responded to my touch, licking at my fingers and whispering around my ragged wings. The tease and flow of hot, sweet air. Air laced with the taste of grit, of baked asphalt and *demon*. The air was too thick, and the smell…

I opened my eyes and saw farther than a few yards for the first time in months. No more six steps. No more pacing. A glance over my shoulder revealed my cage. A semi trailer unit, parked up and unhitched on a vast lawn.

A grassy area stretched ahead, ending in a pedestrianized road, and beyond that, an empty highway. The subdued light seemed wrong for the time of day. Or was it night? The lack of people suggested it was late, but the sky was lit and glowed despite the heavy cloud cover.

I stepped down from the trailer and onto cool, wet grass. Such delight in the little things. Freedom spread out before me. I pushed my element farther and stretched my mind to clear the numbness.

I could feel it, the crawl and itch of a familiar touch, a familiar place that had no right to be here. Above, clouds pulled apart, and behind, pulsing veins of color danced silently in the sky. So beautiful, and so very, very wrong in the skies over LA.

The veil.

What have they done?

CHAPTER 10

*W*e walked from my trailer across the dewy grass to the science museum. The sprawling building's windows were dark. Trash had gathered in doorways, and the once manicured lawn was a tangle of grass and brush.

The veil's colorful ribbon of light writhed limply in the sky. The last time the veil had been visible it hadn't taken much to bring it down. Sprinkle in chaos to upset the natural balance of the elements, and it would fall. If the demons beyond the veil knew it was weak, they would rally, and they would come again. After time holding no meaning for so long, I felt its passage keenly.

All the sacrifices over the years, all the lives lost, and now history was about to repeat.

I followed Ramírez up a flight of steps to the museum entrance and paused in front of the doors. Inside, silent escalators led to a first-floor gallery area. Christian climbed two stairs at a time toward the higher vantage point.

I hung back, eyeing the empty building. How long had it been like this? Where were the people? "Tell me everything."

Ramírez hesitated at my tone. "I will, but we need to find shelter. It's… worse at night."

"I'm not cowering inside that building." A breeze hissed through the grass, carrying the familiar smell of demon woven with hot asphalt. A purplish hue painted my view of the lawn. It was happening again.

Facing the window, I pulled my element close, wrapping myself in what it meant to be wholly and completely me again. Seized half open, my wings hung like rigid burdens on my back. I couldn't stand the agony of breaking them to stretch their bones wide. But I needed to. I needed to do many things to remind myself of who and what I was before being locked away.

Shadows slid through the grass. I could smell them. *Lessers*, probably stirred by the reappearance of the veil or driven through from the netherworld.

Foolish humans. How could they have let this happen over their pursuit of clean energy?

They would never abandon the potential of the veil. The veil falling all those months ago hadn't been an end. It had been a beginning. The beginning of humans and their curiosity.

"Li'el?"

Fools. All of them. Their world was perfect, and they were risking it all for power? Did they not know what they already had? Could they not see the perfection surrounding them? If they had witnessed the destruction in netherworld, if they had seen Hell in all its devastating glory, they would not have sought the power of the veil.

"Li'el?"

I whirled on Ramírez. "I leave you alone for a few months and this is what happens? How could you be so reckless?!"

The colors of the veil rippled across her face, smoothing

away those new lines. She turned her face away as though ashamed. "It's been two years."

Years.

Years in my box.

The waste of it ignited my carefully controlled rage but I quelled it. Years—months—the past was of no consequence. "How long has the veil been visible?" Despite my control, venom dripped from each word.

She swallowed. "A few days."

Good. There was still time to stop this. They had come for me in the last hour when all else had failed. "You should have asked me to help long before this."

"I know," she whispered. "Li'el, I'm sorry."

I ignored her useless words and stepped closer. "During the Fall, when the demons came, did your species learn nothing?"

She bristled and lifted her chin. "We learned we had to protect ourselves from *your* kind."

My laugh was brittle. "By opening the door and inviting them back?"

She rolled her lips together and looked across the grass. "It wasn't like that. They said they had found a way to harness the veil and use the elements—"

"Harness chaos?" This time when I laughed, she flinched. "You are apes playing with nuclear weapons. We must stop this or there will be nothing left of your world worth saving. The veil is the first sign. Next, demons will come. Lessers if you're lucky. Higher demons if not. And once chaos has taken root here, the princes will come. And don't think for one second they haven't learned from their mistakes."

Her pulse fluttered in the curve of her neck. "You stopped it before."

Me? If she had hoped to find a savior, she would be sorely disappointed. "Not I. I had nothing to do with the last Fall, and this time…" My wings were broken, my element weak. What miracles did she expect from me? "There was a Court. A King and Queen of Hell. Together, they balanced the chaos energies and restored the veil. Do you have a King and Queen, Ramírez? Do you have chaos and control demons to set this right? All you have is me, and whatever was left of me you helped destroy in that box!"

My wings twitched, the bones grating. My growl sounded low and deadly like something worthy of a demon monster.

Her defiance wavered, and inside the building, Christian started back down the stairs, coming to her rescue like the valiant hero he believed he was.

"The government did this," she said. "We thought they would put it right, but after the first wave hit and nobody did anything—"

"The first wave? Lessers?"

"Many." Concern dug a V into her brow. She looked again at the tall, swaying grasses, afraid of what was lurking in their depths. "You have to help us, Li'el."

Christian loitered in the entryway, his finger resting on the rifle's trigger. They'd asked for my help, yet neither of them trusted me. What did I owe them?

I turned away. "Any demon worth their name would kill you all and welcome their kin through." I smiled, knowing they couldn't see it. "Fortunately for you, this world must survive, even if some of you don't deserve to be saved."

A strangled demon howl erupted across the grasses near the edge of the highway. That sound was not meant for this world.

"Get inside," I told them. "The lessers will not attack with me here."

"Are you sure?" Ramírez asked, referencing my weakened state. "Let me help you."

I inched my wings open, deliberately breaking swollen

sinew and soaking up the jagged stabs of pain. "I'm perfectly capable of crushing the skulls of a few lessers." And I needed it to shake off the decay from being crouched in the box for so long... for years... and to remind myself exactly what I was capable of.

"Please." Guilt drenched that single word.

"No."

She opened her mouth, about to protest.

"I need this."

I started down the steps and stretched my senses outward. Whether Ramírez listened didn't matter. After a few steps, I dissolved into air, moving freely for the first time in years. The constant physical pain from my wings faded beneath the sensation of freedom, becoming more of an echo in my ethereal state.

I flowed outward, spreading into a mist, soaring across the silent grounds. At the fringes of my reach, LA lay too quietly, its roads empty. I imagined many had fled at the sight of the veil, but some would have stayed and holed up in their homes. I would help them where I could, but this moment was for me.

Lessers shifted in the grass, venturing closer, sensing weakness.

They were not meant to be here. This city was mine.

I pulled my element in, making myself ghostly. The pain returned, my wings useless, but wings, even ruined wings, were a sign of status among demons and a basic means of signaling strength. Revealing their shredded expanse, I cast my power outward and trawled it over the lessers.

They knew what demon they faced.

I saw them through the mist, felt them breathing and hesitate. Dozens of eyes peered back and more were coming. In large numbers, they were formidable, but no match for my rage.

I smiled. It had been so very long since I'd given in to my most demon desires. Not just the years kept in the box, but farther back to a time when I'd ruled as one of the Seven. To kill, to master, to own, to be demon. I hadn't always been Li'el. I'd once been a creature of power and wrath.

The lesser to my right inched forward, snout huffing close to the ground. On all fours, it stood as tall as a man. Its crescent claws were designed to rip its prey apart. The tail lashing behind it bore three spikes. Power trembled through its muscles. It was not like the weakest demons left over from the Fall. This lesser had come straight out of the nether-world. Bigger, hungrier, stronger.

I looked it square in the eye. A challenge. It saw my lessened state and smelled the decay on my wings, and instincts told it to *take*.

"Let's dance."

The beast launched through the air with its jaws wide and claws extended, and fell through the ghost of me, stumbling to the ground. My laughter sailed through the air. The beast turned in time to see the real me—a creature made of mist, of smoke, of the very air it needed to breathe—and faced its death.

"I am air and everywhere," I whispered, sending the words into the mist.

The beast sprang a second time. I whirled away, and before it could land, I yanked the air from inside its lungs, choking it. It tumbled and clawed at its throat. I pinned it beneath my foot, wrapped my hand around its snout, and snapped its head back. An audible crack ricocheted through the silence like a gunshot.

The swarm of lessers bounded forward, spilling out of shadows, from beneath parked cars, and dropping from rooftops. Hundreds.

The lust for the kill burned fiercely. Yes, this would be a slaughter, and I welcomed it.

I flung my wings open, hearing them crack and feeling old bones shatter and mend. Pain strummed and beat and throbbed, and it felt *good.*

Yes, come to me. Remind me of who I am, what I am, and what I can be.

They sprang and clawed and rushed and snapped. I flung them back, struck some, suffocated others. Countless came and died beneath my hands until demon blood soaked the ground and their stink filled the air. The more I killed, the easier it became and the less of a hold the pain had on me.

I am demon. This city is mine.

The veil throbbed above, its push and pull a reminder of the netherworld and what I had been—a warning and a promise. The netherworld was close, and given the chance, it would come, it would take, and it would turn this world ugly. But I would not give it that chance. LA was mine. Its people were mine to protect. *Mine.* No one would take the City of Angels from me.

Claws dug into my right wing, dousing me in agony. I arched the skeletal framework high, flinging the beast off, but another landed on my back, clawing and biting to maintain its grip. My growl shook the air and earth. I whirled and flicked the creature off. Another rushed in. Another tore at my wings. Teeth sank in, yanking me down.

No, not my wings...

They should not have been this strong. The veil hadn't fallen. They should have been weaker and disorganized.

I turned to air, let the beasts fall, struck them down by suffocating them, and tore through their numbers. When it was over and no more beasts came from the mists, I stood alone, my shredded wings dripping blood and painting my now solid flesh with their gore.

Stretching my element far, more demons scurried away. Hundreds—no, thousands. There shouldn't have been so many. This was not a normal force. Had the princes beyond the veil driven them through, or was something else drawing them here?

"I need you to tell me everything that's happened in my absence," I said.

Ramírez had approached near the end of my killing spree, her rifle poised, first on the lessers and then on me. I had wondered if she might shoot, but she had hung back and watched me kill. She had seen me in an alleyway once, my wings intact, my vessel perfect, *civilized*. She might have believed then that I was good. Now she saw a creature, skin wet with blood, wings virtually destroyed. I stood raw and exposed as completely demon. No more facades. No more charming Li'el. I tossed her a smile, revealing sharp teeth, and she witnessed why humans had once named me the devil.

I saw fear on her face, fear and horror. She was right to fear me. Just because I played at being human, it didn't mean I wasn't everything she knew of demons.

"Am I everything you thought I was?" I turned, letting the wings fizzle away, washed the blood from my body with a gesture, and rebuilt the magnificent male vessel with his Hollywood smile and perfectly tailored casual clothes. By the time I'd crossed the blood-soaked ground, my shoes were shining and my cuffs were perfectly aligned with the jacket I'd created. She saw the suave black man, the clever camouflage that had helped me blend in with humans for centuries, and the honest fear in her eyes grew. Now she understood the creature she had bargained with.

The stinking demon carcasses scattered around us could have easily been humans felled by my claws. Once, they would have been.

"Remember this scene the next time you consider betraying me," I said, passing beside her through the parting mists and up the steps to the museum.

"I..."

I didn't know what she would have said. *I'm sorry,* perhaps. *I didn't understand.* I didn't want her excuses. The past was done. Now I had to salvage the future, if there was one for this world.

CHAPTER 11

"*P*ublic attractions—where people gathered in large numbers—were the first to close," Ramírez explained. "Fifty-two people were killed at the city zoo. That's how we knew more lessers were getting through."

Ramírez and I sat in the large cafeteria on the ground floor of the science museum. Chairs and tables had been abandoned. A discarded kid's coat was draped over a nearby ice cream counter, but the quiet was thick and telling.

Christian patrolled the building out of sight, moving through the air on the first floor.

"Once the city issued a curfew and the military got involved, people started leaving. Then the government issued a notice to stay, saying we'd be safe in our homes. My department was supposed to help keep order. The city had to keep functioning. It barely survived the first Fall, and now this…" She trailed off. "Then they closed the roads."

"Why?" I asked.

She regarded me warily as though I might leap across the table and kill her. She had nothing to fear from me, though I had no intention of telling her that—yet.

"The official line was, *For our safety*, but… I don't know. It feels different this time. Last time, it happened fast, and it was over in days. This time…"

"Because this time it's not coming from the netherworld. It started this side of the veil." I leaned in. Ramírez stilled, not wanting to flinch away. "Christian said the government was hoping to harness the veil. What do you know about that?"

"Right before this started, the governor announced there had been a breakthrough in clean energy, right here in California." She shrugged. "Californians are used to big claims. If it's not batteries, it's solar. We've heard it all before."

"But this time?"

She pressed her lips together. "I'm not even sure there's a connection."

"Unfortunate timing if not."

"Ask Christian. Maybe he knows more."

While my blood was running hot, the best place for Christian was far, far away from me. I had my control reined in for now. "How did you meet up with him?"

"He was with the team that swooped in as soon as Catherine gave the green light to have you… dealt with."

"Dealt with… like a stray hound." I arched an eyebrow and relaxed back in my chair. "Delightful."

"I searched for him when I figured you could help us. Turns out, once there were no more demons to catch, he started freelancing as a private demon hunter. I was already in touch with him when the lessers started attacking."

"So, he told you where I was."

She nodded and picked at her thumbnail, focusing there instead of on me. "They closed your attraction after the earthquake—Look, I'm just a cop. I don't make the decisions. I couldn't stop them from capturing you or what they did… afterward."

"Sure you couldn't."

She threw her hands up. "What was I supposed to do?"

"Come visit," I replied, the picture of calm.

"I..." She hesitated.

"Hmm?" I encouraged.

"It wasn't right..." She scowled at her chewed-up fingernails.

"I appreciate the sentiment." I could have told her how I had searched the thousands of anonymous faces for hers and how I'd looked forward to seeing her, even just once. Strange how one human woman had spent so much time occupying my thoughts. Strange and curious. She had lost her family to demons. She was firmly on the side of the righteous and hadn't sought me out until she'd needed my help. There was nothing between us but misunderstandings and curiosity. At least that was what I told myself.

"We have no right to ask you for help," she said and finally met my gaze. "But you're the only one who understands what's happening."

"I wouldn't say I understand it, but I am the only one who can help control it and find a solution. What has Christian said about my helping?"

"That you'll use us, then kill us the first chance you get."

That would be the *demon* thing to do. "He's right." I hid much of my smile but let a little show through. "*You* don't have to worry."

"Will you use us—him?"

"I haven't killed any people in a long time, despite how strategically removing many of your lesser specimens from the gene pool would greatly improve your species."

"That wasn't what I asked."

Clever. She knew how I played with words. I had forgotten that about her. I placed my hand over my heart. "I solemnly swear I have no intention of killing any human beings."

"Thank you." She frowned. "I think." Then she held out her hand across the table.

I looked at it, adopting my own frown.

"Marianna Ramírez," she said. "My friends call me Anna."

Friends? I closed my hand around hers, finding it small and warm. "Prince of Pride and restaurateur, among other things. You may call me Li'el."

Her smile twisted up my insides in strange and unusual knots that weren't entirely unpleasant. I released her hand and leaned back in the seat, making a mental note to incite that smile more often.

"So, Li'el, where do we start?"

"Most man-made disasters begin with one person and cascade down to the general population. We find that person who has all the answers."

"And how do we do that?"

"We go back to where it all began."

"Li'el?" Noah launched himself from one of my many couches as though the cushions were on fire. He bounded toward me but pulled up short, noticing Anna and Christian at the last second. "I... What the... I didn't think I'd see you again." He puffed out a sigh and rubbed the back of his neck. "Damn, you're okay. You're really okay?"

"You doubted it?" I scanned the clothes, empty takeout cartons, and beer cans strewn about my apartment living room and what I could see of my disheveled bedroom beyond.

Anna and Christian drifted forward, toeing through the mess.

Noah trailed after me. "Yeah, I doubted it. What they did—"

"It's done." I turned. Shallow depressions darkened his eyes. In my absence, he had turned into a shadow of his former self. I knew how that felt. Frankly, I was surprised to see him. As far as I could tell from the dust and disarray downstairs, the restaurant had been closed for some time. Noah should have been with his family, not crashing on my couch.

He looked me in the eye, and when he spoke, he lowered his voice. "When they took you, it happened so fast. I tried to tell them what happened to Rosa wasn't you, but they—"

I squeezed his shoulder. "We have more pressing matters."

Anna picked up a slip of a little black dress from a chair arm and raised her eyebrow.

Noah blushed. "Er, that's erm... that had nothing to do with me. Some people stayed here months back, and I... it was... I didn't have anywhere else to go." He sighed and ran trembling fingers through his hair. "You're not pissed?"

A smile touched my lips. I patted him on the back. "It's good to see you."

He gulped, but concern and guilt tightened his smile into a grimace. Two years had passed, I reminded myself. Much had happened. We all had regrets.

In the kitchen, I opened a few cupboards and found them sparse. We had seen market stalls on the way into Hollywood. The military was allowing supply vehicles through the roadblocks to keep the city functioning, but prices had crept up. LA was barely clinging on by its fingernails.

"Is this cocaine?" Christian asked. He knelt next to the coffee table beside the window and pushed around the dregs of some white powder.

"That's not mine," Noah immediately denied. "I found it. Erm..."

All eyes turned accusingly to me. "I'm demon." I dug out a

dusty bottle of bourbon and a glass. "It's the bodies in the basement you should be concerned with."

Christian's rifle rattled.

"He's joking," Anna said. "I think he's joking. You're joking, right?"

"Yeah," Noah offhandedly replied for me, but his tone had an unfortunate question behind it. "Yeah. I've been down there. There aren't any bodies."

The quiet got awkward, especially considering the last time I'd set foot inside my restaurant I'd been accused of murder.

I smiled to myself, poured the last of the bourbon, and lifted it to my lips. All three watched me, one frowning, one about to shoot, and the other eyeing me as though I might vanish at any second. Entertainment would be scarce over the next few days and weeks. Playing with these three would do nicely.

"You'll be staying here while we search for the source of recent events," I told them, leaving no room for discussion. "There is one main entrance that can be easily fortified, and a fire escape that is quite secure. You'll be safe here." More muted silence. "Unless you all have somewhere better to be?"

"No. This is good," Noah agreed.

Anna nodded, and Christian glared.

"That's decided, then. Get yourselves and this place cleaned up." I set the glass down on the counter. "You're all hungry. I'll be back shortly with sustenance." At that, I snapped out of my human vessel into smoke and mist and funneled through the air vents, all pretenses of being human going up in smoke.

From above, LA lay wounded, its once throbbing heart barely ticking under the midday sun. Few cars used the roads, and fewer people walked the streets. The city would not survive for long. I reached through the air, feeling far and wide, touching fear, hunger, and anger. There were demons here too. Their dens had turned the air rancid. But they were all lessers. That was good. If we could stop this before the higher demons came, LA might quickly recover. I reached farther, seeking anything unusual or out of place.

The veil beat down alongside the midday heat, distorting my elemental feedback and distracting my mind. The nether-world. Home. So close.

No. My *old* home.

LA was home now.

The Dark Court and its princes were beyond the veil. How many had survived the Fall? Most had perished, hadn't they? The king had survived. He always did in some form or another. The queen was a chaos girl trapped and driven mad by her element. Those two must exist beyond the veil for it to still be intact. Without them, the veil would have fallen. But we did not have a Queen of Chaos or a King of Control on this side of the veil. Humans barely knew about the elements, yet they believed they could harness the veil and siphon its power? Human beings couldn't touch the veil. They did not exist on the same plane as the elements. Only elemental demons could draw from it. That was the way it had always been. But something had changed. I needed to find out what, to find the source, the beginning.

There could be no end without the beginning.

With my airborne search proving fruitless, I poured myself back into my vessel, purchased supplies and a dispos-able phone from a nervous market stall attendant, and put in a crackly call to an old friend.

Upon returning to my apartment, I found the mess cleaned up enough to move around freely. After handing over the supplies, I left the humans to refuel and entered the bedroom, closing the door quietly behind me.

Reaching under the bed, my fingers brushed the edges of

the wooden chest. Hauling it out, I set it down on the bed and breathed into the lock to flick it open. Forty-four feathers were nestled inside. I didn't need to count them. I knew their number the same as I knew my many names. The same way I knew there were other feathers out there, given to chosen individuals over the years. Tokens. Promises. Pieces of me.

I lifted one of the smaller feathers out, turned it over under the light, and checked the trailing edges for imperfections. Satisfied, I slipped it up my sleeve, closed the chest, and pushed it back under the bed.

When I returned to the living area, Anna was standing sentry at the windows overlooking the street outside, Noah was eating a home-made burrito made of nothing more than processed chicken and cheese, and my element told me Christian was lurking in one of the back bedrooms. Each was capable of looking after themselves and surviving, but we had to do more than survive. I had to make it right. Would any of them follow a demon?

"Noah, is the internet still accessible?" I asked.

He set the burrito down, and after wiping his hands on a towel, he dug his cell out of his rear pocket. "Yeah. It drops out sometimes. Same with the cell reception…"

"Good. Search for all the locations and dates of demon attacks. I want a timeline of the escalation." I handed over my newly purchased phone and quietly added, "Download the security footage from the restaurant cameras the night I was captured. Transfer it onto there and keep it safe."

He blinked and hesitated, keeping his gaze down.

"We still have the footage?" I asked.

"Yeah, I…" He scratched his unshaven cheek, his attention flicking to the windows. "I might have watched it a few times, I guess."

"Not just the capture. Save as much of that day as you can find."

He looked up and nodded, pressing his lips into a determined line. Whatever had caused his doubt wasn't there now.

Anna turned away from the window. "I can't wait around any longer. It's driving me crazy. Tell me you have a plan…"

More than one. "Are you still working with the police?" I asked her.

She frowned, her mouth twisting. "After the military took command, most of the department left before they could close the roads. I don't even know if there's a PD left. Nobody is answering their radios."

Then she was all-in with me. Good. I needed her focused, not running off at every call from her station. If we didn't act soon, there wouldn't be much left of LA to police. "You mentioned how lessers attacked public places?"

"Yes. The city zoo was the first."

"There's a reason they swarmed that location. When exactly did it happen?"

"I'm not sure. About six months ago. They planned on reopening, but I don't know if they did." Her gaze drifted along with her thoughts. "We could go take a look?"

"I'm coming with you," Christian announced, striding into the room from the rear hall.

"Neither of you are coming," I said, shutting him down. "I travel faster alone, and it will be dusk soon."

The hunter folded his arms and made a dismissive sound at the back of his throat. "You're just going to go off and do whatever you want?"

"That's generally what adults do."

Noah looked up from the phone I'd given him, dark eyebrow raised, likely wondering if Christian had bitten off more than he could chew. Shrugging, Noah took a bite of his burrito and got back to work. A fluttering muscle in Christian's cheek gave his frustration away. "We had a deal."

"I haven't forgotten our deal, demon hunter."

Noah spluttered, choking on his last mouthful of burrito. "Now I remember you! You're the soldier who caught Li'el! I saw you on the security footage." He huffed an incredulous laugh, the ironic kind, and shook his head, muttering, "You are one lucky son of a bitch."

Christian frowned at Noah. "We have a deal," he repeated, jabbing a finger at me while speaking to Noah. "One that demon won't wriggle out of."

Noah didn't rise to the bait. He stood and headed for the elevator. Under his breath, too lightly for anyone to hear but me, he muttered, "Jackass."

"I don't wriggle," I corrected Christian. "And you're welcome to try to stop me from leaving." I opened my arms, presenting a demon-shaped target for the rifle slung over his shoulder.

He opted to glower instead. "I don't trust you."

Clearly.

Sauntering after Noah, I added, "Help yourself to the cocaine. What's mine is yours, *demon hunter*." I purred the last words, adding a seductive lilt, and chuckled at his disgusted grunt.

CHAPTER 12

$\mathcal{T}$he Los Angeles Zoo sprawled over one hundred and thirty acres. It wouldn't take me long to sense something unusual if I filtered through the grounds as air, but on arriving, I noticed a small European car parked by the entrance, its engine running.

Anna was behind the wheel.

I remade myself into a man and took a few moments to ground myself in flesh. Traveling as air was my natural state, but every time I crafted my vessel, I expended energy I couldn't afford to use. How else was I supposed to get around? I was not designed to pack my magnificence into tiny vehicles.

Anna scanned the overgrown entrance, likely looking for me. I should have realized she wouldn't let me come alone. If I found anything of use, she would want to see the evidence herself. Christian wasn't the only one who didn't trust me.

"Did you leave the trigger-happy sidekick at home?" I asked as I stepped from the bushes.

She scowled through the window at my sudden appearance. I much preferred her smile. "How long were you hiding out in there?"

"Hiding out?" I snorted. "Girl, you have much to learn about me."

She blinked at my easy tone. The casual accent had thrown her off balance, as I'd known it would. The clothes threw her off too. I'd crafted jogging pants and a slim-fitting shirt. I knew exactly how I looked without having to read the surprise in her eyes. As I'd told her, everything I did was an art. That included how I looked and talked at any given second. None of it was a happy accident.

She climbed out of the car, still frowning. That wouldn't do.

"I just arrived," I admitted.

"Did you er... fly all this way?" she asked, falling into step beside me as we made for the entrance.

"Fly? Yes and no."

A few more steps, a few more seconds for her to consider her words. "Do you ever answer straight?"

"When you ask the right questions."

Police tape sealed off the entrance gate. Ramírez ducked under it and approached the chain binding the gates closed. "Do you have a key?" she asked, lips tilting up at the corner.

I took the padlock in my hand and blew into the keyhole. The lock fell open.

Her slightly raised eyebrow was a step up from her frown.

"One of my many, many talents," I explained.

"Uh-huh." She walked on ahead through the abandoned tollbooths and into the plaza. Trash and fallen branches cluttered the pathways. The power was off, leaving various vending machines and booths cold and dark. To our left, the path veered off toward the Sea Life Cliffs exhibit. Crickets chirped. Gulls called, and far in the distance, something howled. Not demon. Likely a dog.

Ramírez shrugged off her rifle. I considered telling her the most dangerous thing in the park was standing right behind her, then reconsidered those words.

"They moved all the animals on," she explained. "The ones that survived the attack."

"Animals were killed as well as people?"

"Yes." She glanced behind her. "Is that significant?"

"It could be. Do you know which animals were killed?" I drew up alongside her.

"No, not really. The news reports were all about the people, but there was mention of big cats being killed."

"Do you know where their enclosures are?"

"Sure." She smiled, and that curious flutter tickled me somewhere inside. "I used to come here a lot, you know... when I was little."

"You were a little girl? I don't believe it."

"It's true."

"Next you'll tell me you had dolls and played dress-up."

"Kinda. My sisters did the dressing up. We played cops and robbers."

"Ah."

"I always got the bad guy."

I did not doubt that. We walked on, passing through the abandoned elephant enclosure. Many fences had fallen or been pulled over. Claw marks on some of the enclosure walls didn't go unnoticed by either of us. Anna tightened her grip on her gun.

Daylight had faded to a warm orange hue as the tiger enclosure came into view. Much of the fence was buckled and bowed. A section had been completely torn away, the links severed by claws sharper than those belonging to the enclosure's former resident. The information board proclaimed the enclosure had been home to a four-year-old Sumatran tiger.

I leaned against the concrete barrier and counted at least fifteen pairs of claw marks breaching the walls. Lessers had gotten in and out. But a young tiger in its prime would have been a challenge for lesser demons to take down. Why had they attacked this animal?

"Do you remember if any other animals were killed?" I asked.

"The elephants, I think. There may have been others, but the reports were chaotic." Her gaze drifted down to where dark stains had been baked into the pathway.

"And this was the first attack?" I asked, keeping her thoughts on track.

"That I'm aware of."

"Wait here…" I vaulted over the concrete wall and landed inside the enclosure in a crouch. The air carried a mixture of smells to me. The pungent odor of a big cat and the equally overpowering smell of lesser demon, but something else inside all that was difficult to separate. I straightened and passed through long grass to where blood and fur lay crusted in the mud. Much of the tiger's body was gone, either removed or decomposed. Its lower jaw lay in the grass. Crouching, I picked up the bone and examined it. The bone was smooth, no signs of any breaks or fractures. Something had torn it out. A lucky strike by a lesser, perhaps. Or by something bigger, with far more strength and coordination?

"Li'el…?"

Straightening, I turned to see Anna leaning over the wall.

"What is that?" she called.

High in the tree behind her, demon eyes glowed through the foliage. Instinctively, I reached outward with my element, swirling air through the branches to get a feel for what was watching Anna, but the air current rustled the leaves.

Anna turned.

Fear jolted through her. She lifted the rifle with a shout.

The lesser leaped, jaws wide.

I reached for the air it breathed, but the beast had too much momentum. It slammed into Anna, jaws closing around her throat, going straight for the kill. Part mist, I spilled into the air between them, wrapped my grip around the beast's upper jaw, and yanked, pulling both it and Anna against me. Claws dug into my side and dragged downward. Pain flared and was just as quickly extinguished. As long as I was between the lesser and Anna, she was safe. My vessel could be rebuilt. Hers couldn't.

I twisted, slipping free of flesh and turning fully into air, and yanked the lesser back, away from Anna. It clawed and screeched and writhed, teeth flashing and gnawing against my hold. I flung it aside and whirled. Anna had stumbled against the wall. She was fine. Shaken, but—

Another lesser sprang out of the undergrowth, a *scorsi*— part hominid, part scorpion—accompanied by a deafening hiss. It arched its stinger high. I poured all of myself into the space between the demons and revealed my true demon form, damaged wings spread wide. Agony snapped across my back. I shunned it and bore down on the scorsi.

A warning growl rumbled through my chest. *Mine.* The scorsi shuddered. Its rattling scales hissed louder. *Back down.*

Gunfire raked the bushes, and a quick glance revealed why. The flora writhed with lesser bodies. So many. Too many.

"Run," I barked at Anna. "Go, now!"

"I'm not leaving you." She swept her rifle in an arc but didn't fire. The lessers held back.

Foolish human. "Go, Anna. I'll distract them."

Anna's glare locked on mine. "I'm not leaving you again."

Why, when she had been so keen to see me captured before?

Whatever her reasons, it didn't matter. I was immortal. Whatever they did to me, I would heal. She was fragile and precious. There was just one Marianna Ramírez, one of her among billions of people. I couldn't protect her from all the lessers. One might get through. She could get hurt or worse. Already, blood soaked her shirt, but there was fire in her eyes.

Stubborn human.

The lessers surged forward. Anna fired her gun. And then all around there was a volley of beasts, all clawing, snapping, charging.

"Go," I hissed, seeing an opening.

Anna darted through, but the lessers spilled in, blocking my line of sight. With a snarl, I reached into their bodies and yanked out the air from inside them. They stumbled and collapsed. I sailed on through, down the path to where I expected to find Anna. She wasn't there.

Lessers howled into the dusk.

No, no… She had to be here.

A lesser landed on my wing. I whirled and roared into the wave, blasting them back. Wings spread, I presented all of me, filling the path and blocking the way.

"You want me?" Arms spread, I summoned my element, yanking the air down from above and mixing it with LA's warmth, stirring up a storm. "Here I am."

A surge of air tore up the pathways, bowing trees and rattling abandoned cages. It scooped up the lessers and swept them back on themselves, and with one final push, they washed over the side of the tiger enclosure.

A horn honked, and a car engine revved.

The wind settled. I turned to see Anna's car plow through the barrier and skid into a turn. It rocked to a halt. "Get in!"

Get in? Was she insane? I flicked out my wings, frowned, and thumbed over my shoulder. "You do see these?"

"Li'el, get in this car right now. Don't make me shoot you."

"Baby, I don't do cars."

She narrowed her eyes. "Look behind you."

I did. Lessers. The paths, the borders, the bushes, the trees. Demon glares everywhere. I wasn't strong enough to fight them all. I would survive, but they would hunt Anna down.

But a car?

"Li'el! Move!"

In a blink, I'd funneled in through the window and into the front passenger seat, turning my wings to air to avoid the logistics of packing them into the tiny vehicle.

Anna planted her foot on the throttle, spun the car around, and launched it out of the plaza, leaving the zoo and the lessers far behind.

I slumped in the seat and pinched the bridge of my nose. The engine rumbled, the metal shell rattled, and outside, the almost empty city blurred by.

"You okay?" she finally asked in a quiet voice.

"Am I okay?" I wanted to spread my wings, to turn to air, to leave the car and sail through the air. No, I was not okay. "I'm fine." Opening my eyes, I looked at her, and didn't acknowledge how we were hurtling along the road in a steel trap. Her hair was a knotted mass of darkness strewn about her shoulders. Her cheeks were pale, lips touched with pink, and her eyes were a startling blue. Cuts dashed her chin and several deep gashes raked over her collarbone. "Are you hurt?"

"I'm… No, I'm okay." She glared ahead. "Was that normal? All those lessers there like that?"

"No, not at all normal." Her grazed knuckles turned white

as she gripped the steering wheel. "Are you sure you're okay?"

"Yes." And then more firmly, "Yes, I'm okay. We got out."

"Yes, we did."

Finally, she glanced over and then flung her glare back to the road ahead. She waved a hand in my general direction. "Can you er... can you do anything about that?"

I looked down. "About what?"

"You're er... you're naked. It's... I mean, you know, it's... you're..."

"Socially unacceptable. Yes, I realize that, but I did just wrangle several hundred lesser demons, and now I'm riding in a car, which is on my short list of things I don't like, right up there with campfires, so if you don't mind, while I concentrate on not filling this tiny car with my wings, you can either admire my nakedness or ignore it."

A moment passed, and then she snorted the laugh she'd been holding in. "We survived."

I smiled, dropped my head back, and thought, *No demon will ever hurt you, Anna Ramírez.*

CHAPTER 13

"*T*hey attacked. I've never seen anything like it," Anna was saying. Her voice carried to me as I "rested" out of sight in the bedroom. It wasn't eavesdropping if I had no choice but to hear—words carried astonishingly far on air. "Not since the Fall. There were so many, and Li'el... he was..." Chips crunched and a bag rustled.

"Was what?" Noah asked around a mouthful of food.

"He was everywhere. I couldn't keep track of him. When he's like that, all demon, it's like I can't understand what I'm seeing, you know? But he stopped them. He drove them back. I... He was light and air and..." She laughed the kind of feminine laugh I hadn't been sure she was capable of. "It's really hard to explain."

"Sounds awesome," Noah said. Awesome was surely too small a word for me. Magnificent, glorious, resplendent— those were adjectives I could get behind.

"The first time I saw him, yah know... the wings and *him*... was when he got caught. I knew what he was, but to see it—"

"It wouldn't have been awesome had Anna died, which

103

was a real possibility," I said, striding in from the bedroom. Unable to summon enough power to materialize clothing, I'd taken a fresh pair of jeans and sweatshirt from a closet and dressed like a human would. A ridiculously complicated process when one was accustomed to cladding one's vessel with a single thought.

"I was about to say the same." Christian emerged from the back hallway, timing his arrival perfectly with mine. The hunter had probably been waiting for me to emerge. "She could have died." And clearly that was my fault, seeing as I was the only demon in the room. Never mind that Anna had decided to meet me outside the zoo.

I tossed the tiger's jawbone on the table in front of Noah. It skidded across the polished surface and bumped against his glass of water. "What does a lion do when it sees off a rival male and claims the pride for itself?"

Noah swallowed. "Did that belong to a lion?"

"He kills the males in the pride." Christian stopped behind the couch, placing himself behind Anna and Noah in a position of power. They were looking at the bone and didn't notice Christian fold his arms and rake me over with one of his holier-than-thou challenging gazes. It was possible he wasn't conscious of his body language, but the protective posture was a clear warning. If this hunter had been demon, his wings would have been embarrassingly small and hardly worth mentioning.

I strode to the windows, showing Christian my back. Two could play the posturing game. Humans weren't as far removed from demons as many assumed, especially human males. There was a dance here, one of strength and non-verbal warnings. It was pathetic that he believed he could compare with me in any way.

"It's not a lion's jaw," I replied. "It belonged to a four-year-old male tiger. The lion, in this analogy, ate the tiger."

"Wait, there's something out there that's... bigger?" Noah asked.

I let that question fall unanswered. LA barely glistened beyond the glass, where once the city had dazzled. There was enough of my city left to save, but what if I couldn't? As Christian had once rightly pointed out, I was not the demon I had once been despite the posturing.

"The lessers were either driven to the zoo or compelled to go there," I said, admiring the sprinkling of lights. "When lessers gather to that extent, it's usually from a surplus of chaos energy. Unfortunately, we didn't have enough time to investigate the grounds, but I didn't detect any rogue chaos element." That kind of power would have been difficult for me to miss, even in my reduced state. But I also hadn't noticed the lessers until it was too late. An unacceptable mistake.

"You're saying there's a bigger demon out there?" Anna asked.

"It's possible."

"If it's going after rivals, why hasn't it attacked you?"

"Have you forgotten where I was for the last two years?" I turned in time to catch Christian's incensed nostril flare and Anna's flash of guilt. "Until recently, I was concealed inside a box with my element suffocated by a barrier of glyphs. The demon couldn't detect me, the same way I couldn't sense the shift in the veil. You benched me, taking me out of the game entirely."

Noah leaned away from Christian and toward me. "Wait, so... it'll come now?"

"Perhaps. But this behavior, killing wild animals, is not normal. If a higher demon breached the veil—"

"A what?" Noah asked.

"A prince, for example."

His face paled.

"Killing caged animals is very… unprincelike. And the princes don't often act alone, not when the stakes are this high."

"I thought they were all solitary hunters?" Anna asked, checking over her shoulder with our resident demon hunter because he knew more about demon princes than the prince standing a few feet in front of her.

"They are," Christian confirmed. "Unless it suits them to combine forces. That's why they waited until the veil fell before coming through in force. They're higher demons because they're capable of complex strategic planning. They're also very capable of getting along when they all want the same thing. After they have it, they go back to trying to slaughter each other."

"Just so." Christian had paid attention in hunter school. "The lessers I killed were all fresh from the netherworld." The wounds they had inflicted still smarted. "It takes a concentration of chaos energy or a higher demon to organize them that way. Since we don't have a surplus of chaos, we have to assume they're gathering at the command of another demon."

"Can't you, you know…" Noah waved a hand, suggesting I should somehow be able to pluck answers out of the air. "Do your thing and find this bigger demon?"

"I've been doing my thing. There are no higher demons in LA."

"Unless it's shielded like you were," Anna said.

I nodded. "But unlikely. No demon likes to be caged."

"Aren't you a higher demon?" Christian asked rhetorically.

"It's been a while since I checked."

He leered like he'd gotten one up on me. "Wouldn't that make *you* the prime suspect?"

"It would." I paused, adding a few seconds of silence for

dramatic effect. There's an art to silences too. "Do I look as though I enjoy wrestling tigers and collecting lesser demons in my spare time? There's also the fact you had me neatly packaged in a plastic box while the lessers first attacked. You, Christian, are my alibi." His face fell like I'd taken away his favorite toy. "Sorry to disappoint," I drawled.

"Maybe one less demon in LA would be a start," he suggested.

"You tried that," Anna snapped, "and all you did was take our best defense against the demons out of play. If Li'el had been around when all this started, he could have stopped it."

The hunter laughed. "Don't let him fool you. You think that when he wipes all the demons off the city map he'll just sit back and give us LA back? Look at him."

I spread my arms. "Please do."

"He wants this city. For all we know, his presence is attracting this other demon. He could have started it!"

"If there is another demon," I reminded him. "And you're right. I do want this city. But what use is a war zone? I've been there, and it didn't work out. If you spent as much energy searching for the source of these attacks as you did trying to turn me into your killer, you may actually be useful to us."

"I don't need to turn you into a killer when you already are one." He glared, waiting for me to deny it. He failed to understand I had never denied or hidden what I was. "You almost got Ramírez killed—"

"Are you done?" Anna interrupted.

"I told you this was a bad idea, and I stand by that. I'm here to put him down when the time comes, and that time will come."

I smiled at my hunter's outburst. "I do hope so."

He shook off the combined stares of Noah and Anna and retreated to the kitchen where various glasses and plates felt the hunter's wrath. Such a wasted opportunity. He'd be good at his job if he could get past his prejudices.

With Christian attacking the cutlery and Noah examining the tiger's jaw, Anna approached me and asked, "How does this help with the veil?"

"According to Noah's timeline, the attacks became more common right until the veil started to crumble, and then they stopped. It's not much, but at this point, all we can do is assume the attacks and the appearance of the veil are connected."

"What does it take to weaken the veil exactly?"

"An imbalance in the elements. The last Fall originated in the netherworld when those elements were grossly swayed toward chaos. When chaos reigns, the veil falls. That's how it's always been."

"But how? What unbalanced chaos to begin with?"

I hesitated. The answer wasn't simple, and it cut close to home. "The princes killed the demon queen—the chaos queen—unleashing chaos in the netherworld." I remembered it well. With demon civilisation built on a survival of the fittest mentality, killing the queen had been our greatest achievement and worst mistake. It had been glorious and terrible and wonderful, and everything I despised about my kin—about myself. Power corrupted in both worlds, demons just took corruption to a whole new level.

Anna must have seen some of those thoughts on my face. She quietly asked, "Did *you* help kill her?"

"I remember it well." I kept my expression level. Smirking while discussing murder was something Ramírez didn't react well to.

"Why?" she asked. "Why did you kill her?"

"It seemed like a good idea at the time. She died. The princes split her power. Win-win if you happened to be an upstanding member of the Dark Court."

"Only it didn't happen like that, did it?"

I remembered the flood of strength spilling into my veins and being able to stretch my senses far throughout the netherworld. I had been air and everywhere, in everything. I had known all, felt all, heard all.

"The power was divine," I whispered in reverence, careful to keep the others from hearing. "It didn't last. The king objected to having his queen slaughtered. He doled out punishments, and with chaos unleashed, the netherworld went to hell soon after. It's been dying ever since. Then, during the last Fall, another queen was..." How to describe the Mad Queen's forced ascension? "Well, the king *found* another queen. The veil was put right. And humans and demons all lived happily ever after." *Until humans screwed it up again.*

She paused and considered the irony dripping from my tone. "You talk like you're not a prince, but Christian said you were the Prince of Pride."

Oh, Christian and his unsurpassed demon knowledge. "He believes he knows me. He is mistaken." I hesitated in saying more. It was one thing to think of how far I had fallen, but quite another to admit it. I had told Anna enough.

She fell quiet and admired the subdued city alongside me. As an expert in silences, I knew this one was soft, undemanding, and didn't need to be filled.

"It's dark out. We should close the blinds and turn the lights out. Get some rest," she told the others. "We'll approach this fresh tomorrow."

They retired to their rooms, Christian tossing me one last look that said he'd be sleeping with one eye open. I might have delighted in haunting his room if talk of the old queen hadn't doused my mood.

Rest. Yes. They would need it. I, on the other hand, had another flight ahead of me.

Once my humans were secured in their rooms, I took to the air and spread through LA, stretching farther and wider, seeking any sign of another higher demon in my city. As I sailed on the breeze, the conversation with Anna played over in my mind. Over two years ago, the veil had fallen when the princes had disrupted the chaos elements. The same had happened here, but could the cause be human? I needed to find out. Christian had worked for the Institute and the military. It was time he and I had a heart to heart, apex demon to demon hunter.

CHAPTER 14

Subdued morning air had crept over the roof when I pulled myself back into the illusion of a man and approached Christian. He stood three feet from the roof edge, rifle slung over his shoulder, his back to me as he observed the street below.

It would have been simple to push him off the edge, but where was the art in such a clumsy kill?

"Careful—" He jumped at the sound of my voice. I caught his shoulder before he could do something foolish like trip over the lip and plummet to his death by accident. He stumbled and whirled. "Wouldn't want to fall."

"Fuck!" He reached for his rifle but paused when he realized I could have killed him and hadn't. "Fuck," he muttered again, shaking the shock out of his hands.

I leaned out over the edge. "You would have made a terrible mess."

"Why didn't you?" he snarled.

I rolled my eyes. This again. "Come inside. You and I need to talk."

He followed me in through the fire escape to the back of my apartment. It was early. My element informed me, by the pitch and pace of their breathing, that Noah and Ramírez still slept. I led Christian into the elevator and soaked up the prickly silence as we rode down to the restaurant level. The doors opened, and a memory flashed of the hunter standing over me.

"Sit," I told him at the bar. He considered arguing, but common sense prevailed, and he slid onto a bar stool. "What's your poison?"

"I'll take a whiskey. Make it the best you have back there."

He set the rifle down on the bar, within his reach, while I dusted off two glasses and a bottle of fine whiskey. He watched me pour two glasses, set the bottle aside, and push his drink toward him.

Lifting my glass, I saluted him. "To enemies. May they keep us honed and true."

He arched a brow but went along with it and downed his whiskey in one. The kick hit him, and he spluttered, but he offered up his glass for a refill. I obliged. We could get along like civilized males.

"I'm not buying it," he said, scratching his chin.

"Buying what?"

"You." He swept a hand at me, and I assumed he was referring to my general appearance, currently wrapped in dress pants and a V-neck sweater. "The whole *normal* act. I know what you're doing."

"Perhaps you can enlighten me?"

"Noah idolizes you. Probably has Stockholm syndrome since he's worked for you for so long." He took a generous gulp of his drink. "Ramírez is smarter than that, but after the zoo, there's something…" He pointed a me. "Something happened, and now she's warming up to you. But you

112

already know this because you're playing them both like guitars."

"Fiddles."

"What?"

"Never mind. What's *your* interest in Ramírez?" I hadn't planned to discuss our four-person group, but with Christian so enamored with me playing the bad demon mastermind, I decided to play along.

"Me and Ramírez? Nothing," he replied firmly. "She came to me. I helped her out. That's it."

His downturned gaze told me he wasn't, but if he wanted to lie to himself, that wasn't my problem. "You've often been right during your life…"

"Sometimes. Most times," he agreed. "And when it comes to demons, I'm always right."

Well now, there was a challenge if ever I'd heard one. "So, what happened? What made you Christian the demon hunter?"

"I suppose you would have to ask since you don't experience life like humans do."

Only about 3.4 million lives I'd encountered, loved, lost, admired, feared, hated, misunderstood, and more, but sure, whatever Christian said, because naturally, he was right, being the demon hunter and all.

"Pops fucked off before I can remember him. Later I figured he was in jail. Ma raised me and my brothers to be upstanding American citizens. Daniel, my youngest brother, died of an overdose at sixteen. Right after that I went into the military. I know what it's like to lose someone. I wanted to protect people. Protect America. Do the right thing. I was young and stupid."

Was?

"It toughened me up. And I was damn good at it."

"Joining the forces had nothing to do with the desire to kill to feed your hero complex?"

That earned me a burning scowl. "You wouldn't understand. I don't even know why I'm wasting my time talking to you. Your demon brain can't wrap itself around human values."

"And you know that because you know everything about demons."

"Damn straight."

I downed my drink in one. The alcohol wouldn't affect me the same way it would him, but the warmth briefly combated the heated beat from my phantom wings. "Who taught you everything you know about demons? Was it the Institute?"

"I started there, sure. Bagged and tagged a few hundred demons until the veil fell and it all went to shit. Then, I got recruited somewhere else."

"By the elite military team you mentioned?"

He shifted on his stool and chuckled a dry laugh. "See, it won't work on me. You sweeten me up and then ease in a few subtle questions, and before I know it, I'm telling you everything you want to know? I don't think so."

"Or I could be trying to help like you wanted me to. Like our bargain suggests."

"The bargain is a joke, and we both know it."

"I keep my word."

"Of course you do. Whatever." He finished his third glass. I poured another. "Why did you bring me down here?"

"To ask you about the military outfit you worked for so I can determine where and when this all began. It's difficult to get a grip on events when you sealed me away for much of it."

"We should have put you down the second we captured you..." He scanned the abandoned restaurant floor. "Right over there, wasn't it? A bullet to the head. PC-Eighty in your veins. You wouldn't get up from that. Not if I had my way. Boom, dead demon. It would have been a nice demonstration to all those idiots clinging to your reputation like you were a god. You're a killer, a predator. You can dress in human clothes all you like and talk like you're an English movie star, but you'll always be a demon underneath it all."

I gently set my glass down.

"It was my job to do it," he went on. "I could have. Could have pinned you under my boot and added you to my kill count. Maybe I'd have taken those wings of yours and hung them on my wall like a fuckin' trophy—"

I moved in a blur. Solid one moment, air the next, and solid again with my hand around his throat, forcing him down over the bar. His arm flailed, knocking his glass to the ground. It shattered into pieces on the floor beside me. He scrabbled for his gun.

I leaned in, using my entire body to pin him down, and bowed my head so my lips touched his cheek. I could breathe in and steal the air from his lungs. He would never talk again.

"Let's get something perfectly clear," I whispered across his rough skin. Threats were often more dangerous when issued with perfect restraint. "I am a patient demon, probably the most patient of demons. My kin would have punched your heart through your chest and made you eat it long before now. Fortunately for you, I'm not like them. However, you need to understand this, *hunter*. My patience is great, but it is not infinite."

His breaths came faster. Blood pumped hard, flushing his body with the strength it needed to fight. But he wouldn't fight, he knew I had my prey trapped under my claws. Not so stupid now. Fighting would get him killed.

"You caught me because I allowed it. You walk freely because I allow it. You're alive because I haven't killed you.

It's really quite simple. I am the predator here, and you are my bitch." I ran my tongue along his jaw and up his cheek, careful to make it slow, drawing out every shudder and pant. Tasting the heady mix of sweat, whiskey, and fear inspired the best and the worst of me. Instincts clamored. *Mine.* "There's a good boy."

"Li'el?"

Ramírez stood in the elevator car, the open doors affording her an uninterrupted view of me hunched over Christian. From her vantage point, it likely appeared as though I'd been about to eat the hunter alive. Which was, in fact, accurate. She wasn't armed, but she'd reached for where her sidearm had once been.

I freed Christian. He sprang for his gun. I snatched it up, snapped the rifle in half, and shoved the pieces into his chest. He stumbled backward. "The words you're looking for are, *Thank you, Li'el, for you are indeed the most patient and reasonable demon I have ever met. My life is in your debt.* Now you try it."

"F-fuck you!" He stumbled, almost falling over a table, and staggered toward Ramírez. "You see… You see what he is? He could have… Jesus, he could have…" He rubbed his face where I'd licked him and hurried into the elevator car. Anna followed him moments later. I didn't need to look to know she wore disgust on her face.

The elevator doors rumbled closed.

"In that analogy," I told the empty room, "I was the lion."

~

ANNA HAD PUSHED her bed away from the windows and set up a watch point over the street outside. She glanced at her rifle, resting against the wall, the moment I stepped inside.

She believed her gun could stop me should I turn on her. I had no intention of ruining that fantasy.

Words were balanced on her tongue. Accusations too, probably, but she kept them to herself and turned back to the window. From our vantage point, LA looked untouched, basking in the sunlight, until one looked closer and saw that the streets were devoid of people and cars. Above, virtually invisible behind the sunlight, the veil rippled.

"I feel like we're all trapped here. Like the world forgot about us and left here for whatever might come through the veil." She looked to me for answers. When I offered none, she asked, "You keep saying you're different, but why should I believe you?"

"You shouldn't." I stopped beside her. Movement on the street caught my eye. A solitary dog snuffled down the sidewalk. Someone's pet, lost or abandoned.

Anna's lips turned down. "That doesn't help." She shook her head and faced LA once more. "He was just following orders. Don't hate him."

"Christian is one man. I've met many far worthier of hate." She rolled her eyes at my evasive answer. "I went into that conversation with the best of intentions."

"Unless your intentions were to terrify him, I doubt you succeeded."

"Perfection takes a degree of trial and error."

"Perfection, huh?" She arched an eyebrow. "I think you have a ways to go."

I leaned a shoulder against the glass and studied Anna. She peeked at me from the corner of her eye but kept her gaze ahead. She didn't fear me. She didn't hate me, either. She seemed comfortable with me standing beside her, and I found myself content to be next to her.

I still had the feather I'd selected from the others. This would make a fine moment to hand it to her, but I hesitated, thoughts tripping over oddly placed doubts and concerns. What if she wouldn't take it, and why did her response even matter to me? I brushed off the strange insecurities. "Christian will not speak with me, but he will with you. Ask him about the military outfit he worked for. Find out where they were based. I want to get to the root of our current situation, and we have little time."

She nodded. "I will. He just needs some time alone."

"All I did was lick him. Where I come from, that's foreplay."

"You traumatized him."

"He shouldn't have insulted me."

She studied me the same way I had studied her. Having her gaze roam over my vessel in such a slow, deliberate manner sent a delightful thrill through me. I wanted to strip down the feeling and study it until I understood why this woman's glances and words entranced me and muddled my thoughts. I wanted more of her looks, more of her words, more of her, but not in the way I usually sought out the company of humans. This was different in ways I had rarely experienced before.

"I almost wish I could meet another demon," she said. "Just so I can see how different you claim to be."

"No, you don't." Any other demon would have killed her and Christian as soon as they became liabilities. That thought soured my mood, reminding me how fragile human lives were. Perhaps now was the right time to offer her the feather? If she kept the feather close, I would always know where she was. I could find her, help her. *Mine*.

I had felt these curious emotions before. I knew these feelings for what they were, and no good could come of them.

"Is everything okay?" she asked, facing me.

I smiled, masking the crack in my expression. "Of course."

Noah leaned into the room. "There's a guy downstairs knocking on the shutters. Should I let him in?"

I reached out with my element and recognized the newcomer. "Yes. We'll be right there."

Noah disappeared while Anna continued to read through my carefully constructed exterior. She probably wasn't aware how her gaze stripped me bare. Or maybe she was, and that made her as cool and calculating as me. What did she see when she looked at me? A demon pretending to be a man, or a demon who had learned what it meant to be human?

The feather would have to wait. I started for the door.

"Li'el...?"

I paused. "Yes?"

She swallowed her first words, then pushed away from the window. "I'm coming with you."

The elevator carried us silently to the ground floor and opened on Noah and my guest. I approached, instinctively keeping Anna a step behind. Demons and humans alike had reason to be wary around our newcomer.

He had filled out since I had last seen him in Boston, but he still commanded a formidable presence, like he threw off his own gravity. He turned away from Noah and smiled his typical friendly smile.

"Li'el," Adam Harper greeted. "I was surprised to hear from you."

I offered my hand, expecting him to hesitate. He didn't. Instead, he closed his hand around mine, giving it a firm shake.

"Anna, Noah, this is Adam Harper," I introduced. "He's an Institute specialist." They exchanged puzzled expressions. "He's here to help."

Noah escorted Adam into the elevator as they discussed the flight over from the east coast.

Anna hung back. "You brought in another demon hunter?"

How to describe Adam Harper? He was more of a general than a hunter. At one time, he might have been Christian's superior.

Anna caught my wayward smile before I could mask it. "What are you up to?"

"Just fulfilling my end of the deal."

CHAPTER 15

*N*oah, Anna, Christian, and Adam Harper were positioned around a coffee table, chairs pulled in close, with an array of city maps, official-looking documents, and news articles spread in front of them.

I deliberately hung back, reining in my element to hide my presence from their senses. My participation would only distract them. They discussed the veil, the moment it became visible, the events leading up to it, the attacks, and more. Adam asked all the right questions. He kept the group on track and focused their efforts in a way I could not emulate. These people knew I was demon. Every word I said, every move I made, they had been trained to distrust. Our odd group needed Adam Harper's people skills and experience inside the Institute.

"Li'el." Adam lifted his head. "Looking at all the evidence, it appears there are several possible sources and a number of leads worth following, including the offices of the energy firm quoted in several press releases. I suggest we split up and investigate. Would you agree?"

Christian spoke before I could reply. "Anna and I will take the EcoZone offices—"

"I'll investigate EcoZone," I interrupted.

Christian bristled. "Alone?"

"I can look after myself."

"And how are we supposed to trust the information you return with?"

"Because I'm helping you."

"Helping me?!"

"Christian," Adam barked in a voice familiar with issuing commands. "Trust Li'el or walk out the door right now. The veil is weakening. Demons will come. It's those demons you need to worry about, not the one on our side."

Annoyance flared in Christian's eyes. "And how does a pencil pusher like you know anything about demons in the real world?"

Adam leveled his stare on the hunter. "I've worked with demons my entire life. I spearheaded a classified Institute program to create, raise, and train half-blood soldiers. I've bargained with higher demons. There are few people who know more about demon-kind than I do."

"I worked at the Institute too. They were all accountants playing at being scientists. It was a joke."

Adam removed his glasses and wiped them with the edge of his shirt. "I have a half-demon son and a half-demon daughter. You may have heard of them. Projects Alpha and Gamma, also known as Stefan Harper and..." He stalled, likely still getting used to the idea of Gem as his daughter. "Gemma Harper."

Christian stilled, mouth open, grasping for a reply. "*You* spearheaded Project Typhon?"

Anna leaned in. "The half-blood girl is your daughter? Is she okay?"

"She's doing fine." Adam caught my eye, nodded once,

replaced his glasses, and continued, his crowd more rapt now that they knew his credentials. "This doesn't feel like the kind of coordinated attack Boston experienced," he said. "Official reports around the time the lesser attacks escalated are unclear on where they came from. Most of LA's nether-world zones collapsed months ago, so it was assumed by the Institute that the lessers must have survived the Santa Monica incident, but you only have to examine the photographs to know these lessers are stronger, hence the amount of damage they inflicted in such a short time. There's no doubt they came from beyond the veil, but as to why or how, we don't know. It could be demon coordinated, but if that were the case, events would have escalated by now."

"How much more can they escalate?" Noah asked.

"Higher demons—princes—on this side, cultivating chaos. That hasn't happened. Let's hope it doesn't. I believe there's another force at work here, possibly related to the rumors of EcoZone harnessing the veil for clean energy, but at this stage, it's pure speculation. Whatever happened, it appears to have stalled. We hopefully have time to find the fault and stop whatever is causing the imbalance before the damage becomes irreversible."

My opinion of Adam Harper aside, he was good at his job. He looked at me, waiting for my input. There was a time when he would have gladly driven a stake through my heart and filled me full of whatever new drug the Institute had concocted. He and I were enemies, but Adam Harper had lost loved ones in the war against demons. His ambitions at the Institute had cost many lives, some of them deliberate sacri-fices in his desire to *win*. Now, he was trying to make amends. This trip to LA was an opportunity for him to prove he could do more than screw up the lives of those around him in the name of his beloved science.

I nodded for him to continue.

"Li'el will take the EcoZone office," he confirmed. "Anna and Christian should visit here." He jabbed the street map. "The site of the second lesser attack. We suspect the lessers struck and killed what they saw as rival predators in LA, but let's expand that theory by visiting this site too."

"Where is that?" I asked.

"Marina del Rey."

"There aren't many predators at marinas," I thought aloud. "Unless the lessers considered Sunseeker yachts a threat."

Adam agreed with a nod. "Which is why we need to investigate. There's a reason they swarmed the marina. Noah and I will stay here and search for more evidence of demon activity."

Following the attack, the zoo remained a hot zone of lesser activity. I didn't want Anna walking into another ambush. "I'll take the marina."

"Then I'm going to the offices, right?" Christian queried, happier now that he felt he had his finger on the root of the problem.

"Try not to get a paper cut. Anna, you can come with me or go with Christian to EcoZone."

Naturally, she would choose me.

"I'll go with Christian."

Or not. She clearly had to make sure Christian was up to the task. What other reason could she had to choose him? The hunter's expression warmed at her choice.

"Be careful," I warned. "We don't know how many lessers are out there." I hadn't detected the first swarm at the zoo, and my reach was thinning with each passing night. We were virtually blind.

"You too," Anna said. "We'll be back before dark. The lessers are worse after dusk." She smiled, though it was tinged with sadness, or was I reading too much into it? I couldn't read her the way I could others. Why was that?

I needed to focus on the task, not on Anna. Focus and ignore the thoughts that a demon of my caliber should not be having over a fragile human whose only interest in me was more akin to morbid fascination.

Damned humans and their distractions.

If I gave her my feather, it would keep her safe and keep me close, but she was already walking toward the exit with Christian. She would be fine without it. Of course she would. Her actions at the zoo had confirmed she was more than capable and didn't need me shadowing her. So why couldn't I fight the urge to turn to air and ghost after her?

"What's Project Typhon?" Noah asked Adam, drawing my attention away from Anna.

I wondered if Adam might stall there. He was protective of the Institute's work, but the man had changed. "We—the Institute, I mean," he began. "We wanted to raise a demon in captivity and control it, turn it into a weapon. To do that, we had to mix demon DNA with human DNA." Adam sighed, sounding regretful, but pride gleamed in his eye. His projects had been the man's crowning achievement. "Unfortunately, initial tests failed, and then... well..." He was likely thinking how his half-demon son had given in to his demon side, and how his daughter, Gem, would forever despise him for removing her ability to love. Yes, Adam had much to atone for. He would do everything he could for us. "The project was doomed from the beginning."

Noah quizzed him some more. While they talked and Anna and Christian readied to depart for EcoZone, I took to the roof, where I let my vessel dissolve and lifted the ragged bones of my wings high, under the warmth of the sun. Pain crackled. It never stopped hurting. Some wounds never healed. The sooner I fixed the veil, the sooner everything would go back to the way it was before. But not for me…

I stepped to the edge of the building. My pretend life was over. The act had been exposed. I could craft another life, but not yet. This city and its people, those still inside their homes, deserved to be saved. They had lost much, and I knew loss. I felt it every time the air touched my featherless wings, and I remembered it every time I recalled the deaths among the ashes of my past. *Human lives—so frustratingly short-lived.*

I stepped off the rooftop.

~

THE MARINA WATERS glistened under the sun. The sight would have been pristine if not for the masts of sunken boats protruding at odd angles from the water and the layers of bobbing trash.

I coalesced at the edge of a dock or tried to. Pulling all of me back into flesh, muscle, and bone proved more difficult every time I switched from solid to air. I clumsily rebuilt my demon form, grateful I was alone when I fell to a knee, wings draped low. For the longest handful of seconds, I knew only pain. I couldn't banish my wings, didn't have the energy, so I gritted my teeth and embraced the waves of heat. There was no other way through it.

I had always been able to heal most wounds, but not anymore. Healing took effort, switching forms took effort, and I'd once done these things without thinking about them.

I forced myself to look at the remains of my wings. Could I lose them entirely?

Boat rigging clanged nearby. I straightened and bunched my wings close against my back so the agony wasn't so intense. There was no need to craft my human vessel. By the amount of debris scattered around the pontoons, the marina had been abandoned for weeks.

I walked along the dock's edge. A rotting lesser carcass baked in the sun, a white mass of maggots writhing inside its remains. Twenty more had been left to decay. The remains were too decomposed for me to ascertain what had killed them.

Why had they swarmed here?

A smattering of boats remained afloat. Some bore claw gashes in their hulls, but a couple had survived the assault unscathed. Most yachts had been covered and abandoned. Clutter and trash had collected on and around those. But one boat, a superyacht named *Reely Nauti,* had its rigging pulled tight and the decks cleared.

If someone was living inside, they could have witnessed the lesser swarm. I probed my element inside first, finding it empty, and boarded along the gangplank. Beyond the normal signs of habitation—discarded blankets, water bottles, even a well-read copy of *Moby Dick*—nothing hinted at why lessers had swarmed here.

Outside, once more at the marina's edge, I watched the water lap serenely at the dockside wall. Between the gaps in the debris, the water darkened.

My element couldn't breach the water's surface. Something below the water could have drawn the lessers, but it was unlikely. It's one thing for lessers to be driven through the veil, another for water-bound lesser-demons to swim through.

The rotting lesser carcasses, the location, the boat…

"Will you save him?" the little icy half-blood girl had asked me right before I'd said goodbye in Boston. She had meant Torrent. I had told her I would do all I could.

Nothing here suggested any of this was connected to

Torrent, but nothing ruled him out either, other than the demon's presumed death during the Santa Monica event.

Ignoring the familiar pain, I turned to air and headed back to Hollywood.

∾

"WHO DOESN'T HAVE a phone in LA?" Adam's gruff voice traveled through the apartment.

"It has something to do with the way he travels," came Noah's reply, tight with anxiety.

I entered my living room, the all-over body ache and exhaustion weighing me down. The two men looked up. Relief flooded Noah's expression, but Adam's face only tightened into a deeper frown. I wondered if I'd let the pain show on my face and then noticed Christian out cold on the couch.

"What happened?"

They stepped back, letting me get in close. The hunter's face was deathly pale and wet with perspiration.

"He got back early from EcoZone. As soon as he stepped inside the restaurant, he lost consciousness," Adam explained.

Christian's chest rose and fell. Pressing two fingers to the pulse point at his neck confirmed his heartbeat was strong but fast. I saw no signs of obvious injury. "Did he say anything?"

"No," Noah replied. "He was out of breath. He said your name and then dropped."

"Where's Anna?"

"She er... she didn't come back."

I should have given her the feather.

"Watch him," I told Noah, pointing at Christian.

I approached the coffee table where the maps and files were scattered and dug out the EcoZone address. By air, it would take me five minutes to reach, but the thought of dropping my vessel and rebuilding it again blurred my vision. If I rushed out there, I might not be able to turn back into something solid for hours.

"Adam, did you hire a car to get here from the airport?" I shuddered.

"I borrowed an abandoned one."

Was I really doing this? "Let's go."

He knew my aversion to human vehicles, and the man was too observant to dismiss it. There would be questions. He was likely already forming a theory in his head. I was weak. It was the last thing I wanted them to know, but I had no choice.

Adam drove the borrowed rental—a compact SUV that smelled of mildew—through LA's streets, his silence deafening. I knew all the questions burning on his tongue. He had spent his life studying demons, using them the same way he used anyone and anything as a means to an end. He had supposedly changed, but I understood humans like he believed he understood demons. Few of us changed for long.

"I should thank you," he said, steering the car through an empty intersection.

"Yet you haven't." This was not the time for talking, or reconciliation, or whatever he believed he could get from me.

"No. I guess not."

The minutes dripped by as slow and painful as molasses off a spoon. No car journey lasted forever. It would end. Everything ended eventually. Best not to think about the metal cage or about folding myself into such a tiny space.

"Gamma wouldn't have survived without you." And he was talking again, filling a perfectly good silence.

"You underestimate her."

"No, I don't think so. As tough as she is, she's also fragile."

"What you see as fragile, I see as strength."

"We will have to agree to disagree."

I chuckled dryly. "As humans go, you have the unenviable talent of being able to infuriate everyone and everything around you. How have you survived this long? I genuinely want to know."

His lips twitched. "I know demons."

"Maybe you should try knowing humans. You might learn a few things."

"Ironic coming from you."

"Isn't it just."

We turned at the end of the street, and up ahead, Anna's car was parked against the curb. I was out before Adam had brought his rental to a complete stop. "Stay here." Approaching the steel-and-glass façade of the EcoZone building, I sent my element probing ahead. Lessers were crouched out of sight nearby. Their gazes crawled over me like tiny insects. They wouldn't approach, not without huge numbers. I sensed only lessers, no highers. Nothing I couldn't handle.

The front doors had been jimmied open, likely Christian's work.

"Anna?" I called.

The building was empty. From the layers of dust, it had been empty for months. I searched anyway. Why hadn't I given her the feather? I never hesitated, but with her... Damn her and the ridiculous doubts she caused.

"Li'el?" Adam's summons traveled through the empty hallways.

I found him in an office, rifling through paperwork. "Look, all these sheets refer to the immediate termination of something or someone called Katrina B."

"Anna isn't here."

"What's Katrina B?" he asked.

"We have other priorities."

He set the sheets down and picked up some more. "I'm sure Ramírez is fine... Here, this spreadsheet documents increasing numbers. They were measuring the output of something in megajoules over consecutive months."

"She's not fine. She's missing."

"She's a competent young lady." He picked up a laptop, bundled up the files under his arm, and headed for the door. "This is important."

Before it crossed my mind not to react, I had the man by the throat. "Anna. Is. Important." My façade shimmered, my control waning. Teeth sharpened, their tips brushing my tongue. I snarled, showing Adam the teeth that would tear out his throat. "We aren't leaving until we've found her."

Adam glared back, disturbingly lacking in fear. He'd seen it all before. Nothing surprised him. "She's not here," he replied calmly. "Let's not return empty-handed."

It wouldn't take much to kill him. A twitch of the wrist and he'd be gone. I wasn't the first being—human or demon — to think about killing Adam Harper, but this man served a purpose.

"You are weak. It's almost dusk," Adam said. "I know you are capable of rational thoughts and actions. Don't let Noah, Christian, and Anna down by doing something stupid because your instincts have you wrapped around your own claws. You are in no condition to fight another lesser ambush. Be smarter. Or are you just one step above the lessers hiding in the bushes?"

The itch to kill Adam Harper grew almost too acute to bear. I released him. A second longer and I would have crushed his windpipe. The insufferable Institute man was right. Anna wasn't here. No good would come of me scouring the building for breadcrumbs. Once Christian woke, we would have a solid lead to follow. *If he woke.*

Adam nodded. "The information on this laptop could help us determine what weakened the veil. You understand that?"

"Don't patronize me, human. The world won't miss you should you experience a fatal accident."

He pressed his lips together. "You're probably right. But I know what to look for in these documents, and we all want the veil closed before your demon kin can come through. None of the princes like to share. In your condition, they'd kill you because they could. How many debts are outstanding? How many rivalries and battles have yet to be settled?"

Correct again. After millenia, when the veil was put right, I finally had what I'd wanted all along. This world to myself. And now, the appearance of the veil threatened all that was mine.

"I'm beginning to understand how you've lived this long."

As I passed him, heading for the exit, he muttered, "By the skin of my teeth, mostly."

CHAPTER 16

The ex-Institute man hurried up to my apartment with his laptop prize, eager to crack open its secrets. After checking Christian's still comatose state, I returned alone to the bar, the city curiously silent outside, and poured myself a drink. It warmed my human vessel, filling in empty holes. I spread my hands on the bar and bowed forward, stretching the muscles in my back, my phantom wings aching. Why did I feel as though LA's slow demise was also mine? I had been part of this city since humans had settled it. Perhaps its heartbeat was also mine?

Something was very wrong with the world, and it wasn't just the veil or the lessers or all those obvious things. *I* was wrong. Inside me, in the parts that had existed since humans had huddled in straw huts, the parts that made up my immortal being, they were coming undone. This weakness, it crippled. My wilted and barren wings were just the outward symptom. Ever since the veil had been restored, trapped me on this side, I'd changed. I'd fought for the half-blood girl. I'd briefly had the strength of a Dark Court shoring me up, but without it, without my title, without my *name*, I was crumbling.

Was this… mortality?

What a strange feeling to have time slip through my fingers and wonder if it would stop today, tomorrow, next month. How did humans manage the impending end? How did they function knowing the next day might be their last?

No, I wasn't dying. I was just… sick. I would get my strength back. There was always the veil. I could reach into it and tease off some power. A little wouldn't hurt.

"Li'el?"

"Anna…" She stood on the other side of the bar as though she'd been there all along, waiting to be served. My relief at seeing her alive was short-lived. I'd seen that glassy look before, right before the reporter had pressed a gun to her head and scattered the insides of her skull all over my bar.

Anna held her rifle at her side, the barrel aimed at the floor.

"I… I feel… strange." She cocked her head, listening to something only she could hear. Her eyes unfocused as though she were looking through me, through the walls, at someone or something else.

"Anna?"

She blinked. "Li'el, there you are. I've been looking for you…" She looked around. "I thought this was a party. Where is everyone?" She set the rifle down on the bar and took a seat. "Never mind. If it's just you and me, I have a lot of questions." She laughed easily and scooped up my drink. "While researching you, I came across an article that said you're one of LA's most sought-after demons. There were only two demons on the list."

"Only two?" I settled my hand on the rifle, intending to stow it away behind the bar, but Anna placed her hand on the stock and smiled sweetly.

"That's mine," she warned, still smiling.

"Who was the other one?"

"Oh, he's right over there."

The cool, smooth crawl of a water elemental demon brushed against my air, the warning coming too late.

Torrent emerged from the back hall. His leathery wings hung partially open and relaxed as he moved between tables. Fully open, their spread would rival mine in size. Scales shimmered across patches of his armored skin. A Prince of Hell's Firstborn, he had been honed in the netherworld where he would have used the horns sweeping from his skull to gouge his enemies for sport. As one of the finest demon specimens the netherworld had to offer, few could match him.

Torrent had never hidden his raw demon appearance, but now that the mental lies fed to him by his father, Prince Leviathan, no longer constrained him, he had embraced his demon heritage.

Anna still smiled up at me. Torrent had adopted his father's talent for human mind control, making Anna his puppet. With a single thought, he could make her place the barrel of the rifle to my head or in her mouth. I kept my hand on the weapon, pinning it down.

The reason the reporter had killed herself was no longer a mystery.

I fought the instinct to discard my human vessel and reveal all of me. My broken wings and ragged weakness would do more harm than good. Whatever plagued me, Torrent had no such weakness.

The smile on the demon's lips was painted with malice.

"Torrent." Even as I said the name, I knew it was wrong by the way he held himself and his unforgiving glare. "Or should I call you Kar'ak?"

"Kar'ak." He gestured, unfurling long black scythe-like

135

claws. The kind familiar with gutting lessers or his higher kin if he caught them unawares. "Torrent was an inconsequential byproduct of my father's attempts to control me."

His invisible element probed mine for weaknesses. It was customary for elementals to feel each other out almost unconsciously, but Torrent's—Kar'ak's probing was deliberate. He suspected I was weak, othrwise he wouldn't be looking for it. I held myself in check, giving nothing away. It had been months—years since I'd faced another higher in combat. Words were my usual weapons, but claws would suffice if it came to that.

"I seem to recall the mind games were punishment for trying to murder your father. He imprisoned you too. You would still be imprisoned if not for luck."

Kar'ak's ocean-blue eyes narrowed. No demon liked to be reminded of their failures. By mentioning it, I was also reminding him of my status as a prince alongside his father. Hopefully, it would be enough for him to submit. If it came down to a physical battle, Kar'ak was strong enough and elementally powerful enough to win. I couldn't afford for him to realize that. He probably assumed I hadn't dropped the human vessel because I didn't consider him a threat, not that it cost me too much to constantly change forms.

"Is there anything of Torrent left?" I asked.

He bowed his head—the first time he had taken his eyes off me since arriving. "When my father broke and rebuilt minds, his work was designed to last."

That was a yes and good to hear. I had told Gem I would do everything I could to save Torrent, and I'd meant it. If anything of the water demon was left in there, I might be able to draw him out. But right now, I had more pressing concerns, like keeping myself and Anna alive.

He cruised closer like a shark drifting through its territory, and all the while, his elemental touch closed in. He would keep pushing until he broke through or I snapped.

"You killed the reporter?" I asked, keeping the strain from my voice.

Humor glittered brightly in his eyes. "Human minds are so easily molded. I had wondered what my father's fascination was with his playthings, but they really are entertaining. Besides, what else is there to do on this side of the veil?" A snarl sneaked through, indicating he wasn't enjoying being trapped here. Was he behind the weakening of the veil? He was powerful, all firstborns were, but he wasn't a Court all unto himself. To bring the veil down or remake it required a Court. One demon with delusions of grandeur was not sufficient.

He placed himself behind Anna with the front entrance at his back, blocking that escape. With his wings partially open, he didn't need to flare them wide to make his point. Unlike Christian's posturing games, Kar'ak knew exactly the threat he presented.

"What's your interest in this girl?" I sounded casual, though my heart pounded.

Anna's gaze had drifted over my shoulder. She was probably unaware of anything happening around her.

He studied Anna with all the emotional attachment of a shark eyeing its next mouthful. "She has an interesting array of thoughts. Most are occupied by emotional nonsense. But when I discovered images of you inside her short-term memory, I recognized an opportunity."

"Oh?" I closed my fingers around the stock of the rifle.

"I'll admit to being impressed. I searched for you after Santa Monica, but you hid your presence from me and from marauding lessers. Even now, you hide your power."

Yes, hiding it, that's exactly what I was aiming for.

"The veil is weak," he went on. "You feel the netherworld

calling. My rightful place is among the Dark Court, as is yours. I do not know how to weaken the barrier further, but you do."

Ah, so that was why he was here. "You want to go home?"

"I want what is mine. When my father died, the princes denied me ascension. The others rule over the netherworld in my place. I want that power. I want what is mine and what was taken from me. I am a prince in all but name."

Envy. He was his father's son. It was embarrassing how predictable my kin were.

"Let the girl go and we'll discuss the veil, the netherworld, the Court and your place in it."

"Release my leverage over you? I don't think I will." He tilted his head. "You said her name was Anna... Humans rarely think of their own names. However, she often thinks of you. I admire your work, *Pride*. Seeding yourself into her thoughts, making her believe you're almost human. It's admirable. Even my father would be impressed with your art. She's smitten with her dark prince, though she paradoxically hates herself for it. The human capacity for self-hatred is an unusual evolutionary trait, but an interesting one to study."

Humans adopted that same gaze when pinning butterflies to corkboards. Anna was nothing to him. Just a means of getting to me. He lifted his hand. "Anna, come to me."

She obeyed, slipping off the stool like a puppet on a string.

Rage burned hot and fast inside me, seeking a source. If I betrayed my feelings, I'd betray my weaknesses. Demons didn't feel and certainly not for puppet-humans. If he knew I was weak, he would likely kill Anna, Noah, and Adam, and I was in no condition to stop him. Kar'ak was of no use to me. He epitomized everything I was trying to save the human world from. But I'd promised Gem I'd try to save Torrent. Even if I could kill Kar'ak, I couldn't.

Anna strolled toward the demon. In two steps, she would be close enough for him to tear her heart out of her chest. She would be dead and gone, and I would have done nothing to prevent it. Gem had often berated me for my lack of action, but hers wasn't my life to toy with. This was different. Anna had no defense against Kar'ak. I couldn't let this happen. Anna was *mine*.

I snatched the rifle, lined the sights between Kar'ak's eyes, and pulled the trigger. The Institute-etched round punched into his forehead and flung him backward through a window, shattering the glass and bending the shutters. He collapsed in a heap, left wing twitching.

Vaulting over the bar, I aimed loosely and emptied the clip into the demon's body. It wouldn't kill him, but it would buy us time.

"Holy shit," Anna gasped, Kar'ak's hold on her mind broken. "What the... what is that?"

"That is our cue to leave." I snatched her hand and yanked her toward the elevator. "Gather the essentials. Leave everything else." I shoved her inside and handed her back her gun. "Get the others out. Now!"

"What—who is that?!"

"That's the demon you never wanted to meet." The doors closed, and I let out a weary sigh. Battling Kar'ak was the last thing I wanted to do, but what choice did I have?

I returned to Kar'ak's limp body and watched the head wound tug itself back together. It would take time for him to regain consciousness, but when he woke up, he'd come for them.

Noah hurried by, arms filled with their research. Adam carried the still unconscious Christian. I helped them through the doors and outside to Adam's waiting car. Anna climbed into the front passenger seat.

"There's more…" Adam said after stowing Christian into the back seat. He tried to head back inside.

I blocked the door. "Leave it."

"There are important documents—"

"LEAVE IT."

Behind me, air sailed over Kar'ak's tongue and down his windpipe, inflating vast lungs.

"Go!" I ordered.

"It won't take long—"

I snatched Adam's shirt and shoved him into the driver's seat. "Do you want Leviathan's son to turn you into a puppet? No, I didn't think so. Do not argue with me, Adam Harper."

He paled and stammered what was likely a protest.

I slammed the car door closed. "Listen to me and go. I'll catch up with you."

Noah jumped into the back. "Go, go, go. He's waking up!"

"You're not coming?" Anna asked through the open window.

"I am…" I checked behind me. Kar'ak's wing twitched and lifted. "Go." I had to delay him. He was too close. He could track them. If I bought them enough time, he'd lose their scent. I plucked the feather from my sleeve and reached in through the window. "Take it and go as far as you can. Use elemental glyphs to shield yourself. Adam knows how."

The engine sputtered to life and roared under Adam's foot.

"How will you find us?" she asked.

I tracked the feather in her hand and watched her lay it against her thigh. Good.

A growl sounded behind me. "I just will. Go!"

Adam slammed the gas pedal to the floor, and the rental

car sped away. Air shifted behind me, recoiling from the mass of demon inside the restaurant. I discarded my human vessel and twisted, fully demon in one fluid motion. Steeping back inside, my wings snapped outward, barreling pain through me.

Kar'ak was on his feet. He saw my wings first. His eyes widened. Shock. Horror. They must have been quite the mess for a firstborn prince to recoil. I grabbed a half-finished bottle of bourbon and smashed it across his face. He staggered, wings sweeping forward to balance him. I had him weakened from the headshot and on his back foot. If I was going to beat him, now would be the time. I couldn't let up. Couldn't give him an opening. I leaped over the bar and yanked open the drawers. It had to be here.

Kar'ak's snarl rippled the air. An explosion of pain shattered my thoughts and stole my breath away. Claws had cut through my wing. Didn't matter. I needed... There. The lighter glinted on the bartop. I snatched it up, twisted and came around laughing. "You think that's pain?"

Claws extended, I raked them forward to catch his chest, but he flung a wing in. I tore through the membrane instead, wrenching a furious cry from him. He swatted his wing outward, shoving me back, and sprang. I flicked the lighter, summoned a tiny flame, and threw it at his face.

Fire whooshed across the spilled bourbon. Air rushed in, feeding the flames.

Kar'ak roared and staggered back.

As air, I shifted sideways, appearing to vanish. In a blur, I was behind him. I hooked my arm around his throat and punched claws into his lower back. He arched away, wings spread, and bellowed his rage.

Brutal. Savage. Everything inside of me that I'd fought to escape. It all came back, stronger and harder than ever.

He bowed forward, trying to pull me over him. He would

have succeeded had I not dissolved. Pain snapped and flooded through every insubstantial piece of me. Sparks of light exploded in my vision. Kar'ak whirled. His wings sliced through my insubstantial form, but it didn't matter. I was air and everywhere. I yanked on my element, pulled it in through the broken window, under the doors, and through every gap, and pushed it into Kar'ak, crushing him under its sudden, deafening onslaught. It was all I had to give, and when the air died, Kar'ak knelt, wings shredded and skin sanded raw, but he was alive. The flames had spluttered out.

You will save him...

I could finish him off. He was stunned, on his knees. *I should tear his throat and heart out and be done with him. Without a Court, it might kill him.*

I had given a feather to Gem and made a promise to help Torrent. I couldn't break it.

I backed up, scooped up the lighter, dissolved my wings, and funneled into the air vents.

In my bedroom, I pulled out the chest of feathers. I had to do this. The extinguished lighter burned in my hand. I looked up at the room in which I had spent many a day and night being worshipped and worshipping those in return. It was just a room, wasn't it? Just an apartment. Just another act.

I opened the chest of feathers and looked down into their gleaming mass.

I knew how fire liked to consume them. I'd once had my feathers burned from my wings—every single one.

I flicked the lighter alight and swallowed.

This life as Li'el. This apartment. This restaurant. More than any of my personas, this had been the one I could have lived for centuries to come.

Not anymore.

I breathed in, summoned my element, and blew. Feathers

flew into the air and sailed through the door, out into the living room. I lifted the lighter.

Keep the fire from my door.

I could never have imagined I would be the one to light that fire.

The little flame caught a dallying feather and instantly turned blue, flaring hotter. It spiraled to the bed, spilling flames where it landed. Fire licked across the sheets. More feathers caught, each one bursting bright, and each one delivering shredding agony. Fire raced across the floor and up the walls.

I backed away. Fire would slow a water elemental.

The elevator pinged, and Kar'ak thundered into the living room. Air swept in too, lifting the ash and blasting a cloud into Kar'ak's face. As the fire raged and the water elemental roared his fury, I turned to air and vanished.

CHAPTER 17

Somewhere inside, I registered standing on the doorstep of Anna's little canal house, staring at the feather left out on the window sill, and thinking that being surrounded by so much water wasn't the best place to hide from a water elemental, but I never spoke the words. Exhausted and barely able to hold a physical form, I heard Anna invite me in and then nothing but the beat of my heart and the ebb and flow of voices. Or were those voices my courtly kin from beyond the veil, calling to me as they called to Kar'ak? That power was so close, yet so out of reach. That old life, that old me. Prince of Pride, one of the Seven. A killer, a manipulator, a demon at the height of evolution. I'd lost my life in LA. I'd lost my wings. My feathers were gone, as was my strength and my power. What was left for me here?

"Hey there."

Her hair is dark, but her eyes are blue. Defiance.

Anna was in the room, I realized. She had been here a while. I had felt her hand on my arm, her fingers caressing my shoulder.

"Noah answered the door," she was saying. "You were naked. If he didn't have a crush on your before, he does now."

Color touched her cheeks. Her darker skin hid it well, but I felt the warmth kiss the air. I ran my gaze over the outline of her lips, along her jaw to the braid draped over her shoulder, then up to her eyes. She looked down at me, the humor in them fading away.

I was naked now too. Someone had tried to toss a sheet over me, resulting in something of a tangled mess with glimpses of dark limbs. "You kept my feather?"

"Adam said I should." She bit her lip. "He said there weren't many left." She swallowed and settled back in the chair beside the bed. I appeared to be in a woman's bedroom, sprawled on a woman's bed. The sheets smelled of Anna, of soap and something like hand cream. My winged burdens throbbed, sprawled beneath me and hanging off the bed, one tucked at an odd angle. It didn't matter. I had no desire to move.

"Your wings." She caught herself peering over my shoulder and tore her gaze away. "Did that demon do that to you?"

"No."

"What's happening to them—to you?"

I propped my head up on a hand and consciously worked to heal what I could. "There was a time when I reveled with humans. Demon-kind find humans revolting and weak. I never did. I admired you and loved you, and when you admired and loved me in return, when you worshipped me over decades, I loved you more. Eventually, that love turned into Pride. Not just for myself, but for you and your kind."

The sheet slipped down to my waist, inviting Anna's gaze. I let it happen and watched her attention drift. I still had the dimple where her bullet had sailed through me. She noticed and arched an eyebrow at me.

146

"Humans helped me become more than just demon. Once I had that power, I didn't want to let it go. I sought more worshippers, more love, more admiration. It changed me, and when the Prince of Greed—Mammon—ended my life here, the power I had gained turned bitter." My skin itched. More scars would remain, but I didn't have the energy to care. "I no longer have that pride, and without the Court, I find I am becoming something else again. Something weaker. I fear I may lose my wings entirely, and after that... I don't know." It didn't hurt to tell her. I'd thought it would, but all I felt was relief at sharing my concerns. She knew more about me than any human ever had. It should have been a weakness to reveal so much, but the more I told her, the more I wanted to tell her. Every truth I gave her she measured, weighed, and embraced.

"Is Kar'ak gone?" She looked out the windows. They'd hastily scrawled glyphs on the walls, blocking out all demons besides me. I had been invited.

"For now. Thank you"—I gestured at the bed—"for this."

"Thank you. For everything. He would have..." Her eyes narrowed. "I guess that's how he got the reporter."

"I'm sorry." The sight of her at Kar'ak's mercy was one I wouldn't readily forgive or forget.

"When he was inside my head, it felt... it felt like he could have done worse. Like he was being careful. But he showed me things too. He showed me you in your world. It was... I didn't truly understand who you were before, but I do now."

The things he could have shown her. Massacres, the power I'd wielded, the games I'd played. I had always been different, but I'd always been demon too. The netherworld was not the human world. We ruled by claw and tooth.

"He showed me things, but he got it wrong." She looked down at her lap and picked at her thumbnail. "He showed me what a demon would consider weaknesses. He showed me

147

how you helped the half-blood girl, Gem, and others. There was a girl made of fire and a prince made of ice. They needed you. He wanted me to see you as weak, but I saw something else instead. He showed me what makes you different, what makes you stronger than all the others, but he couldn't see it because he's just demon."

"I'm sorry you had to see all that."

"And that's the difference." This time her smile meant something more. Rising from her chair, she admired the parts of me on display. She chuckled at her own thoughts and left the room.

My smile faded.

Kar'ak, the veil, the lessers, the pain, the weakness. There was one solution. Almost too dangerous to consider. I could tap into the veil. I could regain the power I'd lost. But with power came the lure of the Dark Court beyond the veil, and it would call to me, just like it called to Kar'ak. *They* would call. My brethren. I was not immune to the Court's temptation. I had left that world behind long ago, and I had been forced from its embrace when the veil fell. But I hadn't known the cost. Recent events had reminded me of exactly what I'd lost. Would it be better to wither away by choice or become the creature hundreds of thousands of demons feared? Become the prince once more? Should I become the devil to save the City of Angels?

I drew air through my teeth, over my tongue, and breathed it in.

~

"HERE." Adam tapped at the map, pointing to a green field near Hidden Springs in the Angeles National Forest. "It won't be easy to get to. Roadblocks are everywhere. We'd

148

have to hike on foot. But that's where EcoZone was running their tests."

"And these tests were what exactly?" I leaned against the counter separating Anna's living area from the kitchen. The bungalow was bijou, with quaint windows and timber nooks. It was perfectly Anna.

The group had gathered around a low coffee table, looking oddly comfortable among soft furnishings and potted plants. Christian was among them, curiously serene. He hadn't once insulted me in the forty minutes since I'd emerged from the bedroom, now clothed and none the worse for my run in with Kar'ak. I made sure it appeared that way.

"In the absence of more information," Adam replied, "we can assume they were trying to harness the veil for clean energy. At least that's their public remit. Behind closed doors..." He shrugged. "The military had an interest in the netherworld long before the public was aware of it and demons. Had EcoZone succeeded, the possibilities would be endless." His tone drifted along with his thoughts.

"But something happened?" I said, bringing him back on topic.

"This isn't my area of expertise, but from what Noah uncovered on the laptop, it looks as though they deliberately or unwittingly latched onto an element they couldn't control or contain. My guess is Chaos. They got what they wanted: a massive spike in energy production. The results are off the charts, and then there's nothing. The reports all stop. That happened two days before the lesser swarms started. Considering the relatively short time that's elapsed between now and when the veil was last opened, it's a wonder they didn't tear a hole through it and let all the demons through. Perhaps they had fail-safes in place, which is why we're looking at a weaker veil and not a second collapse. Astoundingly foolish. But with high risks comes high rewards."

"Foolish like breeding half-human demons?" Christian said matter-of-factly. He didn't look up. He wasn't interested in making Adam a new friend.

"Remind me again why you're here," Adam asked. "All I've seen of your performance so far is your talent for becoming a liability."

"I'm here…" He looked at me and then reconsidered whatever he was about to say. "I can get you into that facility. A squad I know worked security there before an accident shut the whole place down. It'll be locked up tight, but I can probably get my hands on some key cards. If not, I can at least get you there. I also know where to get guns since we're all out."

"And you didn't think to mention all this before?" Anna asked.

"I didn't know that place was EcoZone. It's called something else. But that's the location. I dropped off a few of the squad guys there once after we went out drinking. The whole place is wrapped in razor wire and twelve-foot-high electric fencing. I didn't ask questions. Even if I had, they wouldn't have answered."

Anna asked, "If we can get inside that site, maybe we can reverse what they did?"

It was a leap. Beyond a switch that said "press here to avoid apocalypse," none of us knew what to look for. Adam was the only one who might, and he had admitted this wasn't his area of expertise. "Why didn't the staff reverse it if they could?"

"And we still don't know what or who Katrina B is." Noah chimed in. "It crops up in the reports as a source, but nothing else. It could be a person. Maybe Katrina was in charge?"

Too many questions. "We need to get on the ground and see."

"And what do we do about Kar'ak?" Christian asked, looking at me accusingly.

"Aren't you the demon hunter?"

He smiled an insincere smile. "How many enforcers did it take to bring down a prince in Boston?"

"Not including the snipers?" Adam paused to think. "I believe it was around thirty, each armed with etched rounds and equipped with PC-Thirty-Four injectors. Although, in the interest of honesty, we later discovered Mammon wanted to be caught to get access to our half-bloods."

Mammon, the Prince of Greed. My phantom wings throbbed. He had barred me from this world, stripped me of my title, and attempted to burn my wings to cinders. I recalled precisely how I had tried to kill him. While the two worlds had been peeling apart at the seams, all I'd seen, all I'd wanted was revenge. That had been a mistake that had cost me.

I unclenched a fist I hadn't realized I'd clutched tight. Mammon was gone, locked beyond the veil with the other remaining princes where he belonged.

Carefully, calmly, against a backdrop of bad memories, I asked, "You have PC-Eighty, the same drug you took me down with?"

"Yeah," Christian drawled. "Not much, though."

He probably had a stash tucked away especially for me. "We'll need it. Inside this house, you're all safe, so long as Anna doesn't invite Kar'ak in. However, he will eventually find us, and he'll use anything and everything to manipulate you. He is the demon you all believed me to be. Don't underestimate him. And don't kill him."

"What? Why?" both Noah and Christian asked together.

"It's complicated."

"I don't think it's complicated. I think it's because you know him," Christian replied. "He got inside our heads. We need to take him out."

"I do know him, but it's not what you think." Explaining how Kar'ak was also Torrent and how I'd promised to save him wouldn't convince Christian of anything. The man had already made up his mind. Demons equaled bad.

"If I can bring him down, I'm killing him," Christian declared.

"If you kill him, it won't be me you have to answer to. It will be a pissed-off half-blood with a penchant for ripping out demon hearts. She's not as friendly as I am." Gem would chew Christian up and spit him out again. For all his demon-hunter talk, he was not ready to tussle with an angry half-blood.

"She's also my daughter," Adam added. "If you can subdue this Kar'ak, Li'el, please do. Rendered unconscious with the help of PC-Eighty, we can bind them for a limited time."

Christian cursed under his breath, muttering about how I would get them all killed.

"What happened to you at EcoZone?" I enquired. "You know, the place you left Anna to be captured by Kar'ak…"

He glared. "I'm not explaining myself to you."

I could guess. Kar'ak had caught the hunter and sent him on his way with instructions to return to me. Christian had led the demon to my front door, leaving Anna exposed.

Perhaps Adam was right. The hunter was a liability. He had yet to prove his usefulness. Perhaps getting us to the EcoZone test site would be his opportunity to shine.

"It's ten a.m.," Anna said. "If we leave now, we'll have a few hours to visit the site and get back before dark."

"We all go," I agreed. "I want Adam there to decipher what we see. Anna on guard, Christian as our guide, and Noah, you're the second driver. We'll pick up Anna's car on the way." I could survive another car journey. After burning all my feathers and Kar'ak almost tearing my wings off, a road trip didn't seem so bad a prospect.

~

WE PULLED off the road a mile before the roadblock and hiked from the highway through the gardens of several sprawling villas and upward onto oak-lined trails. Christian led the way. I followed behind the others. Both him and Anna were armed with small handguns, scrounged on our way past an abandoned police substation. Their rounds might slow down a lesser if they were good shots, but it wouldn't keep demons down for long. Fortunately, Christian assured us he also had several PC-Eighty injectors on him.

Heat beat at us from all sides. The sky stretched a brilliant blue toward a backbone of tree-speckled hills, and above it all a ribbon of light twitched. The veil. This could almost be the netherworld. All it needed was a few demon howls and the purplish hue coating everything. Home sweet home.

Anna dropped back, joining me at the end of our train. "How are you holding up?"

Sweat beaded at her hairline. She'd bunched her shirt around her middle and tied it in a knot, revealing glimpses of her curvy waist. I would have rather enjoyed running my fingers along those curves.

"I am quite fine," I assured her.

"Quite fine, huh?" She arched a brow. "Are you really English?"

"Not in the least. I adopt any accent and language to suit the circumstances. *Chi cerca mal, mal trova.*" Italian rolled off my tongue as easily as Arabic or Russian. Some languages had died out centuries ago, their spoken variants living on in my memory alone.

Shielding her eyes from the sun, she studied my face, puzzling out my motives. "What did you say?"

"Roughly translated, *He who looks for evil will find it.*"

Christian stalked ahead. Anna caught my glance and understood without a word.

"So, why English?" she asked. "Why not speak Italian the whole time?"

"Because in LA, English attracts attention. It sparks conversation and is easily understood. I am designed to attract and seduce. English is the most economic language."

She stepped around brushwood and wiped perspiration from her forehead, thinking on my explanation. "Everything you do is minutely manufactured, right down to what you're wearing?"

My trousers and shirt were a simple enough illusion. All part of the act. "Yes."

"So, what's the real you?" She swept a few loose strands of her hair back.

"The real me?"

"Yeah. If it's all an act, then there's another you underneath. The real you. Say something in demon."

A human had never asked me that before. I wasn't sure what to say that wouldn't sound as though I was threating to slaughter her offspring. I settled on a few words, the most basic terms, and ground them out. The tone was off and the words were too smooth to be true demon. I preferred Italian.

"That sounds complicated." She cleared her throat and attempted to speak it back.

I winced, stopped on the trail, and pressed a finger to her lips. You wouldn't think you could butcher the demon language, but you'd be wrong. "Human tongues aren't designed to speak it."

It occurred to me that we had stopped walking and I still held my finger to her lips. An urge to trace that finger around her heart-shaped mouth proved almost impossible to resist. But I wouldn't stop there. I'd slip my hand into her hair, free her braid, and tilt her head back. By the agreement in her gaze, she would let me.

I switched my touch to brush my thumb across her lips, relishing their softness. Their corners gently lifted, a smile peeking through.

"C'mon…" Noah called from around a bend in the trail.

I withdrew my hand and stepped back. Now was not the time to indulge in pleasurable detours. I left her with a smile of my own and nodded ahead. The others were leaving us behind.

She cleared her throat again and matched my pace through the brush. "I'm afraid to ask what it meant."

"It's probably best you don't know." I may have suggested she and I get personal in all the right ways, and many of the wrong ways too. Especially the wrong ones. "I suggest not repeating it in demon company."

She laughed loud enough for Christian to shoot us a scathing glare. "Did you teach me how to *swear* in demon?"

I tempered my smile. "Something like that."

"And your demon form is what I saw last night?"

"I have two. What you saw last night, with the wings and my splendid nakedness on display, that's my natural state, and my second state is purely as my element. I occasionally merge them. Wings and air, half there, half not. It's suitably dramatic."

"So, you can appear just as air?"

"You've seen me as air several times."

"It's difficult, though. I mean, for me to really understand what I'm seeing."

We trudged on, catching up with the others. I pushed a branch aside and let her through. "Your human mind says it isn't possible, so it doesn't see all of it. A shame, really. I'm naturally a delight to behold as air. That confusion you experience is how demons who came here in antiquity could hide as myths."

We fell quiet for a few strides. I enjoyed silences with her. They were comfortable. She had my feather on her person, pressed somewhere close to her skin. Its warmth molded with mine. That too was a comfort. "I am pleased we met, Anna."

My words or a root tripped her stride, but she recovered and brushed her braid back. "Me too. You are... erm... interesting."

"*Interesting*. Hmm. I will have to work on that."

We walked in that silence for a few strides more. "Do you think we'll fix the veil?"

"We will." *One way or another.*

"I believe you. I shouldn't, but everything you've done to help us can't be a lie. Does that make me crazy?"

"No. It makes you reasonable. Unlike some..." I nodded at the demon hunter striding ahead.

"Christian is trying to do the right thing." And she couldn't help defending him.

"Someone's right is often someone else's wrong."

She mulled over those words for a while. "I think, when this is all over, I would like to know you. Not your acts, just you... wings an' all."

"I would like that." When this was over, it would probably be too late for me, but I wasn't about to dash her hopes. She needed a little hope. All humans did. It kept them moving forward and inspired them to achieve seemingly impossible things.

The beginnings of a fence glittered in the undergrowth. The closer we got, the more obvious the fence became. We joined a road that had been abandoned for some time. Christian wasn't wrong. The fence was too high to climb over, and it was topped with extended razor wire. The ten thousand volts warning signs were disturbing.

"Holy shit." Noah whistled. "What were they trying to keep out? T-Rex?"

The warning lights weren't active. I couldn't feel an electrical charge around the wires. The fence was dead, but it still proved a formidable obstacle for anyone who couldn't turn themselves into air and filter through the links.

We walked along its outer edge toward a smaller personnel gate, but the keypad was dark.

"Can you do your lock-whispering thing?" Anna asked.

"Not on electronic locks."

"Nobody brought wire cutters?" Adam asked.

"Right, like any of us own wire cutters," Noah snorted. "Damn, I must have left my breaking-into-top-secret-government-facilities kit behind."

"Over here." Christian had wandered farther along the fence where it curved away toward a creek. He stood back, admiring an obvious bow in the fence. Something had wanted to get inside badly enough to open a wide gash in the wire.

"Maybe it was a T-Rex?" Noah mumbled.

The hole stretched almost to the top of the fence. Its edges had frayed and buckled. Parts had been cut clean through, others stretched and torn.

"Lessers, perhaps?" I thought aloud.

Whatever had gotten inside had left no tracks in the leaf litter. *Impossible.*

"Or maybe something wanted out?" Adam mused. "The edges are curled toward us. That suggests something broke out, not in."

"Not necessarily," I said. "Lessers could have pulled it open."

"I'm starting to wonder if power wasn't the only thing

EcoZone was working on," Anna said, scanning the trees around us for threats. There weren't any. I would have sensed anything large moving through the air.

"Whatever it was, we still need to get inside." Christian clambered through the hole.

It took another twenty minutes of walking before a squat and unassuming EcoZone building came into sight. Considering the dramatic fencing, the building looked like nothing more than a single-story warehouse tucked into a natural quarry.

"The bulk of the facility is likely underground," Adam said as we approached the entrance blocked by industrial steel doors. "Especially if their activities weren't publicity friendly."

"Are we walking into an Institute situation here?" Christian asked. "You experimented with all kinds of shit. Made half-demon kids, merged different demons together, all kinds of illegal BS. Is that what EcoZone was doing? Are we gonna find demons in there?"

"I don't know," Adam replied, making it sound like *maybe*. "When the Institute's true nature became public, the government or the military could have created another branch."

"Because the Institute failed at everything it did?" I enquired.

Adam's mouth tightened. "We didn't fail. If it weren't for us, you wouldn't have etched rounds or the PC drugs to bring down demons. If it wasn't for our research, the Fall would have been even more catastrophic. Like it or not, one of our half-bloods helped restore the veil—"

"I sincerely hope you're not talking about Muse," I interrupted. "For one, she was never *one of yours*. Her sacrifices and choices were hers to make and had nothing to do with you." I managed to keep the growl from my voice—barely. But the threat was threaded through each word. I'd left Gem with Muse in Boston for a reason. More than any human or demon, Muse had fought for what she believed in. She had won, saving countless lives, but at a great cost. For Adam to claim her victory as his, he would soon discover how natural selection worked, and that my being the dominant predator demanded I finish him off and feed his remains to the lessers.

"All right, boys." Anna's voice of reason broke through my murderous throughts. "Let's all put our claws away. How do we get through this door? I don't see a lock."

I revealed my actual claws, thrust them into the centre of the door, and pulled, popping it off its hinges. We were met with a clean and sparse foyer, complete with security booths and one-way glass to observe staff coming and going. Hot air wafted out, carrying the unmistakable smell of rotting flesh and emptied bowels. The fetid odor of death.

The group recoiled and spluttered.

We soon found the first body. Something had torn a security guard apart, painting the floor with his intestines—now shriveled and dried. No insects had gotten in to accelerate decay.

Noah retreated outside to sounds of heaving. Anna had paled, and Adam had merely paused to peer grimly at the carcass. Christian sniffed, commented "lessers," and continued.

The air in here was hot and ripe. There would be much worse to come.

Noah stumbled back inside and leaned against a security table.

"Stay here," I told him. "Keep an eye on the trees. If you see anything suspicious, call out. I'll hear you."

He nodded, relieved, and pressed the back of his hand to his mouth. "I'm not made for this shit."

Few people were.

Deeper inside, tight corridors and numbered doors lined

our route. We came across more bodies, torn up and tossed around the hallways in a manner that could only be demon.

"I think we know why nobody tried to fix the veil from inside," Anna said. "This place is a tomb."

Emergency lights flickered and buzzed, illuminating a path to a central elevator hub. A floor plan on the wall showed a conical-shaped structure beneath us. It narrowed to a point like a stake in the ground. The subterranean building had three levels. None were named or marked, just numbered.

"Guess we're going down," Christian mumbled.

There were only four of us, and the building was vast. As air, I could extend our search perimeter, but it would still take hours. "We can't search the entire facility before nightfall."

"Then let's go straight to the bottom," Adam suggested. "Whatever they were working on, my guess is it's there."

Christian jabbed the elevator call button. It didn't respond. "Stairs it is, then."

I delayed by a few strides and fell in behind Anna. "If you need help, touch the feather."

Her hand went to her hip, betraying where she had tucked my feather away. She managed a smile. "I will."

More bodies littered the stairwell. Some were armed but few had freed their weapons in time. Whatever had hit them had hit them fast. The deeper we descended, the heavier the air became. Anna coughed into her sleeve.

Down and down and down we walked, until the air cooled and stilled.

At the bottom, a red emergency light blinked over a closed steel door.

"Wait," I warned them.

A low hum emanated from beyond the door. My elemental had stalled in front of it and invisibly lapped at the seams, unable to break through. Whatever was beyond was perfectly sealed inside. I reached farther, sending tendrils through vents, but all were closed and sealed tight.

"What is it?" Anna asked.

"I think we found what we're looking for." I shook off the "handsome man" and revealed all of me, keeping the bones of my wings tucked in close. "All right."

Anna stepped back and cupped her gun in her hands. "Get behind me," she told Adam.

Christian tested the grip on his handgun and slowly pressed down on the door handle. The seal cracked. Air breathed through the slim gap like the inhalation of an enormous beast waiting in the dark. He kicked the door open.

Power.

It slammed into me, bowing me over, tearing out my thoughts. I had no choice but to crumple around it, but its beat rode up and over me, down my back, and scattered across my wings, yanking them open. I dropped to my knees, numb, stripped raw, and ravaged, but also alight with... *the veil.*

Shouts. Anna's. Christian's. *Help him—Leave him—Oh my god...*

Slowly, so slowly, sensation crackled into my fingertips, danced up my arms, and fizzled across my barren wings. I blinked, found I was propped up on my hands, facing the floor, and lifted my head. Inside the chamber was a glass dome made up of triangular segments, all interlocked, and around it throbbed the blues, purples, and greens of the veil. Right there. So close. Close enough to touch. Close enough to *take.*

"Stay back."

I was moving, walking. I wanted—no, I *needed* to touch it. *Power.* So much. So close.

"Li'el?" Anna. She didn't matter. Nothing did but the

sweet whispering promise of power. One touch and everything would be right again.

"Stop him. If he reaches it—"

Voices. They meant nothing. I lifted a hand, claws shining. If I touched it, the veil would become part of me. Chaos, control, ice, air, fire, water, earth. All the elements. *Mine.* I wouldn't be a prince. No, I would be more. So much more. I would be a king.

I stretched my wings, their pain insignificant. Yes. It was always meant to be this way. This world was mine—would be mine. None could challenge me.

The hunter blocked my way. He pointed his little gun at my head, snarling, showing me blunt human teeth. "Do it. Make me kill you."

So small and fragile. It was a wonder their species had survived evolution. Bone and flesh. They were not even attuned to the veil and the elements that made up everything they saw, heard, experienced. They were cattle. Lesser creatures. And this one would learn his place.

"He doesn't know what he's doing. It's the veil... Help me." The human woman was at a control panel. The panel controlled the dome, the veil's anchor. She couldn't stop it, could she?

"Not her, me!" the hunter barked. "Look at me, you ugly-ass fairy. Yeah, that's right."

I yanked the air from the man's lungs, buckling his chest inward. He collapsed. Dead or alive, I didn't care.

"Anna!" A second man. This one stood back, watching, not stopping me... studying me. He was a coward, this man. I knew him. He was no threat. The woman though... *Yes, she must be removed.*

"Stop," I ordered.

She didn't. Her hands worked across the panel, flicking switches. Lights flashed. Alarms sounded. I pulled the air from her lungs like unspooling a thread. She choked, clutching at her throat, and turned to me. Pain haunted her expression. A strange kind of pain, as though she hated herself, not me. Her little cross pendant glinted.

"Stop," the coward begged. "Don't do this. You're better than this. You've fought your instincts for centuries. You can overcome them now. Fight it. You're more than demon, Li'el. You know it."

I moved in. The colors of the veil played across the female's stricken face, sparking in her glistening eyes. Yes, she had already given in. She had known this would happen. None of this surprised her. But she had hoped a demon could change. I understood now. She had hoped her human feelings were right, and perhaps they were, but I had always been demon, and I would always be demon no matter what disguise I crafted for myself. And the veil, the power, to have it so close, to have it become mine. Wasn't that what I had evolved to become? Wasn't that my purpose?

"Oh, little human, did you think me tamed?" I moved in close, brushed my lips against hers, and breathed in, pulling the last of her life with it. There was an art to killing. An art to everything I did. I was the master of my element, and soon to be the master of this world.

The veil stuttered. Power shuddered. *No!*

I shoved the girl aside and plunged my hands into the stream. It sparked and licked at my touch, and then it was gone, dissolved beneath my hands. *No, no, no!*

The coward stood at the panel, hands on the lever. "You'll understand why I did it when you're yourself again."

I saw the reflection of a monster in his glasses, wings aloft, claws extended. All this coward had done was invite death upon him.

"Li'el!" a male called from high above in the building. "You need to get up here." Noah.

No. What I needed to do was kill Adam Harper, and Christian, and...

Anna lay on the floor. Her chest didn't rise. Her breath didn't stir. Her blue eyes stared at nothing.

I'd done this.

The veil, the power. I'd needed... I...

"Help her," Adam urged, still clinging to the lever.

The lever. The veil. The power. I could still take it. Push the coward aside and—

Anna.

Strong, defiant Anna. What had I done?

"I can't be here..." I scooped up Anna's lifeless body and fled the level. Inside the foyer, I set her down on the security table and pressed my lips over hers. *Breathe. Breathe again. I give you air, life. Breathe again. Please.*

Noah was close, hiding in the corner of my vision. The others were coming. Distantly, a storm stirred against the air, a storm made of hunger, and power, and desire, and worse. But I couldn't think of that.

Anna, please. I'm sorry. I am so sorry. Breathe. I pushed air into her lungs, kissed life back into her body, but she didn't take it. She couldn't. *I'm sorry. I'm sorry I proved them right and you wrong. Please, don't let this be the end for you. There's so much more to love, to live.*

"Li'el..."

I shook off someone's grip. The kid's, Noah's...

Don't make me a monster.

"Get away from her, you son of a bitch!"

A hunter's gun fired. Pain bloomed in my wing.

I didn't care.

Breathe.

"He's trying to help her!" Noah yelled.

"He's the one who killed her!"

Breathe, Anna. I'm sorry. You know I am. I was always differ-

ent. I was always the one who had hope, who could do more, who was more. I'm sorry I did this. I'm sorry it had to be you.

Sobbing. Christian's. "Why not me!?" he demanded. "Not her. It shouldn't have been her."

"Something's coming," Adam boomed. "We have to go now! Leave her. Leave him…"

They listened, moving away as the storm outside drew closer.

"I'm trying," I whispered. Her eyes didn't see me. She didn't hear me. Not anymore. Never again. The feather I'd given her poked out from under her belt. I'd given it to her to keep her safe, but it hadn't saved her from me. "I'm trying to be better, to be different, to be good. I'm trying, Anna. But I'm demon. And I'm sorry."

She was gone, and I couldn't bring her back. The woman who had trusted me, seen hope in me, and against everyone, against herself, she had believed in me.

I'd killed her. For all my games, all my acts, all my pretenses, I was demon. My actions defined it.

"My child."

I was no longer alone. I lifted my head and looked into eyes colored with the veil. A demon like nothing I knew was possible. She was light and dark, power and control, hardly there but everywhere, and she looked down at me, crafting a smile onto lips that weren't real.

The veil, my fragmented mind realized, *given form and thought and life and consciousness.*

"*There.*" She touched my face, claws cutting, but I didn't care because her touch changed everything. Power flooded in, power like I'd lost, power like I'd wanted, and feared, and sacrificed, and given up on. Somewhere underneath the maddening ecstasy, doubts huddled together for safekeeping. Doubt and grief for the little police officer who believed I had changed but was wrong.

CHAPTER 18

I woke sprawled on a bed, not in Anna's bungalow but in a bedroom the size of my entire apartment. Impressive wings draped across the king-size, cushioned and blanketed in glossy black feathers. *My* wings. Oh. I lay still, wondering if they might dissolve into air, never to return, should I move. Tentatively, I flexed one tip. The leading feathers fanned wider. *Definitely my wings.* My element spread far and wide, unhindered, smooth and unstoppable. I tasted the sea on the air, tasted the heat, the ebb and flow of life, and mentally rode the currents swirling nearby.

I hadn't felt this good in… I couldn't remember the last time I had been this restored.

Rising from the bed, I approached a wall of mirrors. My wings gleamed, every feather pristine. I flexed their reach and breathed in, expecting pain. None came. My reflection admired me in return. Taut muscle, a body sculpted for strength and stamina. Every inch a marvel, every hard curve exquisite.

Magnificent.

Even my scars had vanished. The one on my chin, given

to me by Mammon, and the dimple on my lower waist...
gone, like Anna was gone.

Wetness tracked down my cheek. I touched the tear, let it
rest on my fingertip, and peered at it.

No. Don't think about her. About how this power cost her her
life. About how your pride killed an innocent, brave, wonderful
woman.

Twisting grief interrupted my thoughts, doubling
me over.

I hugged my wings in close.

Don't think about Anna.

Don't think about what I did.

I had killed others over the years. Too many to count.
Slaughtered hundreds merely because it had suited me,
because I was demon. But that was *before...*

Grief hollowed me out and dumped me on my knees. All
this time, Christian had been right.

He should have killed me.

In the mirror, my wings—my restored glory—mocked
me. But not for long.

There had to be a kitchen, and in it would be knives or
sawing implements, a means to sever the offending
appendages. If I hacked them off, it wouldn't bring her back,
but I couldn't stand to see them. I couldn't bear this terrible
remorse.

I dashed from the bedroom, down a curving hallway, and
strode through an empty living room. No kitchen, but there
had to be one somewhere. Every house had a kitchen. On
and on I searched. Room led into room and corridors
abruptly ended. Was this a house or a maze?

Floor-to-ceiling windows pulled me closer. I pressed my
hands to the glass, almost covering the city sprawl of LA with
my fingers. Then it occurred to me that there were no seams
in the windows, no joins in the polished marble floor, no

kitchen or bathroom either. Human hands hadn't built this house. It had been crafted the same way I crafted my human vessel. It was too perfect.

"She is a god."

I turned, wings sweeping across the floor, and found Kar'ak, in human form, reclining on a perfectly white couch. His shabby jacket and jeans didn't fit the scene.

"As much as I admire your magnificence, Pride," he drawled, "how about you cover up so I can think straight without us having to measure the size of our assets."

My wings vanished in a suitably dramatic puff of air at a gesture, and I built my human vessel and wrapped myself in casual clothing.

"So," he sighed, "you got your mojo back, huh? She does that too."

"Torrent?"

"For now. The other asshole comes and goes. Or he did…"

"That's… unfortunate."

"A pain in the ass is what it is. *He's* a pain in my ass. I have to listen to him snarling inside my head. Like now, he wants to strut around and kill something to prove he's better than you. He's an animal."

A higher demon with a split personality, one pure demon, the other a demon who thought he was human. What an *interesting* development. "He would say the same about you."

"Oh, he does." Torrent tapped a finger to his temple. "Constantly."

"It's good to see you," I admitted. Torrent and I hadn't gotten along, but much had changed. We had changed. "I wasn't sure if you had survived Santa Monica."

"I did, although I'm not sure how…" He trailed off, listening to the thoughts inside his head.

I listened too, hearing the echo of thoughts and inten-

169

tions that weren't mine. The Court linked the princes both physically and mentally. But Torrent and I had no Court... unless we didn't need one. What had she done to me? The effects of the power she had poured into me were similar to an ascension, but so much more, and all from a single touch.

"What is she?" I asked carefully.

"What is she?" he repeated, drumming his fingers on the arm of the couch. "She is everything. She is all the elements. She's a force of nature. She's all the forces of nature. I have no idea what she is."

I'd only seen her for a few seconds, but in those few seconds, she had blown my mind, restored me to my former glory, and rendered me unconscious. Instincts told me she was more dangerous than anything I had witnessed before, but those same instincts wanted more of her. "Where is she?"

"I don't know. I've only been here two days. I woke up in a room not long after you kicked Kar'ak's ass. The fire was a nice touch, by the way."

"It wasn't without its cost." *Like Anna... Don't think about her.*

"She came to the marina, found me on my boat... and offered to take Kar'ak away. I'm... I think I lost my mind for a while. I woke up here, just like you, and now Kar'ak is behind some kind of mental wall. Feels like..." He winced. "It feels like this might not even be real."

"She gave you what you wanted," I thought aloud. She had done the same for me. "We've been recruited. Do you know why?"

"No, but it beats the alternative. She's killed all the other predators she's found." He leaned forward, rested his elbows on his knees, and rubbed his hands together. "We could be recruits—or prisoners."

"Have you tried to leave?"

"Thought about it."

But he hadn't tried it because there were other reasons. "She gave you power."

He nodded. "It's like the Court we made but a thousand times stronger. She *is* power."

"She's the veil," I corrected, remembering the swirl of colors I'd seen in her eyes. Was she tied to the EcoZone facility? Is that why she had been there, or had she simply had time to *find* me?

"How did she get you?" Torrent asked.

I explained about EcoZone, their attempts to harness the veil, and the results near Hidden Springs.

"Well, dayam. It's not every day you find a new energy source, only for it to come alive and eat you." Torrent got to his feet and joined me at the windows, watching LA swelter in the sunlit basin below. "Is your team still out there?"

"Some. Not all of them made it." A new kind of pain tightened my chest and clogged my throat. I couldn't bring Anna back. Death had taken her, as I knew it always would, eventually. Short-lived was the fire belonging to all mortals. Hers burned out too quickly. I'd burned it out. That was my burden to carry, as I'd carried many, many others over the years. Every time I looked in the mirror, I'd see my perfection and feel the kiss I'd used to steal her life.

Never again.

Torrent folded his arms and squinted into the light. "I don't trust myself around her. I see her, and I lose my demon mind. She could tell me to do anything and I would, without hesitation." He blinked as if only now realizing it.

I'd experienced a fraction of her control and assumed more would follow. I, too, would do anything for her to see me again. For her to touch me. I'd ruin worlds, and now that she had restored all of me, I could do exactly that. I had all my power… but she had the control.

"One thing is for certain." Torrent turned his ocean-blue eyes on me. "LA is her beginning."

~

THE PRINCES of the Dark Court had always done as they pleased. The Court was a byproduct of the king's control. The princes were solitary hunters hiding behind the guise of order. When we weren't trying to manipulate our kin, we were outright trying to kill one another. Not directly, though. That wouldn't be the demon thing to do. We schemed, manipulated, and used everything and anything to gain power over others, fighting for the top spot on the demon food chain. The Court created order in chaos. With the king and queen at its head, the elements had been stable for thousands of years. Seven elements, seven Princes of Hell. It had always been that way for as long as my memory served. But the demon whose eyes I'd looked into at the EcoZone facility had rewritten those rules. She was a Court in one demon body. She was the veil. Her power was limitless and intoxicating. It had no boundaries or restrictions. What if she brought down the veil? What if she rewrote the rules of this world, turning the elements inside out? She was a god playing in a sandbox, and as Torrent had said, she had only just begun.

I had to tell Adam and the others. Tell them to get out of LA, get far, far away, and hope this new demon wasn't everything I feared she was.

"Not so easy, is it," Torrent said from the hallway behind me.

I stood in the front doorway, inexplicably unable to step through. Despite everything I knew she could do, I also didn't ache when I moved, my wings were full and magnificent, and my power breathed within me. The last time I felt this alive, humans had worshipped and loved me. And then the demon prince Mammon had ripped it all away. If I walked away, would she take her gifts back? Would I suffer her wrath?

Wasn't that all I deserved?

I gripped the doorframe, claws scratching into the wall. I had never considered myself a coward, but I had also never crossed anything like her before.

"You don't want to leave, not really. She speaks to the part of you rooted in the elements, the primal part. All demons love her. And our love is no fragile thing. It's savage like us."

"Demons don't love," I whispered.

"You and I both know that's a lie we tell ourselves. You can't help but love her. She's hardwired into your soul."

I looked over my shoulder at the water elemental. He leaned casually against a wall, arms folded, expression neutral. "I stood where you are, thinking the same things you are. Tell me I'm wrong. Go on. I want to be wrong."

I couldn't.

"You're too demon to walk away from her gifts."

I stared ahead at the road winding away from the house. I *was* too demon. That would never change, but if I stayed, if I let myself give in to all the things I wanted, what would happen to my city, its people, and to other cities? I could make this right. If I could get to Adam, if he and Christian could return to the facility and destroy it, it might be enough to stop her before she rooted herself in this world—if it wasn't already too late.

I had killed Anna in the pursuit of power and my foolish pride. I couldn't cut that mistake out, but I could use it.

I stepped across the threshold and dissolved into air before I could change my mind.

Find the others and help them before it's too late.

~

I FILTERED in through the gap in the bungalow's window and rebuilt myself, only to come face to face with a gun. Christian fired. I dodged—though I didn't have to, since the round would have sailed through my ghostly form—and grabbed the hunter's face. With the gunshot still ringing and a new bullet hole in one of Anna's walls, I slammed Christian down onto Anna's coffee table, snatched the gun from his hand, and tossed it out the window. It *sploshed* in the canal outside.

"If I wanted any of you dead, you already would be." I spoke to them all, sensing their numbers crowding in close.

"Li'el?"

"Gem?"

She'd grown out her now-blond hair and French-braided it close to her scalp. She'd filled out too, gaining muscle, where before she'd been little more than skin and bone. No weapons. She didn't need them. Ice was her weapon. Her element crackled a warning in her eyes.

"Hello, little icy half-blood."

She scowled at me and at my wings, making me feel smaller under her glare. "Is it true?"

I pulled my wings in close and ruffled them. Her presence here was unexpected, her icy response even more so. "You'll have to be more specific."

"You killed a police officer, someone who trusted you?"

I looked at the others. Noah, Adam, and Christian moved away. They were all wide-eyed and afraid. I'd lost them, maybe Gem too. But it would always turn out this way, wouldn't it? I'd played the human act for a long time, so long I'd believed it was real. But an act was all it was. Whatever I did, whatever I said, the real me would always be demon.

"It's true. And I'm sorry for what I did," I said and meant it. "It's not enough, but I'm trying to make it right."

Gem's icy blue eyes widened. She believed me. At least I hoped she believed me. We had been through enough for her to understand how my words weren't lies.

"What else did they tell you?" I asked.

"Humans are siphoning power from the veil, and that's why it's unstable here."

"It's much worse than that. Whatever EcoZone was doing in the forest, they got more than they'd hoped for. After you left"—I nodded at Adam—"the storm came."

"What was it?" Adam asked.

"Demon. But nothing you know."

"*Who* was it?" Gem asked.

It hadn't escaped my attention how she'd placed herself between me and the others. She was their protector now. And they'd need her. A half-blood was likely the only demon who could resist the demon who had restored me. Gem's humanity would keep her real.

I told Gem and the others everything I knew and suspected. Christian skulked in the kitchen, angry enough to tighten the air around him.

Once I was done, the group sat in silence around the coffee table. Adam poured himself a glass of water in the kitchen. "This is..." He removed his glasses and rubbed his face. "I don't even know where to start. A demon from the veil?"

"A demon *made* of the veil."

Noah had been silent since my arrival, but in the quiet, he spoke up. "That could be the Katrina B referenced in the files. I'll need to go over them again. Maybe there's something that could help us." He averted his eyes, regret and pain shutting him down.

"I'm... of no use to you." I'd been about to say *enthralled by her*, but speaking it made it real and I wasn't yet ready to give in.

175

"You should have stayed away," Christian grumbled, still loitering in the kitchen. "We can't trust a word you say." He thrust a gesture my way. "This creature gave you everything you wanted, and all it cost you was one human life. You're here to mess with our heads by pretending you're on our side." He slammed a fist down on the kitchen counter. "I've said it from the very beginning, but none of you would listen! He'll get you killed!"

"Back off," Gem warned, rising to her feet. "Li'el is different. He's here—"

Christian snorted a dry laugh. "You're half demon and you shacked up with him. Yeah, I know all about you, Project Gamma. You don't get a say in this either."

Gem's eyebrow arched perfectly. The hunter had no idea how that ice he was walking on was getting thinner with every word. "Li'el, can we talk somewhere private?"

We moved to Anna's bedroom, the same room I'd woken in after fighting Kar'ak. I tucked my wings in tighter, plastering them around me like a cloak. Guilt had its claws in me, piercing every thought with regret. *Focus. Help these people.*

"Li'el... Hey, you okay?"

I lifted my gaze from the bed and settled it on the little icy half-blood. Not so little anymore. The woman who looked back at me had lived through too much horror. Raised as a demon-killing machine, she had faced trials that would have broken lesser people.

"I didn't mean to hurt her," I blurted. "I wasn't in control." The words had come too fast for me to stop them, but I'd needed to hear them. Something inside threatened to break. I clutched my wings closer still, holding myself together. How could I be so perfect on the outside and so broken in the middle?

"It's okay..." She settled a hand on my arm, her pale skin all the lighter against the dark of mine. "It'll be okay."

The hope in her eyes, the understanding—I didn't deserve it.

She smiled a sideways grin and threw her arms around me, trapping me inside her embrace. "I missed you."

She smelled like a winter morning, like something alluring but sharp. I brushed my chin against the top of her head and fought the urge to close my wings around her. If any of my half-blood spawn had survived, I imagined they would have matured to be like her. Wonderfully human and demon, the best of both.

"Did Adam call you?" I asked.

She stepped back and blinked quickly, hiding the wet glisten of her eyes. "He told me he was coming to LA. I had a few things to settle in Boston, before I came too. We still have a deal, remember? I gotta keep the fire from your door."

"The stakes have changed."

"Sounds like you need my help more than ever, and don't deny it. Even princes need a friend."

"I'm… I thought I had everything under control. I failed in the worst way. I'm afraid I'll fail again."

Her easy smile faded. "We're all afraid, and we all screw up." She punched me lightly on the arm. "Even you."

"Keep them safe, Gem. Safe from me."

"I will." She touched her fingertips to her chest, right over her heart. An echo of that touch quivered through my wings. I'd given her a feather. She still had it on her. "So, you found Torrent. Is he okay?"

"Okay" wasn't the word I would have used to describe Torrent. "He'll find you when he's ready."

"Oh, I know…" She shrugged. "I—that's fine, I guess."

I opened the window and paused when the glyphs drew my eye. This room still smelled of Anna, like she might come through the door at any moment and ask me how to swear in demon.

"You need to get back inside that facility and destroy everything," I told Gem. "It isn't a coincidence the veil demon came to me when the power was shut off. Maybe if the veil is left to settle, she will return?" It was a longshot and unlikely, but in the absence of any other plan, it was a start.

"What are you going to do?"

I pressed a hand to the window and watched the glass fog around my fingers. When I lifted my hand, the handprint ghosted away. "I'm going to build a new me and hope she doesn't see through my act."

"Li'el...?"

I loosened my grip on my form. My edges blurred, wings dissolving until I was mist on the breeze.

"Burn the feather," I whispered. As air, I funneled through the gap in the window and out over the canals.

She threw the window open behind me. "Li'el, wait! You'll come back, right?"

Be careful what you wish for...

CHAPTER 19

*T*he veil demon was inside the house when I returned. Instincts told me to run, but older instincts, ones I had long ago thought extinct, pulled me forward. My fear fell away like beads of water rolling off my feathers. She stood in the center of the main living area, facing the landscape of LA painted on the canvas of windows. I had never witnessed anything as terrifyingly beautiful in my thousands of years spent maneuvering through time.

The colors of the veil played across her snow-white skin. Her wings, what my limited mind could understand of them, spread in webs of light, impossibly intricate. When I thought I had her in my focus, a subtle shift confused my understanding all over again. My mind told me I couldn't see her because she wasn't real, but she was real and close enough to touch. Tears pricked my eyes, and when they fell, droplets of blood bloomed across the smooth floors.

I bowed my head, looking at those drops of blood. It was true. Demons did love. What other emotion could slay me like this?

She spoke, but not in words, not at first. The sound fractured my thoughts. I was on my knees before I realized I'd fallen. Then her words softened. Understanding crept in one word at a time, either breaking down barriers or building them up.

"Where did you go?" she asked.

"To see some people." Replying happened automatically and without hesitation.

"What did you do?"

"Told them of you."

"*What* of me?" Her tone was neither curious nor angry, merely neutral in a way that made her mood impossible to read. And with her back to me, I had yet to see her face.

I couldn't stop speaking, didn't want to, didn't care. She asked, I answered. It was simple. "That you are like nothing I've ever known, like nothing that should exist."

"How did they respond?"

"Fear and denial. Bravery. Resilience. Defiance."

"Defiance..." She tasted the word and let it linger in the silence. "How?"

"They will destroy the facility that created you." Guilt choked me, and the phantom pains of regret and loss fell heavily on my shoulders. But I couldn't deny her. I couldn't displease her. It wasn't a conscious decision. She had a hold on the most primitive parts of me. Instincts, needs, wants. She was the veil. I didn't stand a chance against her.

"When?"

"I don't know." They hadn't told me, and for that I was grateful. Christian was right. I shouldn't have gone to them. But maybe Gem and the others would succeed. And any chance was better than none.

She moved toward the glass, turning from light, to shadow, to motion, and back into herself. The windows vanished under her touch. A trembling rumbled through the floor and shook the air. In the distance, dust rose in clouds over LA. It looked as though something was tossing toys into the air. But those objects weren't toys. Stone and steel spiraled through the clouds, remaking themselves into a different structure. Higher and higher it climbed, its base crawling outward, absorbing neighborhoods, changing them, twisting them.

Were there people down there?

"Wait…" I began.

Her head tilted, and the vast structure's construction paused.

Tightness clamped my heart. She was remaking LA, my city. Building something out of homes and land people had toiled for decades to claim. It wasn't right. This land wasn't hers.

"Why are you doing this?" I asked.

She blinked. I still hadn't seen her entire face, just he perfect outline of her profile and at EcoZone, the fathomless depths of the veil inside her eyes. Would I lose my mind if she looked upon me? There was only one way to know for sure. Head held high, I climbed to my feet. Stretching my wings wide, I spread each feather, presenting all of me. She might have control of what made me demon, but if she was also demon, then she also had weaknesses. If I could expose them, I could use them against her.

Carefully, I approached. My invisible elemental touch looped ahead, trying to coil around hers, but she stood inside an impenetrable bubble of power, untouchable, unreachable. What would it take for her to see me?

She turned her head, stopping me dead. Light licked along the line of her jaw, the curve of her smooth lips, and a crown of short horns.

She could break minds, break worlds, break me. I almost

wanted her to, just so she'd notice me. What *was* she really? Just demon?

I am Pride. See me. See everything I am. See the magnificence of me.

She reached out a hand. Like her wings, her gossamer skin shimmered, held together by a fabric of light. She touched my shoulder. The power of the veil shocked my veins, burning, cutting, tearing. *Too much.* She shattered my mind into a thousand pieces, wrecking my soul, and she did it all with a smile.

She said, "My work begins."

~

"You touched her, didn't you?" Torrent's voice reached me through the heavy fog muffling my thoughts.

I was sure my skull was in pieces and kept my eyes closed to prevent further damage. Mentally, I ran through all the necessary body parts. Arms, legs, wings—all present and correct, though I had gained an all-over pleasurable tingle. The kind of satisfied body thrill that came after a long night of sexual exploits, only magnified a thousand-fold.

"Feels a bit like touching a high-voltage power line," Torrent added.

"She—" I croaked, and then whatever sentence I'd had planned vanished. Thoughts were tough enough. Talking would come later.

"Be grateful she didn't give you another head or turn your wings to literal ribbons."

I cracked an eye open and found Torrent sprawled in a chair beside the bed. Considering the way he was slouched, as though poured into the cushions, he'd been there for some time. I wondered if he'd brought me into the bedroom, but after rooting around my memories, I found fragments of my stumbling in here and collapsing.

"She did it to lessers." He winced and rubbed his face. "You'll probably see a few of her experiments. It's some weird Frankenstein shit. Why do you think they ran?"

"They ran?" I had assumed the lessers had *attacked* the zoo and marina, driven there with a purpose, but Torrent's words suggested otherwise.

"Fear drove them to swarm." He dropped his head back, resting it against the back of the chair, and sighed hard. "At the marina, they flooded in. I didn't realize they were running from something until it was too late." He blinked at the ceiling.

I propped myself up on my elbows and waited for the room to stop spinning. "How long have I been here?"

"Sleeping her off? No idea. Found you in here after she left."

Swinging my legs over the edge of the bed, I tried to piece my mind back together to coordinate my body and stand, but as the walls shifted and the floor slid away, I bowed forward and covered my face with my hands. Darkness, that was better. But I couldn't stay there. I'd told her about Gem and the others. It had been hours. I had to get to them—no, I couldn't. Every time I tried to help, I made things worse. She —this incredible demon—had my unwilling devotion. Gem would keep them safe.

I dragged my hands down my face and opened my eyes. The room had ceased spinning.

"She was…" I remembered houses being pulled apart and streets turning to dust. Had that been real? "She was building something."

"Yeah," Torrent replied grimly. "A tower of some kind."

"I can't let this happen."

He snorted. "Good luck stopping her."

"You could help," I snapped. "Instead you lounge around here, doing what exactly?"

Torrent rolled his eyes and pushed out of his chair. He crossed the room, threading his fingers through his hair. "Okay, fine, sure. I'll do something. Oh, wait. I must have misplaced my magic demon-killing wand." He turned his sarcasm on me and lifted three fingers. "Let's recap: God is real." One finger went down. "She's an all-powerful demon." The second finger curled inward. "And we're all screwed." He glared, expecting me to deny it. "You've got a plan, oh mighty Prince of Pride? You wanna tell me how I can stop myself from turning into a love-struck demon puppet every time she looks at me? Or maybe you could tell me how to resist answering all her questions about this world and its people, because I damn well don't know how."

I didn't have answers. Not yet.

Torrent blustered a dry laugh. "You can't because you're as screwed as the rest of us. You know, when that wave hit Santa Monica almost three years ago, I was prepared to sacrifice everything. I went on that pier knowing it would kill me. It was my choice."

"I know." I had told Gem not to save him, knowing Torrent had made his last choice as a man. It had been the right choice.

"I couldn't control an ocean, but I could shape it. I could do something good with my pretend life before Kar'ak took it all away. It should have ended there." He laughed bitterly. "But here I am, more powerful than ever, more screwed up than ever, and she's here, a thousand times worse than Delta, worse than the demon I am. And I know I'm her tool. I have no control around her. It's… it's not right. It shouldn't be like this. I gave up everything. *Everything*! But not for this. Not for this, Pride. So, tell me your grand plan. Tell me how to stop her."

I was beginning to understand why Gem cared about Torrent. He would fight for what he believed in.

I straightened, testing my balance. "She gave you more power? You're a prince, correct?"

He sighed. "That was the first thing she did. She gave me power and then blocked Kar'ak. But it's not like the ascension we went through. This..." He looked at his hands. "This is a lot worse and a hundred times better. I mean, I *couldn't* control an ocean before, but now... now I could. It's damn tempting and dangerous. If Kar'ak..."

"I'll deal with Kar'ak. Your new power means we both have substantial reserves. We are princes of a new Court, her Court, but that doesn't mean we have to fall in behind her." I tucked my wings in close and rolled my shoulders, working out the curious tremors. "You don't think the old Court fell in line with the king, do you? We just have to find her weakness. She'll have one. She's the veil. The veil is made up of all the elements."

"Sure. But whatever you throw at her, she'll absorb. She's where our elements come from."

Something he had said earlier sparked a new thought. "The veil... the demon-killing wand..."

"A what now?"

"In the netherworld, there's a blade the princes at the height of their power can summon. It's not really a sword, but a figment of a demon's mind made real by the veil. When wielded, it strips elements from demons. We—the original Dark Court—used it to tear chaos from the first demon queen and kill her."

Torrent, jaw slack, asked, "A magic sword?" He laughed dryly. "You got a unicorn hiding in your wings too, Pride?"

Had he always been this irritating? The elemental blade was no laughing matter. The blade had killed thousand of demons and sundered many princes from their power.

"I really don't know what Gem sees in you." That knocked the grin off his face. "She's here, in LA. If you would stop flouncing around this house at her whim, you could see her again."

His glower made it clear I'd hit a nerve. "Gem's in LA?"

"Yes. She asked after you."

He scratched his neck and drew in a deep breath. "Is she safe?"

"She's Gem."

I couldn't know his thoughts without deliberately prying into his princely mind, but I could guess. They had been more than just close.

"You've seen what this god-demon is." Torrent lifted his gaze, all humor gone. "How can we defeat something like her?"

"We need to find out more about her, what she wants, what she needs. If she is demon, she will have critical flaws. We all have them. Pride, for example. Our weaknesses are our names."

He nodded firmly. "Does she even have a name?"

"All higher demons have names. We need to discover hers."

"And what if she's not demon? What if she really is a god?"

"The bigger they are, the harder they fall. She *will* have a weakness."

I left the room and strode down the hall. It didn't matter what we called her. She was far too powerful for me to deal with alone. "We need backup, the kind that's hard to kill, and lots of it. We need to fight fire with fire."

Keep the fire from my door. I was about to invite it in.

"Backup?" Torrent jogged to catch up. "From where?"

The destination I had in mind was a long way from here, yet not far at all.

The sparse entrance hall loomed, the door closed.

"You're not thinking…?" He trailed off, the implications stealing the rest of his sentence. "How long has it been?"

"Too long and not long enough." I opened the door but didn't step through. Outside, warm air stirred nearby palm trees. Where I was headed, the air could kill.

I was ready to go home.

I had to go back, beyond the veil, back to the demon world I'd left behind. A smile crept comfortably onto my lips.

"I hope you know what you're doing," Torrent said.

"I always know what I'm doing," I replied, distracted by the pull of the weakening veil. I was a prince again. The worlds were my playgrounds, and no demon could bar me from them.

"Do you even know what's left on the other side of the veil?"

I stepped outside onto the dirt path. Air flowed down my feathers, teasing my wings open. "I know there will be nothing left here if we can't stop her." Turning to face Torrent, I met his concerned and somewhat curious expression. "Do what you can to discover her weaknesses."

He nodded. "If she has any."

The veil pulsed. Mentally, I reached out and flexed muscles I hadn't used in years. "I'll be back soon."

He crossed his arms. "She'll know you went through…"

It was a risk. Every step against her was a risk. She could snuff me out with a click of her fingers or make me into something else entirely, turn me into a lesser. My feathers quivered at the thought. "Then use your *talents* to distract her."

He snorted. "Your faith in getting me killed is inspiring."

I stepped back. The veil's presence rippled and twitched, devastatingly tempting. Only princes and half-bloods had the control to step through. Once I did, there would be no undoing it. Whatever lay on the other side would not welcome me. The princes of the Dark Court were just as likely to flock to the veil demon as they were to stop her. But I could reason with Baal, the king—if he didn't kill me on sight.

I lifted my hand and swept my claws in an arc, calling on the control and poise that made me worthy of my name. The fabric of two worlds parted, flickering and dancing, spilling light over me. It pushed against me, trying to scratch me off like an irritating parasite, but I had the opening under my control.

"Say hello to Hell for me," Torrent said.

I stepped through.

CHAPTER 20

*T*he netherworld air rushed in to reduce me into something unworthy. It licked over my wings and lapped at my skin. Air poured down my throat like syrup. It had been so long that I almost stumbled at the sensory imbalance, but I quickly regained my composure. This was *normal.*

The sky bled its purple and black clouds across a midnight canvas sky. I blinked, adjusting my sight to the hues.

The hole in the veil crackled closed behind me, leaving me standing on the landscape of a desolate world. A scorched valley spread in front of me. A lesser demon snuffled through the undergrowth nearby. It stumbled upon my elemental touch, yelped, and bounded off, crashing through the bushes.

I am Pride. I spread my wings. *And I'm home.*

Dissolving into air, I swept over valleys and plains, surveying all that remained. Savage cracks had pulled the land apart. Seas I'd once swam in had dried, leaving basins of dust. Silent lightning flashed in the distance behind a ridge of jagged hills. Scorch marks blackened the earth. A valley of tree stumps projected from the ground. The netherworld had always been on the verge of tearing itself apart. Now it was a slowly rotting carcass. The chaos that had always saturated the air since my brethren and I had slaughtered the queen was absent. Once again, the elements were under control.

A fortress butted out of a hillside. Massive battlements had been hewn from the black rock, shaped by the greatest earth elemental the netherworld had ever known, the king, Baal. The structure dug deeper into the earth than the façade suggested. The last time I'd seen it, the walls had been crawling with lessers summoned by the breakdown of chaos.

Circling on the warm air currents, I saw how the center of the fortress had been sealed and shaped into a dome of rock. I probed its seams with air and found only one weak spot. A prison. The queen would be inside. But it wasn't her I was looking for. Chaos couldn't be reasoned with. Control, on the other hand...

There were hundreds of demons slinking behind stone walls. As air, my phantom touch whispered over those milling around the courtyards, chilling their flesh. I ventured in through arched windows, mapping the best way to the Court's chamber. Lessers perched on ledges, and some scurried around the halls. Their numbers comprised most of the signs of life, but I sensed the throb of considerable power deeper inside the fortress. The king was home.

It occurred to me, as I flew silently and invisibly through the fortress halls, that I was a prince, but not of this Court. I hadn't ascended by traditional means. That made me an outsider. Baal would be within his rights to attack. This homecoming could get interesting.

As I streamed closer, the throne room doors hung open,

elemental symbols flickering inside their construction. I eased inside and assessed the demons crowded around the vast banquet table. A Court, but not of princes. I had arrived during a discussion of sorts. High demons had gathered to petition their king to reinstate a Dark Court. Two thrones sat empty. I hovered above and behind them, no more than a whisper.

Baal's formidable presence dominated his end of the table. Human history spoke of winged monsters, calling them dragons. Baal's scaled wings, long tail, and blazing eyes were certainly the source of those tales.

But there was another demon here. One I had no wish to see unless it was to strip the skin from his bones as he had done to me with fire. He wasn't at the table with the others. He was tucked away beside the wall, almost entirely cloaked in shadows. Contained fire flickered in his black eyes.

Mammon.

Baal looked up. His head swiveled, and his reptilian eyes narrowed on me.

The demons around the table fell silent.

Time to make my entrance. I settled my ghostly self on the dais and made the most of reshaping myself from the air they all breathed, adding a few unnecessary flourishes. A swirl here, a flick of feathers there. Naturally, once solid, I spread my wings, embracing the room. *Read my glorious wings and weep.*

A warning snarl rippled across Baal's lips.

"Hello, darlings," I purred in British English. How delightful it was to see them recoil. Oh, to see the horror on their demon faces and hear their collective growls. Some even bowed their horned heads. How I had missed this.

"*Pride.*" Mammon strode out of the shadows, lava veins throbbing. He reached into the air and pulled a shimmering

191

blade from the veil—*the* elemental blade. He couldn't mean to—

Baal stepped in, blocking Mammon. They shared the visual equivalent of locking horns before Mammon pulled back. His heat lingered on me long after his glare had gone. The blade vanished from his hand, and the Prince of Greed stalked back into his shadows, eyes aglow. Old feuds still burned hot between us.

I retracted my wings and ruffled my feathers. "It seems your Court is lacking in numbers, Baal."

The king's gaze trawled across my form and lingered on my wings. *I am built anew.* His sharp mind would be asking how and why. Where had my power come from? Was I a threat? My warning had been clear without spilling a drop of blood—yet. I was unlikely to get away without a fight, but I preferred to avoid it for as long as possible.

"Leave," Baal ordered his flight. His deep voice resonated through the air, lacing it with control. Of the higher demons gathered, only Mammon had the balls to deny the king's order. The others filed out. Mammon didn't move. He stayed in the shadows, a pillar of everything I despised about my kin.

"Mammon?" Baal urged. It was a curious display—for the king to ask Mammon to leave instead of ordering him. They had always been close. Mammon had hidden the king in the human realm right after the original queen's death—the very same realm Mammon had barred me from. Baal had stayed disguised as human for many years, living a normal life. It was that life I hoped would give me leverage in my petition for help.

The air grew heavy with Mammon's heat. He made sure to drag out his defiance before skulking out the door.

In his absence, the room instantly cooled.

"Pride," Baal grumbled. "You are restored."

"You have questions. I will answer those I can. But know I did not come to fight." I stepped off the dais and joined the watchful Baal at the long table. Elemental glyphs swam beneath the table's surface. In the netherworld, glyphs existed in the same way the veil did. They responded to power, moving to equalize the elements to avoid any one element becoming too powerful. As I pressed my fingers to the tabletop, the glyphs fled, sinking into unknown depths. For the first time in as long as I could recall, the table was blank.

Baal's intake of breath said it all. "It is not possible."

He pressed his massive clawed hands against the surface. Next to mine, his clawed hands were the type to crush skulls. Mine were too, but with finesse. The glyphs didn't return.

"How?" He looked at me with suspicion. Only the king could control the glyphs. They were his language, created by him to control the elements. And I had chased them away. I hadn't done it deliberately, but he didn't need to know that. If I could vanquish the king's language within his fortress walls, what else could I do? Oh yes, I could see the concern in his eyes.

How did I approach this? Threaten him or entice him? Terrify or anger him? Demons didn't respond to threats the same way humans did. If they couldn't tear it to shreds, they usually bowed to it instead. What if I was about to hand the veil demon a demon king?

When I took too long to answer, Baal asked, "The veil is closed. None have been able to open it. And yet here you are, Pride, as if by magic, wielding unknown power. How have you returned?"

I lifted my fingers off the table. "In all your years, did you ever wonder if there was more to the elements?"

"More? Be clear with your words, Pride."

How much of the human male remained in this demon?

Centuries in the netherworld eclipsed a few decades in the human realm. Did he even remember his human life? Would he care?

"The City of Angels has fallen," I told him. "The humans need your help before the rest of their world falls too."

aal listened, asking few questions, while I explained how events had escalated from swarming lessers to a nameless all-powerful demon remaking a city with her hands. By the time I finished, the light outside the throne room windows had turned from mauve to orange.

"And your wings? I witnessed Mammon burn you. How did you come to be so… you again?"

"There were various attempts to create a new Court, but this?" I flicked my claws over my shoulder. "She restored me and more. The power she wields outshines yours."

His expression—always difficult to read behind his scales —flickered. "Why?"

"We don't know."

"We?"

"Kar'ak is there, although somewhat altered. He now answers to the name of Torrent."

"Prince Leviathan's son? His father killed him—"

"Some might argue what Leviathan did to his son was worse."

The king moved around the table, eyeing it and me carefully. "And this demon... she is all the elements?" He trailed a claw along the table's surface. The glyphs still hadn't returned.

"She is the veil."

"How do you know for certain?"

I chuckled. "You would not ask that had you met her."

"And yet you are here, scheming to bring her down, when she has given you everything you desired for so long. You are in your prime again. You could rival any here at my Court, perhaps even me." He gestured at the plain table. "So why do you plot against her?"

"It's the demon thing to do."

"Pride." He laughed, and the sound crept in and around my power, soothing, teasing, trying to work its way into my thoughts and know my mind. The king was not without his mental gifts. His voice could soothe and smother and make lesser minds pliable to his will. "Of all the princes, you always spoke the truth. I found it refreshing. Others, less so. Do not lie to me."

"There are humans there. Humans I... care for. Their world is worth preserving, lest it become a ruin like ours. They have lifted themselves out of the mud and evolved into creatures with dreams and ambitions. They deserve their freedom."

"Yet it was their foolishness and greed that brought this catastrophe upon them."

"I do not proclaim them to be perfect. Evolution is not a straight line. There are false starts and mistakes. We stopped evolving long ago. We could learn much from them." From any other demon, these words would be heresy. But I was hoping Baal remembered. "But only if they survive."

"Perhaps this mistake should be their undoing? Why

196

should I intervene and risk the wrath of this force of nature upon me and my realm?"

"It's the right thing to do."

"The right thing?" Baal laughed again, and it curled the tips of my wings. "You remind me of someone. She would have said the same." He approached a window looking over the battlements. "You are the least demon-like demon I know, Pride. But you are much changed. I do not trust easily."

"Changed, but for the better."

Baal's crocodilian lips turned into a curve resembling a smile or a snarl. "Leave me while I consider your words."

As soon as I left the table, glyphs bobbed back to the surface. Baal noticed and acknowledged the implications with a nod.

Had I done enough? If I failed here, billions of lives could be lost. What would earth become with a demon goddess as its creator? Hesitating in the doorway, I turned and caught Baal's eye.

"I don't know why she hasn't asserted herself on this side of the veil. Perhaps she isn't aware the netherworld exists, or perhaps she's preparing to attack while we discuss what we should do, or perhaps she already knows this land is dead. You mentioned how I could challenge you, Baal. Know I will not stand by while the entire human race and their world are destroyed and remade into something more netherworldly." My claws creaked against the doorframe. "I will not let that come to pass."

"Are you threatening me, Pride?" the King of Hell growled.

I plucked a feather from my wing and tossed it into the air. With a little help from my element, it sailed toward Baal. He caught it, opened his claws, and frowned at the pristine feather on his palm.

"A promise," I said, careful to add the hint of a knowing smile. "Not a threat."

~

THE CHAMBER where the queen had been sealed inside had no windows. Only one heavily glyphed door barred the way in or out. I hung back, not wanting to accidentally unlock the door and release chaos. The first and last time I had seen her, she had been a little girl—a half-blood girl with the terrible gift of the chaos element. *Dawn*, that was her name. She was likely a woman now. Her fate was sealed from birth. Chaos must be controlled. In the human world, Gem had killed her brother rather than let chaos loose. Here, it wasn't as simple. The elements were wilder in the netherworld, not layered and ordered like in the human world. Without a queen to stabilize this world, chaos would weaken the veil. When chaos reigned, the veil would fall. But if the veil was sentient, that changed everything, didn't it? The old ways, the old laws, did they apply anymore?

Turning away from the queen's chamber, I wandered the fortress. Little had changed. Demons didn't change, at least not officially. I knew that to be a well-kept secret and a lie. Demons could change. I was evidence of that. Perhaps the only evidence if the king refused to help. I had hoped he would recall what it meant to be human and find compassion inside that demon head of his. If I was wrong, where else could I turn?

I entered the courtyard and stopped. Mammon's rippling outline scorched the air inside the portcullis. He faced the bridge as though considering venturing into the wilds beyond. From my slightly elevated angle, all I saw were his pointed bat-like wings bunched against his back.

I had much to hate him for. He had taken everything from me and then mutilated my wings with his fire. For that, there would be no reconciliation. Ever. If justice existed, he would have died during the Fall, and yet here he was. The desire for vengeance came back stronger than ever. The last three years were forgotten, and I was back in the throne room. Chaos had surged around us. Half-bloods and demons had tried to save the worlds then, but I'd only had one thing on my mind: revenge. In the chaos, I had planned to kill Mammon. But it hadn't happened like that. He knew my mind, knew my plans, and in one horrible, blinding moment, he had struck. Fire had washed over my wings, lighting them up. *My beautiful wings...*

Lessers shrieked into an approaching dusk, breaking me out of the memory.

Mist curled and licked across the courtyard. And Mammon stood, as still as stone, burning off the mist where it dared touch his black lava-veined skin.

"The king must not leave this fortress," Mammon said. His voice was stone grinding on stone. Startled winged lessers took flight and cawed high above.

There were no other higher demons in the courtyard. Just him and me.

"If he leaves his throne, another will take his place." He turned, black eyes rimmed with crimson flame.

"You, perhaps?" I started forward. I would appear weak if I didn't approach while he addressed me. My wings naturally opened, responding to the threat. I shrugged them back into place, trailing them behind me instead. I would not give him the satisfaction of seeing anything he could interpret fear.

His lips tightened, revealing hints of sharp teeth. "I have no designs to rule this world, Pride."

"No, you want to be king of the human world."

He huffed a disgruntled snort. "That was your desire, not mine."

"Then why take it from me?"

"Your influence on their lives was too great. Humans are better left alone to their own devices."

"Was that all?"

"And I do not like you." His predatory smile grew.

"That's not it." I stopped beside a mound of toppled stones that had once been a well. "You're Greed. You wanted what I had, and when you couldn't have it, you took it from me anyway."

"I *was* Greed. Now I am... just demon."

Of all the demon princes, Mammon was the most dangerous. The fact he was alive while the rest of the old Court had perished said a great deal. His games could last hundreds of years. His words were often lies upon lies spoken with a silver tongue. For a beast that looked as though he could bring down towers with his claws alone, he was notoriously subtle and sly. I wasn't buying his humble act. He was here, in this fortress, close to the king for a reason. He always had a self-serving reason, and he was always three steps ahead of every demon.

"Should I pity you?" I asked.

He lunged. I'd been expecting it, else I might not have shifted into air in time. His claws sailed through where my neck had been moments before. He twisted, wings flinging open, scattering hot embers into the air—into me. Fire lanced through parts of my elemental cloud. Heat threatened to boil me to nothing. The ghost of pain flashed across my phantom wings—a memory of the time he had stripped me raw. *Never again.* I twisted in, tightening around his neck, choking off his air.

Mammon heaved his great wings back and beat down, blasting me with hot embers. Against the superheated onslaught, my grip slipped. I unraveled again and swept around him. From behind, I fell into a crouch, spread my wings, and summoned a storm of netherworld air. *Burn this.* A squall washed in over the battlements and tore across the courtyard. Crouched low, the wave flowed over me and struck Mammon's open wings like wind hooking into a ship's sails. The blast lifted him off his feet and slammed him into a wall. I yanked it all back under my control. The wind dropped. Dust and debris pummeled the ground, my back, and my shoulders.

Mammon landed on his feet, wings bowed, veins alight. He snarled and shook his head, dislodging dust and dirt from his horns.

"How did *you* get through the veil?" he demanded, rising to his full height.

"With help."

"TELL ME." He stalked forward, each step thundering through the ground.

"So you can steal my life again? Do you think I am a mindless lesser you can throw around? I am the Prince of Pride." I flared my wings and bared my teeth. "I am magnificence made flesh. You are nothing but an animal pining over his mistakes. There's no going back for you, Greed!"

Fire flashed in his eyes and danced along the trailing edges of his wings.

A growl erupted—not from Greed, but from the king bearing down on us. The terrible sound trembled through my bones and plucked on ancient strings of command. There was a larger threat than Greed. My enemy and I recoiled, pulling back, tucking our wings in to make ourselves small.

Baal towered over us. "Enough!"

I shot Mammon a glare filled with warning. His top lip curled.

"I said enough!" Baal huffed. He hadn't bothered to open

his wings. Didn't need to. Once he was satisfied we weren't about to tear into each other, he turned, tail sweeping through the debris our battle had scattered. "To the throne room, both of you. Now."

CHAPTER 22

"*H*ad it been any other demon, I would have refused." Baal was standing at his table. Glyphs bobbed close to its surface, rising to their king's touch. "But for all your faults, Pride, you have strengths most demon-kind lack. I believe you. And I agree, we must do something. But I am our queen's guardian. Her respite must not be disturbed. The elements of this world are too precarious for me to leave her side."

Most wouldn't have noticed the king's pause, but I had, and wondered if it might be regret. Regret for his actions, regret for the life he had abandoned, or regret being his queen's jailor? I couldn't know for sure. Perhaps it was all those things. He was trapped here, not unlike his queen, bound by his duty to protect what was left of this dead world. I pitied him like I pitied all demons. They were stuck at an evolutionary dead end I had avoided.

Mammon, a savage beast at the best of times, was the prime example. He stood at opposite end of the table, arms crossed and wings tucked in, shedding an angry beat of heat. I would be glad to be rid of him once back in LA.

Baal had fallen silent. Head bowed, he watched the glyphs swim beneath the table's surface. "These markings are how I learned to control the elements of this world. Perhaps they will help you."

With a sweep of his hand, he pushed power through the table. Mammon staggered, fell forward, and grunted from an unseen impact. Glyphs were painted across his arms, chest, and on the inside of his wing membranes. They throbbed like dying embers, then stilled on his skin. The shadow of agony passed across Mammon's face, but he bore the pain silently.

I knew where this was going and fought to hide a snarl. "He cannot return with me."

"We have no choice," Baal countered.

"I refuse to take him."

"Pride," the king sighed. "Did you not promise to see this through? Not a threat, you said. There is more at stake than your pride."

I lifted my chin. "I would prefer to take the mad queen than that beast."

"The *mad queen*," Baal said, his voice low, "is not a solution."

I turned to Baal, ignoring Mammon's glare. "Chaos may be the only way—"

The king's wings flexed. "Chaos can never be freed again, no matter the cost. You know this. Mammon is what I am giving you. He is all I can spare. He has guarded my reign, and now he guards the elements in yours."

Why did it have to be Mammon? "The veil demon will corrupt his mind."

Mammon finally spoke up. "Many have died trying."

He didn't understand. Neither of them did. But that was the risk I'd taken in coming here. I needed help, and the king was giving me Mammon. I couldn't decide if this was a nightmare or a punishment. "You trust my words, Baal, then trust this: Mammon will seize power for himself. He cannot be trusted with this. He is *greed*. He will take what isn't freely given. That is all he knows."

Baal bowed his head. He missed Mammon's smirk in my direction. By the Court, I would kill him. I certainly couldn't work with him. I couldn't take him back with me. It would be like adding fuel to fireworks.

"Why can't you see him as he really is?" I demanded of Baal.

"Do you believe demons can change, Pride?" he asked.

"No."

"And yet you are evidence of exactly that, are you not?"

I laughed. "I'm different."

He smiled as though humoring a child. "You are not the only one."

I tilted my head at the king. Was he implying Mammon was more than demon? Had Mammon fooled the king with his games? Did he not see Mammon's act?

"I remember what it is to be human," Baal admitted. "I remember regret. I wish I didn't. Mammon, though he'll deny it, remembers as well. I wonder if such things are the way forward for our species, a way to heal our land, but until then, you must use that human thinking of yours, Li'el, and trust that Mammon will help."

That was unlikely. "Why would he help if not for his own gain?"

Baal straightened. "Why do you hope to save those people?"

"I do not wish to see them perish. I do not wish to see my city fall. After everything they have achieved, all that they have strived for, I cannot bear to see it turned to dust." Anna had fought for LA. Just one person and she had wanted to do anything and everything. Humans had their faults, but most were good, and strong, and proud, and brave, and so many good things. "No, I can't lose them."

The king smiled a slow, thoughtful smile. "You are more alike than you realize."

"And if I refuse?"

"Then your pride will seal the fate of a civilization."

Condemn them? No, I'd already made mistakes. I couldn't let this be another. "Mammon." I reluctantly lifted my glare and pinned it on Mammon's smug face. "Can I trust you?"

"You may trust me to do what is right."

Right for whom? For you?! "All right. But if he so much as puts a claw out of place, I will tear the air from his lungs and send him back here with the veil demon close behind."

Baal grunted. "Go, and for all our sakes, refrain from killing each other until this veil demon is dealt with."

CHAPTER 23

*T*he City of Angels had fallen.

There had been a time when I'd only felt the need to thrive and be admired. Life had been easy then. But I had changed. Living among people had changed me. And now, I stood on the hillside beside the Hollywood sign with my heart had been ripped out.

"Were there people down there?" Mammon asked, stepping toward the rocky edge. His wings had sagged, and the glow of his veins had dulled. I couldn't see his face, but I didn't need to. He had once coveted this world, wanting it for himself. *Greed.* He felt the loss too.

"Yes."

"Was it this way when you left?"

"No… This is…" The tower the veil god had constructed covered LA's entire footprint. It rose out of the earth, jagged and cutting. Atop, a crown jutted just like the crown of horns on her head. Nothing of LA remained. Mammon and I looked down at a scene more netherworldly than earthly.

How long had I been gone?

"It's a fortress," Mammon hissed. "A seat of power."

My city is gone... The endless chatter, the sweet heat, and the beautiful people... so many people...

Mammon's veins flared brighter and hotter, lighting his wings like slow-moving lightning across a dark sky. "The king and queen came first. Baal built his fortress and crafted the glyphs to control and shape the elements. Next came the higher demons to wield those elements. *Princes*, Baal named them. This..." He swept claws toward the scene. "She is creating her own world. This is... magnificent."

Magnificent? I knew that look. Greed *wanted* what he saw.

I pulled my claws into fists. It took everything I had not to shove him off the cliff. "Baal says I can trust you. Don't prove your king wrong."

Mammon turned, amused by my words. He gestured at the markings scarring his chest. "I bear his marks. My loyalties are clear."

I ruffled my wings. "All that means is you have Baal where you want him."

"We have unfinished business, you and me. But Baal is right in one thing: I do not wish to see this world fall. Do you agree to put our differences aside until this is over?"

"You wish to strike a deal with the devil, Mammon?"

I extended my hand in the human custom. Mammon extended his, but as he did, he sparked the transformation that peeled open his demon aspect, shrugging off his coal-like skin and horns, and pulled all of him into the body of a human male. The hand that closed around mine was bronze-skinned and soft. An act, of course, but one that was as well-crafted as mine. A man made of dark eyes and promising smiles, packaged in a tailored suit. I was looking at the kind of man my city would have showered with attention. He blended in better than I ever did. I was designed to stand out and be admired. His human guise lured his victims close with suave sophistication. I knew Mammon's human vessel well, having seen it many times over the centuries. Seeing it now only reminded me of how dangerous he was.

"A deal with the devil," Mammon said, but his voice was smooth, his words precise. No longer Mammon, this act, this lie, was Akil Vitalis.

He allowed a slight smile to lift the corner of his mouth. Nothing about his design was accidental, and Baal's comment bobbed to the surface of my thoughts. *You are more alike than you realize.*

The king's markings peaked out from under Akil's shirt collar. A reminder and a warning.

We shook. "A deal." For all his word was worth.

He nodded once and released my hand. "Where do we begin?"

"With a spy."

~

As AIR, I scouted ahead and confirmed the veil demon's house was empty. There was no way of knowing how long it had been vacant, but the wall that had once been windows was just a hole. The mountainous tower sprouting from LA's ruins blocked the light, casting shadows. If Torrent was inside that tower, finding him wouldn't be easy.

"Where are the human military responses? They have formidable weapons." Mammon—*Akil* stopped at the gaping hole and scanned the scene below. "I see no evidence of any human intervention."

"LA was quarantined. The authorities evacuated some, then pulled out of the city. After the Fall, they learned to cut and run. Anyone who stayed was left on their own. That's when I..." *When I was released.* Akil didn't need to know the details of my recent imprisonment. Admitting it would reveal how weak I had been without the Court. "When Anna asked for help."

"Anna?" Akil inquired, turning his gaze my way. Behind his cool expression, he was likely peeling apart my level tone, rooting out the emotion beneath.

"A friend." *Ask me any more questions and our deal is forfeit.*

Akil didn't push and instead sunk into his own melancholy silence. I stood beside my enemy and assessed the destruction we faced. Was I truly going to battle the most powerful demon of all time with my greatest enemy at my side?

"I would like to ask you something." His words had softened with what almost sounded like longing. Like me, Mammon, as demon or man, crafted his voice, his tone, and every word to suit him. Akil knew exactly how to wield the words like weapons. "And given what we're facing, the opportunity may not present itself again."

"Then ask."

"Muse." The name sounded like a hurdle, like it hurt him to speak it. *Curious.* "Is she…" He swallowed, drilling his glare into the tower. "Well?"

Muse was the half-blood I had left Gem with in Boston. She had a history with Akil. A long and complicated history that had abruptly ended when the veil was sealed, trapping Mammon in the netherworld. She had as many reasons to hate him as I did, yet here he was, asking after her. Probably for his own nefarious reasons.

I considered twisting the truth, but it had been too long since I'd played demon games and found I had no appetite for deception. "She is well."

He had barred all emotion from his face, which likely meant there was a great deal turning over in his thoughts. Baal had suggested Mammon had changed. Mammon had spent many years as Akil, living on this side of the veil, living a human life. Could that existence have cultivated *feelings* like it had in me?

"After this is over—" I started.

"I won't be seeing her."

And now it was his turn to shut me down. I narrowed my eyes at the demon prince. Could he have true feelings? Was that why he was staying away. Or was this more lies? This was likely an elaborate trap, probably designed to make me see him as reasonable, when inside, he was a scheming, manipulative demon of the highest order.

"Do not ask why," he grumbled. A muscle twitched in his cheek.

"I have no wish to know." He was a master deceiver. But I already knew that. I would not give his lies any leverage.

Something groaned far below at the foot of the tower and trembled through the earth, sounding very much like a demon howl, but not one I recognized. Torrent had said the veil demon had been working on changing the lessers.

"Creation…" I whispered. What waited inside that tower? Evolved demons, perhaps? That wasn't good. Where on this new demon food chain were Mammon and I? There was only one way to find out.

"Ready?" I asked.

"It has been some time since I sank my claws into a worthy beast." Fire encircled the blacks of his eyes. "Lead on, Pride."

THE TOWER'S roots snaked around and over a network of streets, but the houses were gone, twisted and changed into the veil demon's tower walls. Tunnels fed into the base. Akil and I cautiously approached. Curiously, she had stripped the beach behind us of sand, but she'd left the ocean alone to lap at naked rock.

A grumbling groan rumbled from inside the tunnel.

"Perhaps you should scout ahead as air," Akil suggested.

Right, so whatever trap awaited could snag me while he sauntered in to save the day? I bared my teeth. "Perhaps you should turn back into your demon aspect."

He blinked. "I do not want to reveal the king's *gift*," Akil said, but his tiny delay said more. Demons had few opportunities to play at being human in the netherworld. It must have been years since he'd spoken with a human tongue and walked with human muscles. Yet he had effortlessly slipped back into the role. Did he play at being human while in the netherworld? I couldn't imagine it, but his act was admittedly flawless. I could begrudgingly admire another's art, but I didn't have to like the artist.

We entered the tunnels. Smooth walls arched over us and curved inward, restricting the view to a few meters ahead. At our presence, a subtle white light emanated from below, lighting the way. I sensed no electrical hum and could only assume the light source was organic.

I hugged my wings close, easing my element ahead. Movement nudged my senses, as did the rhythmic push and pull of breathing. "We have company."

What emerged appeared, at first glance, to be humanoid. All the parts were in all the right places, but its smooth, perfectly white skin reminded me of the plastic box I'd been kept inside. The form was too perfect, the body hairless with no male or female genitalia. *Not born, but made.* Striking blue lashless eyes fixed on me and slid to Akil. Neither of us slowed, and the creature stepped aside as we passed. Another appeared ahead, standing motionless as it watched us approach.

Akil's voice touched my mind, using the archaic princely link. *"They seem docile."*

"So do some lessers until they lay their eggs inside your intestines."

More creatures appeared, all stepping aside to let us pass. When we reached an open chamber, I'd lost count of their number. Tunnels broke off with no indication which way led to Torrent.

I turned to Akil and found him eyeing the creatures filing into the chamber behind us. They circled in, pale skin almost translucent. Were they elemental? I couldn't sense any elemental touches. Not human, not demon, something else. The veil demon must have made them for a reason.

"Do you want to say something, or shall I?" Akil asked.

"We come in peace?" I said. One of the blue eyes approached, its attention glued to my wing rising over my shoulder. Its head cocked in a birdlike twitch, and then it reached out with its slim, smooth fingers and touched my feathers.

Akil arched an eyebrow.

The creature purred and ran its hand down my wing.

A shudder ran through me. "As much as I enjoy being stroked—"

Something hissed above. I looked up, saw white feathers and jaws filled with teeth plunging toward me, and ghosted aside. Claws swiped through the air where I had been. Mammon's heat whooshed into the chamber. As air, I spun upward, retracting my wings and all of me, ready to lash out. But I didn't get a chance. Mammon snatched the white-winged *thing* by its neck, slammed it into the ground, planted a foot on its chest, and roared. Our curious blue-eyed gang scattered in a flurry of movement too fast to track.

Don't kill it... I thought.

Mammon's claws came down, tearing through flesh and

PIPPA DACOSTA

sinew. He stepped off the twitching corpse and gave his wings a triumphant shake.

Demons. Reforming, I frowned at the gory scene. "You just had to."

Mammon remade Akil in seconds. Human once again, he straightened his cuffs and said, "We're not here to make friends."

From deep in the bowels of the tower, something large and furious screamed.

"Find Torrent," I said and dashed for a tunnel.

*a*s I poured through tunnels and chambers, mentally mapping every corner, slope, and junction, my element touched hundreds, possibly thousands of life signs. Hundreds were human, but hundreds more differed in subtle ways. Too hot, too cold, odd breathing patterns, the too-small amount of air their bodies displaced. Too many unknowns to count. *She's building an army...* The blue eyes weren't aggressive, but the other creature had been before Mammon abruptly ended its life. What were they?

I spiraled higher, until the cool, slippery sensation of Torrent's element pooled around the tunnel floors. Solid once more, I stepped into his chamber. Cathedral-like proportions soared overhead. Water lay motionless in circular channels surrounding a central island, and on it, with his back to me and wings held closed, knelt Torrent. I'd been gone no more than a day in netherworld time, but a week could have passed here. Torrent had made himself at home. Was he the same demon I'd left behind?

I started toward him. Water rose from the pools in glittering droplets, pulling up a curtain. When it reached halfway to the ceiling, it curled over and rippled outward: Torrent's elemental touch, but *visible*. Mist hung in the air, crowding close but not touching. Was this a threat or something else?

"Torrent?"

"A test, she said," he replied, "of my devotion." His wings lifted as he rose to his feet and turned. "She is disappointed. Demons and humans did not evolve as she had hoped. What she's doing, it's not wrong. She's correcting our mistakes. We lost our way—"

"Torrent." He met my gaze. His eyes weren't glassy or unfocused. He looked at me, perfectly in control. Something had happened to tilt Torrent's mind. "Before I left, we talked about weaknesses, remember?"

I stole a step closer. The water droplets hovered away. Another step and those droplets opened, allowing me through, but they also closed in behind me. The power it took to maintain his element inside my air had to be immense, but he showed no signs of strain.

"She has no weaknesses," he said.

I approached the first channel. Water still lay inside, dark and impenetrable. "What did she do to you?"

"My father tore away my right to rule. He confined me inside a physical cage. He trapped me inside a human mind for hundreds of years." Not Torrent. Kar'ak. I pulled my element in close, ready for the inevitable. "And when I was freed," Kar'ak continued, "I came here, only for the fire elemental, Vanth, to enslave me again." Now seemed like the wrong time to point out how all those unfortunate events had been of his making. Being demon, nothing that happened to him could be his fault.

He stepped off his island and walked through his heavy mist. Water collected on his partially open wings, streamed down his skin, and dripped from the trailing edges. "You princes and your Courts," Kar'ak said. "It's over. You are obsolete. She is the future." He stopped a stride away, squaring up to me. There was no denying his demon prowess, but the strongest demons always kept their strength beneath the surface.

"You're right about one thing," I said.

He tilted his head, wet horns shimmering. "Only the o—"

My knuckles hit him square in the nose to the sound of crunching bone. His mist collapsed, splashing across the floor and sloshing back into its channels. Pain shocked up my arm, but it had been worth it. Kar'ak fell backward and hit the floor with all the grace of a felled tree. He had been so focused on controlling his element and me that he hadn't expected a fist to the face. Few demons did.

I shook out my throbbing hand. *"You're* obsolete. I, however, am absolutely on trend."

That hadn't gone as planned. Now I had an unconscious demon prince to manage and an all-powerful deity to avoid. Wonderful.

A howl sounded deep within the tower and rattled through its tunnels. The blue eyes and their vicious companion weren't the only creatures here, and I had no desire to introduce myself to them until I knew what I was dealing with.

I scooped up Kar'ak's slippery body and hefted him over my shoulder, wings loose and uncontrollable. With a sigh, I misted us out of the tower. Mammon could fend for himself. Maybe she would kill him, but I doubted I'd be so lucky.

"WELL, HERE WE ARE AGAIN." Torrent regarded the marks I'd scratched into the floor around the chair he sat on. He could step across the glyphs, but he wouldn't, not if he wanted to stay as Torrent and not turn into his sociopathic other half. "This is becoming a regular thing, Pride. I'm starting to think you like power games. Is this a demon come on?" He arched a brow, dragging a smirk with it.

I folded my arms. "Precautions. Your alter ego is a pain in my feathers."

"At least you don't have to listen to him prattle on inside your head."

"Is he quiet now?"

Torrent nodded, regarded the markings once more, then slid that look toward the man leaning against a far wall, quietly watching. "Who's the suit?" he asked.

"Unimportant," I replied before Akil could further complicate a difficult situation.

Akil huffed at that but didn't protest. His existence in this world was better kept concealed. Inside the glyphs, Torrent wouldn't sense Akil's true nature or his element. Considering how Akil and his markings might be our secret weapon, I wanted him anonymous for as long as possible.

Akil had been waiting at the cliff house when I returned with an unconscious Kar'ak. While I had secured Kar'ak inside a glyph circle to force him into his human form, Akil had silently observed from the fringes.

Torrent didn't bother to hide his frown. He knew "the suit" was important. "I thought we were partners in this, Pride?"

"We are. It's Kar'ak I don't trust."

"I can't blame you for that…" He sighed.

"What happened?"

"What do you think happened? I started asking questions, and she got suspicious and unbound Kar'ak from my mind to remind me who holds my strings."

Akil sauntered forward. "You allow your father's abuse

218

too much control. The Prince of Envy is long dead. Your current mental affliction is preventable."

Torrent jerked his head. "He talks, huh? Although he knows jack about me and my *mental affliction*. What are you, some demon shrink?"

Akil's brow tightened. "I witnessed your birth and your life at Envy's hands. I know you better than you know yourself."

"Pretentious much."

Akil narrowed his eyes at Torrent, unimpressed.

I shook my head at them and rolled my shoulders, letting my wings sigh for me. "You can psychoanalyze Torrent all you like once I have LA back."

"*We* have LA back," Akil corrected.

"That's what I said."

"It wasn't."

"The City of Angels is mine. The clue is in the name."

"You believe you're an angel?" Akil fought a smile from his lips. "I'd forgotten how full of yourself you are, Pride. It's a wonder you can fly at all with your ego weighing you down."

"Who is this jerk?" Torrent cut in.

"Nobody," I replied. To Akil, I said, "And he'll continue to be a nobody once he goes home. Don't get comfortable *in my city*."

"Oh, I know. You do not need to remind me." The smirk stayed.

I wished I'd punched him in the face instead of Kar'ak. It would have been far more satisfying. There would still be a chance once our agreement was over. I smirked back.

"Is he backup?" Torrent looked as disgusted as I felt.

"Weaknesses," I reminded everyone. "She must have at least one."

"None that I've seen, but when I'm around her, it's almost

impossible to think of anything but her. She..." At a loss for words, Torrent gestured at his head. "Gets inside somehow and screws up my thoughts."

"Apparently, that's easy to do." That gem was from Akil.

"Will you stop?" I grumbled.

"It is a fact," he replied. "Kar'ak, or Torrent, or whatever you call yourself, spent much of the past few centuries being mentally abused. This demon-god knows your weaknesses and exploits them to manipulate you. She is doing what any demon does naturally."

"You believe she's demon?"

"I do," he admitted. "The first demon."

My thoughts stalled. The first? "How is that possible? The king and original queen were the first."

Akil slid his all-knowing gaze to me. "And who told us that?"

The king. "Are you suggesting Baal lied?"

"A dishonest demon. Shocking, I know," he drawled.

"Why would he lie?"

Akil sighed. "Have you really forgotten how to be demon while you've been prancing around this city?"

I recoiled. *"Prancing?"*

"Pride," Torrent snapped. "Listen to the suit."

Swallowing a retort, I nodded for Akil to continue.

"He lied to conceal the source of all power. Had we known about her, we would have tried to exploit her. The Court has something of a reputation for destroying what it gets its claws into. He chose to lie to keep the source safe, to hide her as I hid him from rampaging princes after the death of the original queen."

"And you know this for a fact?"

"No," he admitted. "But it is what I would have done."

"You aren't the king."

"And have no desire to be."

"You never could be."

"You'd be surprised at what I can do."

Ugh, where was Christian? Shoot me up with PC80 now. "No, I really wouldn't."

Torrent rocked back in his chair and whistled low. "Are you sure you two aren't romantically involved? You could cut the sexual tension with a knife."

I growled, low and deadly. "The tension is born of abhorrence and loathing. *If* we are to assume she is the First demon, then she must have a weakness. She is elemental like we are."

"She has a weakness," Akil said matter-of-factly.

When he didn't elaborate, I asked, "Will you share this weakness or keep it all to yourself like your name suggests?"

"Me."

Would Baal mind if I sent him home in pieces? I pinched the bridge of my nose and bowed my head. No more. At this stage, I was proud of myself for not yet trying to kill him.

I moved to the open section of wall where there had once been windows. The tower had risen so high it now collected a crown of clouds. Behind them, an unusual red hue seeped through, giving the changed land a pinkish hue. I wasn't sure there was anything left of LA to save, but there were people in that tower. Buildings could be replaced, but not people.

Behind me, Torrent asked Akil, "All right, I'll bite. How do you know you're her weakness?"

"Because I saw her, but she did not see me."

The glyphs the king had given him—that had to be why she hadn't seen Akil. He really was her weakness.

"Did you feel her push on your thoughts?" I asked, keeping my back to him.

"No."

"What was she doing when you saw her?"

"She was…"

221

When he delayed too long, I turned.

Akil was frowning. He gave his head a shake and gestured, grasping at words. "She was creating."

"How?" I demanded.

"I… It is difficult to explain. She pulled the elements from around her and worked them together, as though she were a maestro directing her orchestra. It was mesmerizing."

If Mammon was our weapon and her weakness, then I needed his allegiances clear. That look of admiration in his dark fire-touched human eyes was not comforting.

"It gives us something to work with," I said. "It also means you can get close to her and perhaps wield the elemental blade?"

He considered it and agreed with a nod. "As a last resort. If the blade fails, I'll be exposed. We need a better plan than brute force and the element of surprise. What happens when *you* get close?"

I drew in a breath and caught Torrent's downward glance. "She gets inside my thoughts. I suspect Torrent's father's ability to mold minds began with this veil demon."

"If that's the case," Akil thought aloud, "perhaps she exhibits all our traits. Envy, greed, pride, and so on."

"That doesn't bode well for a deity."

"No," he agreed, "it does not."

"Torrent, you've spent more time with her than any other demon. Is there anything more you can add?"

He ran his fingers through his hair. "Only that she isn't interested in anything outside her work. I tried to distract her and lure her into opening up, but she's too focused. She seems detached from everything but the elements. Maybe her focus is a weakness too. If we screw up her little science projects, she'll notice us."

"You want to piss off the veil?" I asked incredulously.

"You asked for my opinion. There it is."

"He has a point," Akil said. "It's worth considering. Those creatures we saw, those with the blue eyes, what are they?"

"Lessers," Torrent replied. "Or they were. She's making them into something else. They don't communicate—at least not vocally. They just kinda hang around the tunnels. Some are vicious, and others seem docile. If they have a purpose, I don't know what it is."

"I'll find out," Akil declared. "I'll keep an eye on Mother while I'm there."

"Mother?" I asked, feathers rustling.

"If my theory is correct, then that is what she is, our mother. The mother to all."

I wasn't sure if I was more disturbed by his conclusion or the idea that the deity tearing down and remaking LA was my... mother. Life had been so much easier when all I had to worry about was preening my feathers and attending to the needs of my Hollywood worshippers. Now I had to somehow manage the manipulative Prince of Greed and a prince's son with a split demon personality. How had three demons become the last chance to save the City of Angels?

"There's something else..." Torrent added, his tone making it clear I wouldn't like it. "There are people in her tower. She hasn't killed anyone, that I know of. Just the staff at EcoZone when she broke out. But she has everyone who was left in LA when she started building that tower."

Gem, Adam...

Torrent nodded, not needing to hear my thoughts to know who I was thinking of. "I don't know if they got out in time."

I had told Gem to burn the feather. Had she? I couldn't lose her, not after Anna. Adam, and even Christian—I couldn't lose another human under my protection.

"Who got out in time?" Akil asked.

Akil knew Gem as Project Gamma. He was the demon

who had broken her and her brother out of the Institute before the Fall. He hadn't "saved" them, despite what Gem believed. Mammon had planned to use the half-bloods. He wouldn't hesitate to use her again if it suited his needs.

If he had a half-blood charmed into his service, he would use her to strengthen his ties here. No. Gem was not a bargaining chip, nor was she a tool for him to use. She had earned her freedom. He wasn't taking that away from her.

"Friends," I told him. "You wouldn't understand."

He narrowed his eyes but stayed silent.

I huffed, but I would not let him draw me into another discussion. Mammon was here to stop Mother. That was all. He wasn't staying, and he wasn't getting his claws into Gem. Not while I was around.

Greed will not take her from me too.

"Go, spy on *Mother*," I told him.

"And you?" he asked.

I had every intention of returning to the tunnels as air to find Gem. I'd felt the many, many pockets of human locations. It would take time, but I'd find her. I had found her halfway around the world, albeit with the help of a feather. "I'll work with Torrent on subduing his other half. He's useless to us this way."

"Gee, thanks," he grumbled.

Greed nodded and left the room. When I was sure he'd left the building, I met Torrent's questioning gaze.

"You two have issues," he said.

"Many. Don't trust him."

"Like I would trust any demon. I am one. I know how they think." He sighed at the glyphs still penning him in. "So, how do we deal with my problem?"

"The old-fashioned way. I'll be right back." Half an hour later, I returned with a handful of Sharpie pens, set them down in front of Torrent's circle, and plucked a feather from my wing. "Let's see if we can give you back control. Roll up your sleeve."

"Seriously?"

I flicked out my claws. "I could carve the marks into your flesh if you'd prefer, but you'll likely heal over them."

He rolled up his sleeve, exposing his forearm. "It may come to that."

CHAPTER 25

A soft, fluttering touch told me Gem had ignored my advice—nothing new there—and kept the feather pressed close to her flesh, probably still tucked in her bra considering the warm rhythmic beat of her heart. With Torrent's ink still drying on my hands, I turned to air outside the tower and funelled inside. Gem was alive and calm. It could have been worse. When Adam Harper had taken her from LA to Boston, I'd felt her alarm as though it were my own, and afterward, while attempting to weave through the Institute's underground facility and around the glyphs, I'd experienced her fear and her anger. I had reached her in time then. I would help her now.

My flight along the tunnels abruptly ended when I slammed into a wall of nothingness. I hung in the air, stunned, and tried to probe around the invisible force holding me back. *Impossible.* There was nothing there.

The tunnels rushed by in reverse, flushing me out or up, I wasn't sure. It all looked and felt the same. Over and under I tumbled, unable to stop, unable to claw myself back into a physical form. Then the movement ceased, and I found myself hovering in a hollow chamber similar to the one I'd found Torrent in. Only this one had concentric circles around a central island, upon which stood Mother, as bright and surreal as the veil poured into a female figure. Barely there, but everywhere.

She looked at me, through me, seeing more than air, seeing thoughts, seeing my soul. I couldn't hide, couldn't move, couldn't pull away, and in a blink, none of that mattered because I wanted to be here with her. Where else would I be?

Her grip released me, and I settled on two feet, revealing my wings and all of me. And she was there, so close. Warmth consumed me, and power licked across my skin and spread through every muscle and feather. *She has control.* And I wanted her to have control over me. It was easier this way.

"My child..."

She reached out a hand. I expected the power to over-whelm me and waited, ready to embrace it, but when her hand touched my cheek, I felt only the cool crackle of her smooth skin. I brushed my cheek against her hand. It had been love. A child's love. I couldn't prevent it. It was ingrained.

My child...

Mammon was right. Was he here? Fog smothered my thoughts, pushing them down to where nothing mattered but a mother's touch.

I blinked. She was there, smiling. "This is my fault."

No, it wasn't possible. Mother did not make mistakes.

"I abandoned you. But I am here now, and everything will be right again."

Yes, she was here. Everything would be right again.

"Come..." Her hand closed around mine. She led me to where a ledge jutted from the wall, to where the clouds swirled. I instinctively parted them, pushing the air aside to reveal the glittering ocean beyond. Something else grew among the waters, pushing up through the waves. "Witness creation."

The Pacific receded, waves boiling and crashing, revealing a land I recognized. Sweeping valleys and jagged mountains, all bathed in a pinkish glow. This was the nether-world at the beginning, before the princes corrupted the elements. A paradise. A world I could never have dreamed I would see again.

"Do you see my work?" Mother asked.

"Yes." I saw a world of possibilities, a new world where all our past mistakes had been wiped away. Anna's death, the hundreds—thousands of lives lost over the years. I couldn't get those back, but I could start again. A second chance.

"I am here now," Mother said. "And this world will be perfect."

A sense of rightness chased my doubts away. Of course this was right. It was always supposed to be this way. Demons and humans had evolved in her absence, but we had twisted our worlds into something wrong, taken an evolu-tionary wrong turn, but Mother had returned.

Mother had saved us all… from ourselves.

I had never been more afraid.

"Hello, Christian." I leaned an arm against the cell bars and smiled at the hunter hunched inside. He didn't have the weight of broken wings pushing him down like I'd had, but he looked burdened. Good. "What an interesting turn of events. How many steps is your cell? Six? No, merely four, I see. You'll soon get to know those steps like the back of your hand."

"Pride," he drawled, lifting his head. Dark circles ringed his eyes. "You took your time getting here."

I gripped the bars. Marvelous how Mother had crafted them from the elements. Christian looked hopeful for a moment, as though I was about to yank out the bars and free him. Even if I could, I wouldn't. "Years you kept me caged. By my recollection, you've been here two weeks." I moved away from his cage to admire the picture it presented. Yes, this was immensely satisfying.

"Li'el…" Gem said carefully.

She stood at the bars in the adjacent cell and watched me approach. Her icy blue eyes held wary suspicion. My chest tightened at the sight of her doubt in me.

"You didn't burn my feather," I said.

She swallowed and pressed her hand over her heart. "I tried…" She still wore the same clothes I'd left her in— combat pants and a tank top. Her ragged mop of blond hair curled where it touched her shoulders. "Did you come to let us out?"

I stepped back. No door. No lock. I couldn't lock-whisper them out. From the scratch marks inside, Gem had tried using ice to carve her way out. Mother had sealed them in here. She was likely the only one who could release them.

"Li'el…" Gem lowered her voice. "What's going on out there?"

"Mother is restoring order."

"Mother?" She recoiled, and the tightness in my chest hardened.

"He's talking about Katrina," Noah said from the cell behind me. His was next to Adam's. The Institute man sat much like Christian, beaten and silent, but Noah was alert and curious. "The veil," Noah added. "EcoZone called her Katrina."

"She's your…" Gem began, but couldn't finish.

"She is mother to us all, even you."

She pressed her face to the bars and glared with all her human might. "This doesn't sound like you."

I gripped the bars above her head, tilting my wings back, and leaned in close. When she didn't flinch, I eased my wings around and slipped the leading feathers between the bars to encircle her, blocking out everything else. She let it happen. There was a time when she had done the same, encircling me in ice.

"Gem, careful!" Christian warned. The fool. Gem knew better. She moved closer, pressing herself against the bars so my wings could seal us both inside,

Her icy eyes shone in the dark.

"There is art in everything I do," I whispered.

"What does that mean?" she asked, searching my clouded eyes for reason. She didn't know I'd said those words to Anna. But Gem knew how I created acts to hide behind, just like Mother built her worlds. Gem understood. In many ways, she always had.

"I have never lied to you," I told her.

Her lips gently curved. "You are the most human demon I know, Li'el, but you're still demon. You don't need to lie to manipulate. Is that what you're doing? Manipulating us?"

"*Not you.*" Opening my wings again, I stepped back.

"Isn't it obvious?" Christian grumbled. "He's jumped into bed with that *thing*. Don't bother trying to talk him 'round. Whatever made him different he's obviously given it up. It's their way. Demons all get in line when something bigger and badder comes along. Like the rest of us, he wants to live, so he's put himself in a position of power. He'll do anything to earn her favor." The hunter got to his feet and stood at the bars. "Who's the bitch now, huh?"

I arched an eyebrow. "Your lips are moving, yet you're speaking out of your arse."

Gem snorted a laugh and covered it with a cough.

"Do you still have PC-Eighty in your possession?" I asked the hunter.

He snarled in reply.

"He does," Adam replied.

I thanked the Institute man with a nod. They all looked at me, some believing I was made of deceit, others seeing the truth.

"Do you trust me?" I asked the icy little half-blood.

She nodded.

"You're mine, remember." I smiled.

She touched the spot on her tank top where she'd hidden my feather. "We had a deal."

Good. She had faith. She would need it for what was coming.

I left with a suitably dramatic flick of my wings, and as air, I headed through the tunnels, deeper into the tower. My people were alive and well, as were several thousand other LA citizens. A week ago, Torrent had said the creatures Mother was creating had originally been lessers. With that in mind, I had been spending time monitoring the Blue Eyes, watching them without their knowing, and now it was time to formally introduce myself and find out how much Mother had changed them on the inside, because, as Mother had said, she had been away. She didn't know lessers like I did, nor did she know people like I did. I had lived in both worlds and loved both worlds. Now, all I had to do was save both worlds.

I reformed in the midst of a group of Blue Eyes, careful to keep my wings down and pulled close to make myself smaller and less threatening. Threats would come later. Their smooth white bodies reflected the bluish background hue, deflecting it over my dark skin and feathers. I must have appeared as alien to them as they did to me. As before, they quietly observed me, heads tilting, blue eyes sparkling. These creatures were not aggressive unless provoked. It was typical lesser behavior. They recognized power when they saw it, and like Christian had said, demons fell in line with those more powerful than them, but it wouldn't be enough.

The attack came like before. A sudden rush of movement to my right. The vicious lesser sprang out of the crowd. I caught a glimpse of claws and teeth before ghosting out of its path and yanking it out of the air from behind. The creature scrabbled to twist in my grip. With a thought, I pulled the air from its lungs. Its chest immediately crushed inward. Its elongated muzzle chewed at the air, trying to gulp it down. I held it back until the creature's heart slowed. The Blue Eyes watched me toss the vicious lesser to the floor. It wasn't dead. Any demon could kill another. I was teaching my rapt crowd a lesson. I didn't need to kill.

After eventually regaining consciousness, the wounded lesser whimpered away.

When the second demon came, I effortlessly disabled it, but didn't kill it. A third, bigger and coated in white spikes, met the same fate. When no more came, I made sure to eye each Blue Eye in turn. Satisfied I'd made my point, I vanished.

On the third day, the first Blue Eye knelt in my presence. By the fifth, they all did, and the lessers no longer attacked.

Mother's army was now mine.

THE MEADOW SPREAD on and on, blanketing hills that stretched farther than I could see. Purple-headed flowers swayed beneath the undulating wind. The sky here was a perfect azure. All around, color and light shone in splendor. But no animals, not yet. Mother hadn't perfected the species that would inhabit this new land. It certainly wouldn't be humans. Like demons, we were her mistakes.

Am I doing the right thing?

I walked through her garden, brushing my hands over the flower heads, releasing a sweet scent and pollen into the air. The breeze swept the purple dust around me. Some clung to my feathers, but most scattered.

I must stop her creation before it goes too far.

This five-hundred-mile-long strip of land jutting off the coast into the Pacific was a test. This was Mother's do-over. But the cost was too high. Wasn't it?

Sometimes I envied my demon brethren and their simple minds. I envied their ability not to feel. But I felt it all, felt too much. Mother was creating life, but she was also destroying a world and its people. In her mind, it was an acceptable sacrifice. I could not allow that, no matter her promise of perfection.

What if she's right?

It didn't matter. No civilization born from the murder of another could ever be right.

"Pride... come..." At the whisper of her voice, I turned my back on the new world. The white tower dominated LA's original coastline. But it wasn't too late. There was time to bring it all down. I had played my act. It would soon be time for the curtain to fall.

Returning to the tower and Mother's chamber, I was met with a palace of ice and the small form of the little half-blood girl slumped at its center. The pair of crystal wings sprouting from her back had shattered, leaving jagged edges.

Gem.

My hands curled into fists. I hadn't known. I hadn't felt her distress.

"This..." Mother produced a single black feather. "She says it was a promise. Explain."

Mother had taken my feather from Gem. That was why I hadn't felt her alarm. But why was she here? Mother must have removed her from her cell for a reason. Ice glittered all around us. Gem had fought, but it hadn't lasted. Now, head bowed and shoulders heaving from her ragged breaths, she didn't look up. She probably didn't know I was there. But why had Gem fought? She surely hadn't attacked Mother. She was impulsive, but not foolish. What was I missing?

"It matters not." The feather in Mother's hand turned to black dust. She let the dust fall through her fingers. It vanished before it could settle on the floor. "This... *being*." Mother gestured at Gem. "I did not create her." Mother lifted her hand, and as though lifting Gem on puppet strings, she pulled Gem's limp body upright.

A familiar knot of anger tightened inside my chest. "What is the girl to you?"

"She is not of my design," Mother said. "Where did she come from?"

The full pressure of Mother's penetrating gaze speared into me, dug in, and hooked out answers. "She is a half-breed. Half demon, half human."

"A mistake, then?"

"No." I stepped forward. One, two, three. Mother lifted her chin, halting my advance. "Gem is *better* than us." Four steps, five.

Mother lifted Gem higher in the air. "*Impossible*." Water dripped from her melting wings.

There was another in the room, one I hadn't acknowledged for fear of revealing his presence to Mother. Ink marked his skin, painting him with the same marks that Mammon bore, plus those I'd used to keep Kar'ak at bay, enabling him to move freely around the tower for weeks. Now, the fool endangered everything by revealing his presence with a single word. "Stop."

Mother blinked. Confusion distracted her, her mind puzzling over how her water elemental had appeared so suddenly. "You bear his marks as well."

Also? She had seen Mammon?

"Release Gem," Torrent demanded.

Mother extended her free hand, but whatever she was trying to do didn't work. Her fingers curled in. The air crackled with power. Nothing happened.

Torrent smiled. While those glyphs marked his skin, he was immune to her influence.

"What is this deception?" Mother asked, her flawless face creasing with dismay.

"They stole the marks from me." Akil strode into the chamber. "Stole the king's gift, as I warned you they would."

Time slowed, and all I saw was Akil's smirk. Mother was not surprised to see him. And as he moved to stand beside her, his true motives became clear. He couldn't overthrow Baal in the netherworld, but here, he had something better. Why be satisfied with overthrowing a king when you could become a god? The king's marks showed at his open collar. He wasn't hiding them. He had no intention of hiding from her. That wasn't his way. I should have known. I should have expected this.

"*Greed...*" I stepped forward—my sixth step—but the air between us hardened at Mother's glance. *Turn.* I couldn't. My control was falling into her hands. My act, for all it was worth, was coming undone.

"Perhaps I was wrong to instill you with my power," Mother mused. "This is not the first time my children have betrayed me."

"I have not betrayed you," I defended. "Mammon is manipulating you."

Akil's smirk said it all. "And you have not been turning Mother's army against her? You have not had Torrent feed you information of Mother's creations so you could know which to manipulate to your cause? You have not visited the half-blood girl, asking after this?" He held up the PC-Eighty injector.

No. All my work, everything I had tried to accomplish, he had pulled it all down in seconds.

Akil dropped the injector and crushed it under his heel. "You plotted to stop Mother by using her own creations against her."

How did he know? How could he possibly…?

He had brought Gem to Mother. She had told him. Willingly or not, it didn't matter. He had used her—used all of us. Oh, what a fool I had been to trust him.

"Pride?" Torrent said, concern stuttering through his voice.

There was no way out of this. I had balanced everything perfectly, and Mammon had destroyed it.

Laughter burst free. I laughed so damn hard my wings shook, dislodging a few feathers. The laughter didn't help Torrent's wide-eyed expression, nor did it help Gem. She still hung in the air like a doll. But it felt good. Was I losing my mind? Perhaps. Did it matter? I had lost everything else. The future was insane, and I must have been as well for believing I could stop a deity.

"Immortality has not been kind to Pride's mind." Akil's words struck the touch paper, and I exploded forward, cutting through Mother's barrier, intent on wrapping my hands around Akil's throat. If his human aspect died, hopefully the demon Mammon would too.

"Kill him," Akil purred.

Mother dropped Gem. I knew because I saw the veil light dance through her broken wings as she collapsed. In the next breath, I was swatted out of the air and slammed into a wall of ice. Pain cracked down my back, through my head, and burst through my right wing.

"Discard them," Akil said, his voice like liquid poison.

A force—Mother's—dragged me from the tower. One moment I was inside, the next I was tumbling through air, wings flailing. Air tore at my feathers and howled a storm inside my head. I could fall forever. Would it be so bad? What else was left?

Gem. Gem was left. My little icy half-blood.

Her ice armor cut the light, scattering it in all directions as she fell like a star. An unconscious star that could not—would not survive the impact. Instinct plucked me out of my skin and drove me forward, gathering up the air and making it mine to wrap safely around her. I had her, she was mine, and I wouldn't let her go. Somehow, somewhere, I managed to snatch the plummeting Torrent from a fall that would have shattered his body. Gem needed him.

We landed where the broiling ocean met rocks. I stumbled, dropped my charges, heard Torrent grunt and Gem sigh, and swayed on my feet. They were safe. It wasn't enough, but it was a start. Two lives saved. I had thousands more, hundreds of thousands more to save.

I should have killed Greed.

Anger crackled, burned, sparked my element, churning up a storm. Damn him. Damn him back to Hell.

An engine growled nearby. I turned, dragging my broken wing behind me, and looked into the sunlight sparkling off the ocean surface.

A dark, sleek shape emerged from the sunlit glare. A yacht. From the deck, Adam Harper waved at us.

CHAPTER 26

"*T*hat sure all went to hell in a handbasket," Torrent grumbled, looking comfortably relaxed in the yacht's circular inbuilt couches, especially considering how I'd saved his foolish hide. We were on the *Reely Nauti*, the same boat I'd scouted out at the marina. It was his boat, or at least one he had borrowed and lived on before Mother had invited him to her comeback party.

Pen still marked Torrent's skin, keeping him hidden and Kar'ak at bay, so long as he kept his mouth shut. The past was littered with the bones of heroes and fools. Torrent's heroic blunder in the tower had almost killed him.

I walked through the cabin and out onto the rear deck. Gem was sitting on the edge, pants rolled up to the knee, feet swishing in the water. We were currently drifting miles out at sea. Perhaps Mother wouldn't notice us so far out. That's what Noah had suggested. A few miles of ocean likely wouldn't fool her, but I let him cling to his hope.

I was back in my man-suit, silently nursing my invisible broken wing and wounded pride.

"He freed us," Gem said, pausing to let the words sink in before squinting up at me. "He's freed me twice now."

She could only be talking about Mammon. Bitterness laced my tongue. I swallowed it down. "He's not what you think."

"No? He got us out of the tower. All of us. He came down with Katrina and told her to release us. Said we could be her most prized creations. He pandered to her sense of greed, I think. He found a weakness."

"He also told Mother to kill you. She could just as easily have torn us all apart at our most basic elements. Don't mistake his actions for charity. He'll always be self-serving."

"But she didn't kill us. She swept us out of the tower."

"To plummet to our deaths some thousand feet below?"

"But you were there to save us."

"I won't always be."

Her smile fluttered and died, and I wanted to take her in my arms again and keep her safe from the worlds that would see her dead.

It could so easily have ended differently. Had I lost consciousness, she'd be dead. Had she swept Gem out of the tower, but not me, I wouldn't have reached her in time. "Gem, don't go looking for heroes in demons. They do not exist. And if they did, Mammon would not be one."

She leaned back, bracing her arms on the deck, and continued to swish her legs in the ocean.

"You don't believe me," I said.

"It's not that." Pulling her legs from the water, she stood and padded across the deck to retrieve a towel. "He burned your wings. I know there's a lot of history between you, but he's changed."

"No, he hasn't. He's just making you believe that so he can use you when the time comes."

She approached and settled her little hand on my shoulder. "I'm not some naive half-blood anymore, Li'el. I know demons. You weren't there when he freed us. His intentions were good."

I thought I'd taught her better than this. How could she be so blind? "And you were unconscious when he exposed my entire plan to bring Mother down. Unconscious, I might add, because of his actions."

"I attacked Katrina. I did it to keep her attention off Adam and Noah—not so much Christian, since I don't really care if he dies—"

"You can't make angels of demons, Gem."

She smiled coyly. "Can't you?"

"I am, of course, the exception to every rule ever written."

She chuckled, and I didn't feel much like hiding my smile from her. I wanted to tell her I was sorry for so much, sorry for the past, for my mistakes, sorry for the things I hadn't done, and some that I had. But she was half human and that made her half in my care. I wasn't used to failing, and so far, failure was all I had accomplished.

"How's your wing?" she asked, taking her hand back. I instantly missed the touch.

The phantom bones throbbed. "It will heal."

"Good, because we're going back in as soon as you're up to it." She marched inside the cabin, leaving me alone on the deck.

In the distance, sunlight glinted off Mother's tower. It looked as though a giant had thrust a sword down LA's throat.

Sword... If I could get close to Mother, and if I could summon the elemental blade, it might be enough to strike her down. But then what? It wouldn't be enough to kill her. In fact, killing her could throw both worlds into turmoil. We needed the veil back in its original state. I had to shatter her and return her to the veil. How did one shatter a deity? How

241

could I break apart a goddess that an instinctual part of me loved and admired?

The elemental blade only came to those who knew their own minds and were in perfect control. It came to demons like Mammon, who hadn't wavered in their self-belief, as corrupt as those beliefs were.

I knew what I was. A higher demon who'd evolved. An angel, if ever there was such a thing. The first. I was sure of it. The blade would come to me.

"Li'el?" Gem called.

I entered the main cabin and found the small group waiting. Noah sat at a low table with Adam beside him, and Christian and Torrent loitered at the cabin's edges. Gem stood in front of them, determined as ever.

"You brought a demon back from the netherworld, and you're surprised when he shacks up with the bitch queen from hell?" Predictably, those were Christian's words. Surprisingly, I agreed.

Gem glanced behind her. "That *demon* let you out of your cell. He let us all out. Don't judge demons by their reputation. Some change."

Adam nodded at his daughter's words, a touch of pride in his eyes.

"Did you manage to return to EcoZone before Katrina captured you?" I asked them.

"Yeah." Noah leaned forward. Deep lines thinned his face, reminding me that he and Adam were fragile. This was hard on them both, but they persisted. They did not have elements to control, and they did not heal in hours. On the outside, they were weak and ineffective, but what they had on the outside didn't matter. The human spirit could not be crushed. If anything, in the face of adversity, it soared.

"That's how she found us," Noah went on. "Call it a hunch, but I think she's still tethered to that place. She knew we were there. Anyway, we er... we found something that could be important. The dome you saw..." He hesitated, tripping over the memories. "We think that's her origin."

"They put the veil under extreme stress," Adam explained, "by trying to siphon off power. That exchange of energies summoned Katrina, or Mother, as you call her. Looking through the records, the staff spoke of hearing voices. Later, they realized they had something conscious trapped inside the chamber and called it Katrina. It spoke to them. But by the time the workers' concerns were taken seriously, Katrina had hijacked the engineers' thoughts. Her release wasn't an accident. Katrina manipulated her way out of her cage."

Like a genie in a bottle, only this genie could remake worlds.

"We wondered if there was a way to somehow..." Noah made a pushing motion. "Get her back inside." He clearly hadn't met Mother. "And reverse the power. Send her back to the grid—the veil."

His plan held some merit. If I could shatter her next to that chamber with it open, her elements might return to the veil where they belonged. But the machine would have to be on, and with the chamber charged, I would be unpredictable.

Gem dug into her pocket and held out an injector, exactly like the one Akil had crushed. I frowned. She grinned. "Mammon asked Christian for only one. He knew there were more."

I took it from her. "He couldn't have known that."

Her smile grew. "Will the drug do anything to Katrina?"

"Unlikely." The hope in her eyes faded. I handed it back. "But it could prove useful." *For Mammon.* "Keep it close."

I had to lure Mother back to the EcoZone facility.

There was a way.

Greed had said she might be susceptible to the princes' traits. He had already pandered to her sense of greed. If I could manipulate her sense of pride, she might come to me. But I would have to summon the blade and kill Mother in the same chamber that had driven me mad enough to kill Anna. That close to the veil, I had killed to get my hands on power, to become like Mother. I would likely do the same again. Going back there meant letting go of my control, letting go of what it meant to be me, and returning to the demon I had once been. I had come back from it then, with Mother's help. But there was no guarantee I would come back a second time. I could lose what it meant to be Li'el.

The group all looked at me with hope burning in their human eyes.

Losing myself would be worth it.

CHAPTER 27

*P*urplish clouds hung over the forest and stretched toward a hazy mountain ridge in the distance. The temperature had dropped since we had last walked the trail. The shrubs we passed had wilted on their stems. Leaves had turned bronze. Mother's influence was spreading, subtly altering the seasons.

Gem walked silently beside me. The others weren't in sight, but I sensed them nearby, as planned. I wore my human guise, keeping my wings hidden to avoid snagging them in the foliage.

The huge buckled fence emerged. It had caught a few fallen branches and drooped under the weight.

"We beat my brother…" Gem said, brushing her hair back with both hands and quickly tying the blond mop in a short ponytail. "We can beat *her*."

Her brother's human mind had failed, as it often did with chaos elementals. Gem had killed him despite loving him, or perhaps because of it. The Institute had told her she couldn't love. I disagreed. Half-bloods like her had a way of circumventing the rules.

"When you fought Mother, did you feel her pull on your mind?" I asked.

Grimly, she nodded. "But it wasn't enough to make me do anything I didn't want to do."

Her human half was a blessing in so many ways. "I will need you to keep me *me* once we're inside." She cocked her head, looking at me side-on. "Higher demons can't resist the forces of the veil. Where we're going, I killed a friend for the promise of power."

"The cop? Ramírez?"

I nodded.

"I met her. She was nice. Had a lot of demon hang-ups."

"She had her reasons." But she had learned to forgive. And she had died for it.

"I'm sorry, Li'el."

"So am I." It shamed me to say it. I was demon and would always be demon. I could not escape my nature as Anna's death had clearly demonstrated. It hurt to think about and would for many, many years to come.

We hiked the last few meters to the abandoned facility. "I will be dangerous inside."

She nodded. "I've been training with Muse. She's as freakin' badass as they come. She taught me a lot about managing both sides of myself." Gem's smile was pure predatory confidence. "She made me stronger for being demon and human. So, I can totally take you, Prince of Pride."

I patted her head. "It's adorable you think so."

"Hey!" She ducked and batted my hand away.

I had no wish to tussle with Gem's ice barbs. She made vicious lessers look positively friendly, but it could come to that if I didn't get myself under control. "I am proud of you, Gamma." She laughed softly, but her eyes sparkled a little brighter. "I trust you."

When Mother came, she would not likely be as forgiving

as she had been in the past. I lifted my head and searched the cloud-dappled sky. No storm stirred the air. But she *would* come. This place was her source. It might be the only place that meant anything to her.

It was time to go inside, but I couldn't move forward. I had walked in there with Anna and become the worst of me. I was afraid—yes, that was the chill I couldn't shake. Afraid I would again hurt those I loved.

"I want to thank you," Gem said, tucking her thumbs into her combat pants pockets. The cool breeze whipped a few loose strands of hair across her face. "If it wasn't for you, I never would have found my place—my family."

Pride plucked at my heart. "There is no need to thank me. I merely gave you gentle nudges in the right direction."

"I met my real brother, Adam's son. He lost a sibling too. We have a lot in common. He's kick-ass."

Gem would be safer with them.

"I kinda hated you for a bit." She pursed her lips, nodding to herself. "Leaving me there with them, but it was the right thing to do, I guess."

"It's almost as though I know what I'm doing."

She jabbed me lightly in the arm. "We're lucky." She lifted her face and narrowed her eyes at the EcoZone building. "People, I mean. They're lucky to have you as their guardian angel. If anyone can stop her, you can."

Gem's faith bolstered my pride, but it also reminded me how pride often came before my fall.

Thickening shadows darkened the sky. I turned away and headed inside. "Let's begin."

The security table where I'd tried to breathe life back into Anna's body was blessedly empty. Wild animals or lessers had likely scavenged Anna's body.

I pushed that thought from my mind. "Take the stairs

down. You'll find the control room at the bottom. Once there, turn on the equipment."

Gem nodded and jogged toward the stairwell, building ice daggers in her hands.

Where the air had been dry before, it now smelled of damp and decay. Dead vegetation had blown in, gathering in the corners where it had started to rot. I wondered if, when this was over, I could persuade Mammon to set the building ablaze and reduce it to ashes. But that would mean revealing why this building deserved such drastic treatment, and I would not give that demon the satisfaction of knowing yet another way to hurt me.

Maybe I should burn my wings instead?

I should have done more.

A low hum trembled through the air.

This has to work. For you, Anna. For the mistakes I've made.

I shook off my human guise, unfurling my wings and anchoring myself in my true demon form. Relaxing my hold on my elemental touch, I sent it outward, stretching my touch far. Adam and Christian were close, but hanging back. Good.

I lifted my head, ran my tongue over sharp teeth, and braced myself, facing the forest.

See me, Mother.

The wave hit—a shocking blast of needle-like power that almost robbed me of control. I staggered, but the table where Anna had lain caught my eye, and on it, unnoticed before, her small cross necklace winked in the filth. *Control it. Be better than before. Be everything you can be. Not just demon. Be more.*

The sweet lure of power licked down my back, and a twinge of pain sparked down my newly healed wing, distracting my hungry thoughts. The pain was good. It reminded me of who I had been: the fallen prince, wings

248

burned, pride broken. But I had come back from that. I had learned from my fall, and I was not the same demon that had coveted power. It did not control me.

Before I realized I'd moved, I was at the table, the necklace dangling between my fingers. Its cool touch hardened my resolve. I had control.

I fastened the necklace around my neck and pressed the cross to my skin.

A figure sauntered into sight from the tree-line as though he had every right to be here. Not Mother.

Mammon—Akil.

Power throbbed over me, whispering, *Take it, destroy him, destroy them all. Make this world mine, make myself king.* I closed my fingers around the cross. The voices quieted.

Akil wore that hint of a smile that said everything without saying a word. Which of the two personas had control, I wondered. Here, Mammon preferred to be Akil. That said a lot about the demon if I cared to listen.

I bared my teeth. "Come two steps closer and I will take great pleasure in killing you."

Akil stopped at the threshold, breathed in, and narrowed his eyes on the facility behind me. "What are you doing here?"

"I might ask you the same."

"Then do."

"You betrayed me. Again. Baal was a fool to trust you."

He tilted his head and tugged on his sleeve cuffs. He crafted his words carefully like I crafted my acts. He hesitated only because he intended to build lie upon lie.

"Pride, you and I may not have agreed in the past, but neither you nor I wishes to see this world wiped clean for the sake of a misguided deity's idea of perfection."

My fingers itched to clamp around his neck. I didn't need

to strangle him to choke the air out of him, but it would be immensely satisfying.

He took a step forward. I flared my wings in warning. "I have no time for you and your games, Mammon."

He smiled. I wanted to claw that grin off his lips. "Games are all we have."

"Get out of my way. Go back to her. Go back to Hell for all I care. Just go."

Fire flickered in his eyes. "I didn't betray you. I gave you the weapons you needed. She's coming, and this time, she will not be lenient."

"I'm ready."

"There's another way."

"There was, until you…" I trailed off. A dark cloud moved *against* the breeze. Reaching out with my element, I found thousands of displaced pockets among the trees—all moving closer. The Blue Eyes.

"I have no wish to see you killed." Akil almost sounded sincere.

It was my turn to smile. "She won't kill me. I'm her son."

"No, but I will."

His human appearance flashed away in a blast of heat that singed the tips of my wings. I recoiled. *Not my wings. Not again!* And then a little icy demon was between us. Her glittering, jagged, razor-sharp wings sprang open and speared forward.

"Get away from my Pride!" Gem snarled. Swords of ice extended from her arms, poised and ready.

Mammon stamped backward, embers sailing from the edges of his wings. The king's marks shifted and twitched beneath his skin. "You are fools!"

Gem stalked forward—a shining beacon of light driving him back. "Why are you doing this?"

"Mother wants this," he growled. "She wants the power. She wants it all. You have given her the key to both worlds."

What key? What did he mean? A storm approached, filling the space between forest and sky and framing Mammon's burning wings.

The army of Blue Eyes drew closer, and behind them, Mother's great and terrible power reared up.

The veil's power pushed at my back, luring, demanding, seducing. *Take it and match her in gloriousness.*

Silent lightning forked above, unzipping the purplish sky, revealing the churning, bruised hue of the netherworld.

The veil had opened.

CHAPTER 28

The light from the netherworld spilled into the human world as the veil unraveled.

"Turn off the machine!" Mammon ordered. He spun and faced the oncoming horde of strange white creatures. They slunk from the trees, their whiteness creeping forward as one.

"No." I wasn't turning off the machine. It was opening the veil, but that was good. I needed Mother here. I needed her to see this, to see me. To be proud of her creation.

"Li'el?" Gem asked. "What's happening?"

I took to the air and threw open my wings so the crowd of Blue Eyes could witness all of me. I whispered air across each of them, reminding them of who I was. I could kill them, but I didn't. I could harm them, but I hadn't. I was their king, and they were under my control.

"*Stop*," I whispered.

They slowed as one.

"*Stop*."

Thousands halted. Leaves and dust settled, dirtying up their white skin.

See me, Mother!

I had her army. I had the veil. Now all I needed was the elemental blade. Lifting a hand, I called to it with every cell in my demon body. I was in control. I was the Prince of Pride. I had earned my title. The sword would come to me. It would complete me.

Any second now.

I reached harder.

Power crackled. The veil twitched. Elements churned.

The Blue Eyes suddenly collapsed. Every. Single. One.

No.

The sound of their collapse rumbled through the air like thunder, and behind them, inside the approaching storm, I felt Mother smile.

The spread of bodies dissolved into papery white flakes and stirred into the air, whipped up by a howling wind. Fragments clung to my black wings. *So many...*

She had killed them all.

"Pride!" Mammon snarled.

Thousands of lesser lives, thousands willing to believe in me. What if they were just the beginning? The people in her tower could be next, and then the world, until there was no one left to care for.

The clouds and sky churned and inside it, the weakened veil thrashed. And she came.

"Get inside," Mammon snarled at Gem. "Turn off the machine!"

If Gem listened to him, we would all die.

She hesitated, looking up at me for answers.

I needed more time. I needed to focus. I needed more control. I needed the blade. I needed... *more power.*

Dissolving into air, I poured inside the EcoZone building. The sound of Mammon's howl followed me close behind. More power. The blade was close. I could still do this.

Inside the chamber buried deep beneath the facility, Adam Harper stood at the controls. The rainbow colors of the veil washed over him.

"Pride?" he asked. His grip on the lever faltered.

"Keep it on!" I strode forward, pushing through ripple after ripple of desire telling me to turn and take it all.

The veil captured inside the dome danced and flowed. All the elements of creation, right there. A river of potential. *Mine.*

"Pride, no!" Gem reached for me, her ice shining.

I plunged my hands into the stream. I didn't feel her small hand on my shoulder until it was too late, but I heard her scream. They would hear her scream in the netherworld, because deep inside a stone cage, buried in the king's fortress where no light or air could reach, the mad queen screamed too. I heard her wail as though it were coming from my very soul.

Power. It was too small a word for the avalanche that crashed through me.

I stared into the veil, and Mother peered back at me, pride glowing in her eyes. *We will remake the worlds together.*

The humming slowed, and the throbbing wave of power stuttered.

No, no, no… Not yet. It wasn't enough.

I blinked and watched the flow of the veil thin to nothing.

Adam Harper had his hand on the lever. Defiance as strong as any demon's element burned in the mortal man's eyes.

"This is wrong," he said. Those words would be his last.

Mother appeared in a blast of white light.

With a gesture, she flung Adam backward. He hit a wall with a sickening crack.

"No!" Gem screamed. She flung a lance of ice, piercing

Mother's abdomen, but Mother merely swept it aside. She *was* the elements. Gem couldn't hurt her. None of us could.

Mother fixed Gem in her sights. She lifted her hand and crafted a ball of writhing light.

No, not Gem! I yanked open the veil, snatched Gem's arm, and shoved her through, blocking Mother's line of sight. Gem whirled and froze under my glare.

"Go!" I told her.

Pain erupted down my back and flashed across my wings. Sickening agony threatened to empty out my mind. All my beautiful black feathers curled in and fell to the ground like autumn leaves. *My wings... my wings... not my wings... I need my wings. I need them... They are me. They are my pride.* Could I save them? I scooped up an armful of feathers. I couldn't let them go. Not again. Not after everything they had cost me.

"This is... wrong." Adam Harper's words brought me back. He had gotten to his feet and stood behind Mother. Just a man. Not worthy of her attention while she worked to destroy me. But I saw what this unassuming mortal man held in his hand: an injector.

It wouldn't work.

His eyes behind his crooked glasses met mine. He *knew* it wouldn't work. "*Go,*" he mouthed.

He plunged the injector into Mother's back.

Mother jerked, then she turned and thrust both hands into Adam Harper's chest. In a blink, she turned everything he was and everything he would ever be into ashes.

Mother turned her attention to the control panel. The lever had broken, either by Adam or in the brief battle with Gem. She ran her hands over the controls, rage contorting her face, and then she turned the heat of that rage onto me.

Terrible power built, crushing in from all sides. The feathers in my arms burst into clouds of ash. Her needle-like elemental tendrils crackled against my skin. She had the power to make worlds or destroy them. She would destroy me, but I had control. I was my own demon, not hers.

"This world is no longer yours to remake." I stepped backward through the veil and closed it on her scream.

CHAPTER 29

*M*other's scream rang out across the netherworld's dark plains long after the veil had closed.

I'd fallen to my knees after coming through, shock and fury rendering me numb. I knew all too well how the ragged mess on my back looked, but strangely, it wasn't my wings I mourned. *She took my city and my people. But she has not broken me. No beast shall break me down again.*

I climbed to my feet and spread the shredded mass of sinew, muscle, and bone.

No beast shall take from me again.

Inside, all the rage, the injustice, the wrongness Mother had inspired bubbled up and broke free in a guttural roar.

I am Pride!

As my roar filled the silence, resounding demon cries howled and bayed in answer.

I was done bowing to demon games. It was my turn to reign.

Gem's intake of breath alerted me to her glittering presence. In all the darkness surrounding us, she shone as her demon self. "Your wings?"

"I don't need wings to destroy her. Come. This ends today." I swept Gem up in a funnel of air and tucked her icy body against me as we crossed the broken lands to the king's fortress.

I set her down in the courtyard and materialized solidly beside her. Lessers scurried into the shadows, sensing we weren't to be provoked. Gem kept her chin and wings held high. As a half-blood, she knew how to hide her fear. She had been to the netherworld before as a naive laboratory experiment who had barely known her name, let alone how to survive among demon-kind. The netherworld couldn't hold fond memories for her.

"Follow me," I told her. Lessers crawled along the hallway ceilings, curious and wary of us passing below. Gem's shimmering skin scattered light, sending it dancing across mildew-dripping stones. She dazzled while I absorbed shadows. The Court didn't know what was about to hit them.

Outside the throne room, I pushed my element ahead and flung open the doors. The Court was in session, Baal at its head, presiding over a squabble of bickering demons. As Gem and I strode in, a demon predictably tried something stupid and lunged at me. I choked him without sparing him a glance. Another hissed at Gem. She grinned back, sprouting ridges of ice armor in warning.

"Pride, you will wait!" Baal boomed.

"I don't think so." I shoved a sniveling water demon out of my way and slammed my hands down onto the table, scattering the glyphs to a chorus of gasps. I pointed a finger at Baal. "I made you a promise."

Fury rattled his scales. The king's lips rippled. "What do you want?"

"The mad queen."

More gasps. I scowled at the pathetic excuse for a Court. Half the demons here were barely more than lessers. They only called themselves princes in the absence of anything better. It was a disgrace to the Dark Court and a disgrace to my kin. Baal's reign was a joke.

"Get out!" I snapped.

Baal growled a warning. "The Court does not listen to you, Pride."

"This is no Court, as you well know. The Fall decimated the old way. It is time for you to evolve or die."

Snarls and growls bubbled among their number. I lifted my shredded wings and let them get a good look at the savagery inflicted upon them. "Get out and be grateful I haven't slaughtered you all, you pathetic excuses for demons."

Baal simmered in rage, but he dismissed his flock with a strained nod. "How dare you—"

"Save it," I snarled. "Do I look like I'm in the mood for demon power games?"

"What happened?" he finally asked. His glare flicked to Gem—an unknown demon—and back to me. "Where is Mammon?"

"Mother happened."

Baal's slitted eyes widened. I shouldn't have been surprised. Mammon had told me of Mother's origins, yet I hadn't believed Baal would hide the truth of her for all these years.

"You knew," I confirmed.

"It cannot be—"

"Oh, it is, and she's decided we're all mistakes and she's entitled to a do-over because of reasons."

"It is not possible." He stumbled away from the table—

261

from me—and regarded my wings with awe. "It's been so long, I almost believed my own legends. It cannot be."

"Get over it."

"Mother…"

I rolled my eyes and caught Gem's shrug. *Demons.* "The only reason Mother hasn't started remodeling here is because she can't come through."

"You know that for sure?" Gem asked.

"If she could, she would have come after us. That doesn't mean it'll last."

Gem considered that and asked, "Did my… Did Adam…" She didn't need to finish; the answer was already in my eyes. "He tried to stop her."

"No, he only meant to distract her. He knew exactly what he was doing. He saved us. He did a good thing in the end. You should be proud."

She pressed her frost-touched lips together and nodded firmly. This was not the place to discuss it, but she knew she could if she needed to. "Torrent?"

"I didn't see him or Noah. Only Mammon…" I wet my lips and returned to glaring at Baal. "Mammon is playing fast and loose with his allegiances."

"Mammon," Baal echoed. "The marks… He should be able to at least subdue her."

"Yeah, no. He has his own agenda."

Baal slumped forward, hands spread on the table, and bowed his head. "Mother… She'll destroy everything. We must stop her."

Finally! "And now we're on the same page. Give me the mad queen."

I had never known Baal to be fearful. He had always been a pillar of control. But as difficult as his demon face was to read, just the mention of his queen tightened his eyes. "She is… I cannot."

I knew what the mad queen was. I had witnessed her as a little girl when she had tried to bring chaos down upon us all. *Dawn.* She wouldn't be human now. Years sealed in the dark could destroy the most stable mind. Hers had never been stable to begin with. Chaos abhorred control. Whatever waited inside that stone prison would be unfriendly, but we were out of options.

"You can control her?" I asked.

"With the power of a Court, perhaps..."

"This Court?" I laughed. "Your Court is uninspiring, Baal."

"The Fall decimated our ranks," he grumbled.

"Make a new one."

"It's not that simple."

I snorted a laugh. "The rules we have lived by for millennia no longer apply. Two demon Courts sprang up in LA, albeit weak ones, but they wielded more power than yours does here." I pointed at Gem. "Ice." Myself. "Air." The king. "Earth." Mammon was fire and Torrent water. The king and queen would take their natural places as control and chaos. Voila, a Court.

"It's not that simple. We are not just our elements. You are Pride, Mammon is Greed—"

Again, I pointed at Gem. "Princess of Determination. Torrent is—"

"Resilience," Gem suggested with a shrug. It was as good a suggestion as any.

If demons could give droll looks, Baal was giving me one now. "You can't make it up. You must grow into your name. Become it. Besides, we do not have those goodly attributes in the netherworld."

"You don't have a Court either," I reminded him. "New Court, new rules, and we get to make them. Gem and Torrent have earned whatever name they claim. All we need is the mad queen on our side."

"You make it sound so... trivial."

"Because I've faced Mother and all of this"—I gestured at the space around us and the two empty thrones—"is nonsense. People are dying. My home is changing beyond recognition. A new Court, combined with the mad queen, is our only hope of stopping her. I know what your mad queen can do. She unmade the Prince of Envy. She can *unmake* Mother and turn her back into the elements. After the queen succeeds, we will deal with the fallout."

"She could also unmake the rest of us."

Oh, she could. But I had a hunch the queen wouldn't be so quick to slaughter those who had done her no harm. "It is a risk. But what choice do we have?"

"There must be another way. The sword..."

"The elemental sword is made from the veil. It can't be wielded against itself." At least, that's what I assumed after reaching for it and finding nothing. Or maybe I hadn't been in control enough to summon it. But I did not want to dwell on yet another failure.

Baal bowed his head. "I'll need time to prepare."

That sounded like an agreement, and it was good enough for me. "You don't have long."

~

WHAT HAD ONCE BEEN verdant meadows and ancient forests stretching for mile upon mile had been burned long ago. That didn't stop Gem from pacing the nearby shore while we waited for Baal to come around. Oily waters lapped at Gem's small feet, painting them black.

"When I first came here, everything tried to kill me," she said. A lesser scampered out of sight. A small thing, but its sharp teeth could have made short work of Gem's human appendages. "Now they run."

I had been watching her from afar, but clearly, she knew I was close. I materialized behind her and fell into step.

"A lesser won't pick a fight with something higher on the food chain."

"Is that what we've done?" She stopped and gazed across a lake so black and smooth its surface reflected the purples in the sky. "Humans, I mean…"

"Mother was always inside the veil. EcoZone merely gave her a voice and, eventually, an exit. Baal is as much to blame for keeping her existence secret from us."

"How do we put her back, Li'el?"

The waters swirled around a rock, distorting my already grim reflection. My wings ached, but it was a familiar ache, almost comforting. "With a demon like your brother."

Gem frowned. "Chaos?"

"The mad queen is like Delta. When I last saw her, she was nine years old and incredibly powerful. Now, she's likely your age."

"And the king has kept her inside the fortress all this time?"

I nodded. Gem was likely thinking of her time inside the Institute, reared away from what she called the Outside. She had much in common with the mad queen.

"She's extremely volatile and completely unpredictable."

She smiled sadly. "I know all about chaos."

Of course she did, having been designed to combat it should her brother lose control. "The ritual Baal performed to balance the elements, restore the veil, and contain her may have tempered her." We could hope.

"Baal is… not what I was expecting. The other demons were, but you and him, you almost sounded *normal*."

"What were you expecting? Grunts and growls? Maybe some posturing and a few sliced throats?"

"Well, yeah. *Demons*."

"I'm afraid this Court is not the best example of how the Dark Court once ruled. The Fall decimated the princes, and Baal hasn't forgotten his time among humans. He is perhaps one of the more reasonable demons."

"Like you?"

"There are no other demons like me." I grinned.

A moment passed where only the distant cries of lessers interrupted a gentle silence.

"Back at the facility, you were… were you in control?"

The power, the thrall, had been tempting. "I was."

She nodded and toed the blackened pebbles. "Adam stood up to her."

A great many people hated Adam Harper, but few could argue his death hadn't been brave.

"We will stop Mother." Anna's death would also have a purpose. I had to make this right for her and for the hundreds of thousands of people trapped in Mother's tower.

"You can't know that…"

Before Adam's death, she had been determined. Now, she looked lost. I nudged her wing back and hooked an arm around her waist, pulling her close. "Don't lose hope, little icy half-blood."

Her wan smile was for my benefit.

The surface of the lake rippled, and the earth shuddered. A flock of lessers exploded from their fortress roosts, and the netherworld air breathed out.

The king had set the mad queen free.

THE MAD QUEEN sat rigidly on her throne, smiling the kind of smile chiseled into wooden dolls. She was naked, like all demons, but where her body should have been, a cloak of shadows licked and coiled around glimpses of pale flesh.

A not entirely unpleasant shudder tracked down my spine, urging me to pull my wings close and drop to my knees.

She is the lesser of two evils, I reminded myself.

There was no sign of the confused nine-year-old human girl. She had shed and discarded that part of her. The creature that had emerged from her fortress cocoon was all demon. That was probably a good thing. Demons were more predictable than humans, although chaos would always be notoriously *chaotic*.

Baal stood to her left, guarded and reserved. The king wasn't pleased with having his queen unleashed.

"Pride, yes?" the mad queen asked. Oddly, American tinged her accent. She had spent the first few years of her human life among Institute scientists. If they could see her now, would they be proud or horrified?

I bowed my head and checked on Gem beside me. She swallowed, knowing all too well what it was like to face chaos and survive. "Yes, I am Pride."

"I have you to thank for my release?"

"With... conditions."

The mad queen chuckled. "You were not among those who trapped me, were you?" She pointedly skipped her gaze to Baal, placing the blame on him, but her king didn't respond.

"No," I agreed. "I was not."

"I suppose I am in your debt. For freeing me, I will grant you a favor, Pride. What will it be?"

There might have been a time when I would have asked her to make me her king, but that time and that demon were long dead. "I ask that you unmake a god."

When she laughed, it was the sound of walls crumbling and time coming undone. Madness lived inside her, the unique madness of chaos that repelled and enthralled demon-kind, but also the kind of madness we needed to save both worlds.

CHAPTER 30

*D*ark ringlets fell from the mad queen's head, almost concealing her two tiny spiral horns. She stood, gripping the yacht's rail, and looked at the tower thrusting up from the shore into the churning clouds above. She had probably believed she would never be free, or that she would never return to the human world, yet here she was, free and hopefully about to help us. I hoped her good-will lasted.

Baal stood behind me on the opposite side of the deck, wearing his human guise "Jerry," who was almost as big as his true demon form. Jerry's shaved head and all-over tattoos—similar to those he had gifted Mammon with—marked him as somebody not to be screwed with. He hadn't acknowl-edged me since releasing the queen. I took that to mean I would likely pay for releasing chaos on us all, but not yet.

Through the yacht's windows, I spotted Gem standing with Torrent inside the cabin. They talked too quietly for me to hear without eavesdropping. Gem was probably the only person I could trust to manage Torrent's unique condition, but I did not hold out hope for them. Torrent was little more than a figment of the demon Kar'ak's imagination. Their future was uncertain.

When Noah split off from the group and climbed the stairs to the control cabin, I ducked inside and followed, finding him looking out at an ocean colored pink from the red skies.

"How are you holding up?" I asked.

He tensed and only relaxed when he saw I was wearing my human guise, the man he thought he had known.

"I dunno." He shrugged. "Part of me wants to run away. And knowing what I do about them now…"

We could see the king and queen on the deck below. One stared at what was left of LA, and the other stared at his queen as though expecting her to attack him.

"It's probably best not to think about it."

"Uh-huh. The king and queen of Hell are on the same boat as me, I'm surrounded by demons, and we're about to try to stop some kind of demon-goddess from destroying the world. Sure, I'll try not to think about it." A shrill laugh finished his sentence.

I planted my hand on his shoulder and squeezed gently. "When have I ever let you down?"

"When you let them take you away for two years." I'd expected the sadness in his eyes, but the acidity in his words? "You could have stopped Christian from taking you and you didn't."

"Because I would have killed him and his men, and they didn't deserve that. You forget, I have lived hundreds of centuries. Two years means nothing to me."

His nostrils flared and his lips turned downward. "It meant something to me." The words held more weight than they should have. His feelings went beyond simple friendship.

Ah.

I understood now why he hadn't left. Why he was still here despite the nightmares surrounding him. Why a human, mortal and vulnerable, chose to live among monsters. Of course there was only one reason why he would face such things.

He tried to cover the confession with a smile, but it didn't stick. "You probably think I'm an idiot, right?"

"I don't think you're an idiot. Love is a perfectly natural response when faced with someone as magnificent as I."

His eyes widened. Shock dashed across his face, and then he saw my crooked smile and laughed. "I hate you sometimes."

I patted his shoulder. "I often inspire the whole range of human emotions. It's a talent."

"Gem told me they call you Prince of Pride where you come from. They got that right, huh?"

Prince of Magnificence was taken."

He turned to admire the demons on the deck below. The humor faded from his face. He bumped his fist against the controls. "What am I doing here?"

I covered his fist with my hand, holding it tight. "Reminding us who we're fighting for."

He looked at my hand on his and then up at me.

Over the years, I learned that we do not choose who we love. Oh, we think we do. Humans and demons alike assume they have control of such things, but they don't. We don't. Love is like chaos, wild and unpredictable. It is as likely to destroy as it is to flourish.

I would have spared Noah that fate had I realized his feelings sooner. No good could come from loving demons. I released his hand. "Get us close to the shore and drop anchor. We'll need you."

"Do you..." He swallowed hard with a click. "Do you need me?"

"Noah…" He turned his face away. "I will always need my friends."

He nodded sharply.

I descended to the lower deck. The yacht's engines growled as Noah fired her up.

"Ready?" Gem asked.

"For some things but not others." At her confused expression, I added with a reassuring smile, "Let us hope so."

~

AKIL WAITED on the exposed rocks at the foot of the tower, his tailored attire obscenely human against the backdrop of Mother's tower.

"What's the suit doing here?" Torrent growled.

Gem pressed her little hand against my chest, holding me back. "Let me talk with him."

I glanced back at the mad queen and Jerry making their way up the rocks. Mammon couldn't fail to notice who they were, yet there was no hint of surprise on his human face. But he wasn't the type of demon to let emotions show on his face that he didn't put there. If anything, he appeared mildly amused by our arrival.

Was he Mother's minion, I wondered.

"Li'el…?" Gem asked.

I covered Gem's hand with mine, pressing it closer to my chest. "Do not trust him."

She had grown and changed. She was not the same naive little icy half-blood girl who had let demons control her.

"I can take him." She winked.

Mammon was thousands of years old and an expert at manipulating human emotions, of which Gem had many. She most definitely could try to take him. Many had tried and failed.

Gem met my glare with her own. Princess of Determination, indeed. I released her hand, letting her go.

The king as "Jerry" stopped next to me while the oily touch of the queen's chaos crept closer to my other side. It did not stand between them by chance.

The boat's engines revved as Noah pulled the vessel away from shore, leaving just Christian clambering over the rocks. The hunter had been stubborn in his wish to join us. Perhaps he had something to prove.

Gem stopped in front of Akil, looking tiny compared to the man/demon. Akil lifted a hand and brushed the back of his knuckles down her cheek. The intimate touch set my invisible wings on edge. He said something too softly for me to hear before the brisk ocean breeze snatched it away. I fought the urge to turn myself into air and insert myself between them. Gem would not fall for his tricks. She was better than that, better than him.

The mad queen's cloak of chaos tendrils licked around my legs. I slid my gaze sideways. The look in her eyes spoke of revenge. She had her glare trained on Akil. He, alongside the king, had trapped her in the fortress, and now she had both within her reach. I deliberately caught her eye. Chaos churned in her gaze.

"Revenge will change nothing," I whispered, sending the words to her on a puff of air so only she would hear.

She tilted her head, letting the words sink in. How many times had I sought revenge on Mammon for all he had stolen from me? For decades, I had thought of nothing else. Revenge had become second nature, until the Fall, until all those months I had spent in *hiding*, until Gem had come and everything had changed. I had changed. Could the queen of chaos change too?

"Wait!" Gem blurted.

Akil's arm hooked around Gem, and with a smile tossed carelessly my way, he vanished, taking her with him.

I sprang forward and was met with the king's arm blocking my way.

"Move!" I snapped.

"Mammon has his reasons," the king drawled.

"And what if those reasons have nothing to do with saving this world or its people?"

"Mammon has changed."

I hooked my claws into the king's clothing and yanked him forward, unfurling my wings and discarding my human act. "Change is not always good!"

With a snarl, I flung him aside and dissolved into air.

Damn him. Damn them all. I would not let Mammon take Gem from me.

It didn't take long to find them. Mammon had taken her to Mother's chamber at the top of the tower. I silently poured through the tunnel as Akil threw Gem to her knees in front of Mother.

"Half-bloods are not mistakes," he declared. "They are evolution. They are better in every way. Do not destroy a masterpiece merely because you cannot see its beauty. Build on it."

Mother stood at the center of her chamber, and all around her, mounds of flesh were piled high. The stench of death hung heavy and warm in the air. Limbs rotted, and skin shriveled. Mounds of dead demons. *No...* I drifted closer. Failed creations. Piles and piles of her "mistakes." And Akil had brought Gem here?

"You bring me these gifts, my child," Mother crooned, gossamer wings refracting the light. "But I cannot build on flawed foundations."

Akil had been bringing her demons to work on. These were all his gifts.

But not Gem. Never my Gem.

"These hybrids, half-bloods, they are not like the others," he said.

If I materialized, Mother would likely toss me from the tower or worse. There had to be another way to get to her.

Gem hadn't moved. Her blue eyes tracked Mother, and there, in her hands, jagged icicles formed.

Akil circled the room, drawing Mother's attention *away* from Gem. "What if you returned to us too soon?" he asked Mother. "What if this girl is your masterpiece? Human *and* demon. The best of both of your creations. I do not deny we are flawed. Demons and humans, we are imperfect. The atrocities we have committed, the millions slaughtered in the name of greed, pride, and fear. You look upon us and our history and you see our mistakes, you see how we have destroyed the worlds you gifted us, but the half-bloods are different. Demons will fail. Humans will fail. It is in our nature to destroy ourselves, but among the destruction, your creations evolved. Don't you see, Mother?" He stood with his back to the tower's vast platform into the sky, drawing all of Mother's attention away from Gem. "Human and demon together. They are diamonds in the rough."

Gem lifted her head and fixed her sights on Mother's back. But Gem alone couldn't stop her. Ice was another of Mother's elements. Gem could only distract her.

"Half-bloods..." Mother repeated.

"Look again at what your creations have evolved into."

Mother turned to find Gem on her feet, ice daggers palmed, her demon body aglow with icy crystals. Mother approached, her white skin shimmered and her wings fluttered. "Yes... I see now."

Behind her, Akil stripped his human appearance away, revealing the lava-veined demon beneath and the king's markings aglow on his dark skin. Whatever he intended to do, he had better do it fast.

Mother extended her hand to Gem. "My child, it is true. There is perfection in your construction."

Mammon, hurry.

Why was he just standing there? There had to be a point to this deception. Why else would he manipulate Mother with these promises? Damn him to hell. I couldn't wait for him to screw up.

I sailed over and hovered above Mammon's blazing hot presence from behind. *"Why are you waiting?"*

"These marks did not come with instructions..." he thought back.

The marks had been revealed in his demon form, but nothing had happened.

Gem was on her own.

"Yes." Mother clutched Gem's chin, lifting her off her feet. "Yes, I see the future now. I was so focused on the failures that I did not see the one success."

Gem didn't struggle or cry out. Her gaze was lost under Mother's attention, as mine had been many times before. How could I have expected Gem to survive when I knew how potent Mother's touch was? She was just one half-blood girl surrounded by ancients. Gem would fail.

I materialized beside Mammon and pulled my element in, drawing a storm of air through the tunnels. Beside me, Mammon's fire flared hotter, fed by the oxygen, and so did the king's marks. I staggered away, struck by the sudden influx of power. My power had bolstered his.

We needed more elements. We needed them all!

"Gem, ice now!"

Mother spun, dragging Gem with her. The entire weight of two worlds slammed down on me. Mammon staggered and hunched low against the force, but I would not bow to her. Never again would I bow to any beast.

I flung open my wings and winked at Mother. "I am air and everywhere."

A squall of air and Mammon's fire slammed into Mother, driving her backward. In her grip, Gem's ice flared, dazzling and jagged. Gem brought her ice blades up, angled them at Mother's sides, and grinned. "Survival of the fittest... *bitch*."

She plunged the ice through Mother's ribs, wrenching a scream from Mother.

Mother flung Gem away and whirled on Mammon and me, facing my firestorm. We needed more elements. There were too few of us here to fully subdue her.

"Gem, go!" I called "Get the others!"

Mother lifted her hand and shut off my air as easily as tightening a faucet. I grasped at nothing, stripped of power. *No, not again.* I would not be weak. She had already taken my wings. She would not take my element too. I mentally reached for the veil and summoned the blade.

Mother glanced at Mammon. His fire still raged, and the demon smiled, knowing he was immune.

The blade landed in my hand. Elemental glyphs danced along its length, and the veil energies dripped from its edges.

Mammon unleashed a river of flame. It galloped across the floor and washed over the mounds of dead demons, igniting their carcasses and filling the chamber with smoke. With the blade in hand, sensing her through the air, I lunged forward. Perhaps Mammon and I could do this. At the very least, we could hold her back. Mother yanked the sword out of my hand. It exploded like fireworks. Wayward elements spun into the smoke. Mammon growled a curse. His fire spluttered. This wasn't working. Everything we threw at her failed.

No element and no sword. What other weapons did I have?

The smoke suddenly cleared, revealing scorched carcasses, Mammon on his knees, and Mother looming over him. "You betrayed me. You *lied* to me."

"I told you what you wanted to hear."

She would kill him. Despite the marks throbbing along his wings and chest, without the other elements, neither of us was strong enough to stop her.

"You are no god," he said, lifting his head. "You are the mistake."

She laughed, and the sound made me want to curl my wings around me and hide. But I was not that demon. I was something else, something new. We had all changed. Mother was obsolete.

Chaos entered the room like a hurricane of living darkness.

"Pick on a demon your own size." The mad queen tossed lashings of chaos that sparked and *unmade* everything they licked. Holes appeared in the floor and walls, charred bodies exploded into ash, and the markings on Mammon's chest flared brighter still.

Mother whirled in time to witness the tendrils of chaos hook through her lattice skin and begin to unravel her being. She looked down, watching in horror as the mad queen's black eels ate at her legs, her waist, her wings, plucking her apart, unmaking her.

Yes. Yes! It was working.

Chaos against creation. Chaos *undoing* creation.

I caught Mammon's eye. *"Get the humans out,"* he thought. *"All of them."*

And leave him alone with the two most powerful demons in existence?

His lips turned up. *"You will have to trust me eventually. It may as well be now."*

Trust him?

"Your pride has already killed many. Will you let it be the death of thousands more?"

I had never hated any demon more for being right.

Mother let out an enraged scream and directed all her fury at the mad queen. Chaos tendrils recoiled and unwound from unmaking Mother. They reeled back in. The mad queen blinked suddenly innocent eyes, and inside, the little girl she had once been peered out.

This wasn't working. We needed all of us. We needed a Court.

"Run!" I hissed.

"You!" Mother flung a hand at me.

Air—my air—picked me up off the floor and flung me against the wall, pinning me there. My chest constricted, throat closing. No air. Couldn't breathe.

"And you..." She tried to lift Mammon but failed, his marks making him immune to her influence. That only enraged her more. "You..." She dashed toward me. "You are the architect of all this deception. You deem yourself above me? You, a simple demon of my creation? It is time you all learned to respect your mother's love!" She stopped so close I could only see her. Just her. My entire world. "Love me or die."

A gunshot rang out—such a human sound among all the chaos and snarling elements. Mother's head jerked to the side and fragments of her lattice skull exploded outward. Suddenly, I was back in my restaurant, watching a journalist put a gun to her head. Only this time, Torrent held the rifle, and beside him, Christian grinned like the hunter-killer he was.

Mother collapsed, and a second later I fell to my knees

beside her, gasping all my air back in. She wouldn't be out for long. The wound was already stitching itself back together.

"Anti-elemental-etched rounds," Christian declared, sauntering over and giving Mother's unconscious body an experimental jab with the toe of his boot. "One hundred percent Institute approved."

Mother's body crumpled like paper and collapsed into an ashy mound.

Christian staggered back, alarmed. Had the arrogant demon hunter just saved us all with a single bullet? Maybe I wouldn't have to kill him after all.

"It can't be that easy." I used the cracked wall to steady myself. It was never that easy.

Torrent scoffed. "You call what just happened easy?"

Cracks had appeared in the floors, branching out from the mad queen's holes. My gaze tracked those cracks to where the mad queen stood. She wasn't looking at any of us and didn't even appear to care that we'd disabled the deity. She only had eyes for Mammon. He climbed to his feet and shook himself all over.

"Where's Baal?" I asked. He should have been close to the queen.

"Freeing the people," Torrent replied. "His earth element is the only thing that can break open the tower's cells."

The outline of white flakes dissipated, swept into the air by a light breeze. Was it over? I crossed the chamber to the open section of wall and out onto the ledge. The pinkish light was fading and the clouds drifted like torn cotton candy. I could just make out the black speck of *Reely Nauti* on the mass of ocean below.

A tremble shuddered through the tower. Grit rained from the chamber's ceiling.

"Er… we might wanna leave now," Torrent suggested.

"Where's Gem?" I asked and received blank looks in reply. "Torrent?"

"I thought she was here... with you?"

Mammon narrowed his eyes on the dissipating white flakes. "Deception..." he hissed.

Like all "good" demons, Mother had *lied*.

CHAPTER 31

We didn't have the means to accommodate thousands of refugees. The best we could do was point the freed people toward what had once been the city limits and hope whatever authorities waited on the other side would pick them up. Baal ushered the pale and distraught survivors along, using his sense of control to keep them calm.

Gem wasn't in the tower. I'd searched high and low, found dozens more caverns filled with dead demons, but not Gem.

"Can't you do that thing you do with the feathers?" Torrent asked once I'd joined him in the cliff house.

I paced. One, two, three, four, five, six. Turn. "Mother destroyed the feather I gave her." One, two, three—I couldn't lose Gem—four, five, six. Turn.

She wasn't at the house either. But Mammon was. He stood where the tower filled the void in the wall.

This was his fault. He had taken Gem to make Mother think she was the answer to her creation problem.

As I approached Mammon, parts of the tower crumbled

away, tumbling down its flanks and coming to rest on the old, scarred network of streets.

"Baal is undoing her work," Mammon observed.

"What did you say to Gem?"

The fire demon rolled his broad shoulders, dislodging ashes from the edges of his wings. "I told her to trust me."

My smirk held a razor's edge. *Trust him?*

"I wish to find her as much as you do," he said.

"I believe you because it's what you do. You take what's mine."

He snorted and shook his horned head.

Torrent glowered behind him. "Are you going to stand here bickering or look for her?"

The glyphs scrawled on his skin still held, keeping his demon self at bay, but that didn't make the water elemental any less right.

"I know how to find her." The mad queen stood in the doorway. She had her hands cupped in front of her, and as we approached, she held them out and opened one hand, revealing a single feather sculpted of ice. "Found on the rocks by the ocean."

Partially melted, it lay in a pool of water in the mad queen's palm.

"Water..." Torrent moved and then paused, reconsidering. "May I?" The queen nodded, and Torrent dipped his fingers into the water, then swore. "It's not working."

He yanked up his sleeves and frowned at the swirling marks penned on his forearms. He couldn't use his element without his demon half. Being demon meant letting Kar'ak out to play. "Keep me in line," he said. "Just make sure I find her."

I nodded.

He used his wet fingers to rub out one faded mark, then another. On the third, his hand paused, and his invisible elemental touch slithered into the room. One more mark scrubbed off, and Torrent's human aspect peeled apart, revealing scaled wings and predatory claws.

Kar'ak smiled his slippery smile. "I know where she is."

~

THE WEAKENED VEIL at the site of EcoZone's energy labs let us through into the netherworld and onto its parched and silent landscape.

"The mother is here," Baal confirmed. He spread his dragon-like wings and sniffed the air. "Already she taints my home with her changes."

I turned my head, seeking the direction of the fortress.

I had to get Gem back.

Kar'ak gazed at the netherworld spread before us, his eyes taking on a curious appreciative glow. All he had wanted was to return as a prince. Well, he'd gotten his wish.

Mammon slapped the water demon on the back and huffed a laugh when he stumbled forward. Kar'ak was only marginally smaller than Mammon. They were both formidable demon princes. Did I have Kar'ak's scheming to contend with as well as Mammon's? I couldn't afford to care.

Turning to air strained my already weakening element, but I had no choice. I had seen what Mother's failed experiments amounted to. I would not allow the same to happen to Gem.

"We face her inside the fortress," Baal said. "All of us." His chaos queen regarded him coolly. "And we combine all our elements." The mad queen lowered her chin. "It is the only way."

~

WHERE LESSERS HAD SCURRIED and cawed in the courtyard, they now lay dead in Mother's wake. As air, I followed the trail of rotting carcasses, scouting ahead, spilling in through open doors. The throne room doors hung open. I spilled inside and stalled at the sight I found.

No!

Gem lay sprawled on her back on the glossy glyph-marked table. Frost glittered across the floors and up the walls as though her element were trying to escape.

Ice crystals hung suspended in the air.

Gem.

Her chest had been cleaved open. Mother had pinned her down to dissect her from the inside out. With her body encased in ice, I couldn't tell if she was breathing. I couldn't feel her heartbeat. I couldn't feel her at all.

I was too late.

Shock drenched me. I hung over the scene, hope slipping through my fingers.

I was her guardian.

And I'd been too late.

"Come, my child..." Mother whispered in her sweet, soothing voice. "Come see this creature for what it was... a marvel of two species combined."

How can I claim to be good if all I leave behind are corpses?

I materialized at the side of the table, opposite Mother, and took Gem's hand, freeing it from the ice. Her blue eyes were open, unseeing. What had her final moments been like? Had she cried out for me? Had she held on until the last possible moment, hoping I would come like I had in Boston? But I hadn't arrived in time. I hadn't saved her. What kind of angel was I if I couldn't save the ones I loved?

"You killed her." The words didn't sound like mine. They had taken on an icy edge borrowed from Gem. Mother had taken my wings, and now she had taken my Gem. Wrath burned like an inferno within.

"Of course." Mother's milk-white lips quirked. "But it is no loss. I will craft many more like her."

"They won't *be* her." Words. Distant. Detached. Spoken because she expected a reply, but my thoughts churned with a terrible vengeance.

Mother's expression barely changed. She didn't care that she had ended a life. She wasn't capable of caring, just creating. "Of course they will be the same. You are all my creations. You are all mine to do with as I please."

I carefully let go of Gem's cold hand. She had been the little icy half-blood I'd taught to be human, taught to hope and dream. She had only just begun to live.

I shot out a hand and clamped my fingers around Mother's throat, yanking her close. The touch burned and crackled, pain lashing up my arm. I didn't care. Pain was good. I knew pain. Pain made me real and reminded me who I was.

Mother's glare pulled me in. The lure of her power tried to wrap around me and smooth the pain away, but she would not seduce me again. I was not hers. Gem hadn't been hers. We had evolved beyond what Mother had made us. She had no claim on us, not anymore.

"You're just demon," I hissed.

Her lips twitched, all the colors of the veil swirled in her eyes, and her whispers started inside my thoughts.

"Mammon, now!" Baal commanded.

Vast dark wings opened behind Mother. The king's marks sparked alive, burning across the wings' expanse and tossing out the kind of heat that melted worlds. Mother flinched in my grip and tried to writhe free. Air rushed in through the windows at my silent call. I pulled it from Mother too. She was the veil. That meant her elements were also mine. *Air.* I breathed it in, dragging it from far and wide, washing it over Mammon's wings, flaring his fire hotter, *feeding* his heat.

Mother swung her head back to me. Water bubbled from between her lips. She spluttered and lashed against my hold.

Torrent or Kar'ak. Neither or both. It didn't matter who.

Good.

Stone trembled all around, reshaping, undoing the fortress walls and sealing us inside a cavern. Baal.

But we needed ice to close the circle. We needed Gem.

I shoved Mother backward into Mammon's heat. Stone reached out to embrace her, but where it touched her skin, the rocks crumbled to dust. Mother whirled in a flurry of color, flung open her wings, unsheathed her claws, and screamed at the three demons. Kar'ak, Baal, and Mammon held their ground, each ablaze in their element.

"Gem..." I pressed my hands to her face, melting ice under my touch. "We have a deal, remember?" Her head rolled to one side. I righted it and peered into her shallow eyes. "You do not get out of an agreement with me so easily." I pressed my lips to hers and breathed into her. Her chest lifted, ice cracking. Frost clawed at my mouth, locked on my hands, and climbed up my arms. *Breathe.* Again, I pushed air into her lungs. *Breathe for me. Live.*

Mother raged and yanked on the elements, trying to twist the world around her. Air shifted, stone cracked, and I stared into Gem's eyes. I could bring her back. I'd failed Anna, but I would not fail Gem.

Mother's cackle cut through the howling storm.

The oily touch of chaos spilled in from all sides.

"I will unmake you," the mad queen purred, unleashing a storm of black and purple chaos tendrils.

I curled my ruined wings in close. Chaos whipped across my back. All the elements raged, the veil coming alive all around us, but inside the cocoon my wings made, I saw only

Gem's glittering eyes. My lips on hers, I pushed air into her body, pouring all my will with it. *Breathe, Gem. Live. It cannot end like this. Death cannot have you. Come back to me. You are mine.*

Her eyelashes fluttered.

A gasp hissed through her teeth.

"We need you…" I told her, opening my wings. *I need you.*

Ice snapped and sighed outward. She saw me then, saw the fear on my face and heard the storm raging all around us, and she smiled. *"It's okay,"* she mouthed. Her wound folded inward, closing up. The elements poured in, called from the netherworld around us, and melded together, enhanced, *crafted* into something more than we could ever be apart. That power of the veil rebuilt Gem and soared through every demon here.

Mammon was aglow, barely distinguishable inside a furnace of light. All around, the elements poured and howled, cracked and tore, lashed and beat. I yanked Gem to her feet. "Now!"

Gem's ice wings exploded outward, casting a dazzling net of jagged ice over Mother. Chaos spiraled in, knotting darkness around and through Mother's wings. Fire raced across the floor and surged up her legs. Water bubbled up from inside her, streaming from her eyes and mouth. And the walls closed in, crushing all the elements in close, building pressure until, all at once, the storm they had created snapped tight, wrenching Mother's construction apart.

Mother's scream collapsed into silence. The elements fled. My grip slipped, and the air rushed away from me. Fire spluttered and extinguished with a hiss. Water from Gem's melting ice soaked into the now motionless rocks.

Above us, the colors of the veil dissipated.

Mother was gone.

"We do not have long…" With a sweep of his hand, Baal

parted the stone, opening a window in the rock wall. The veil twitched and danced in the netherworld's purple skies. Its colors had dulled. It was closing once more.

Once the veil was sealed, there would be no passing through. Whatever side we were on when it sealed would be our homes for a very, very long time.

Gem's gaze slid from me to Kar'ak. He stood between Mammon and the mad queen, wing tips dripping water. I knew what Gem was looking for, but he was not Torrent. She left my side and approached him, head up, wings proud. She might have been the smallest demon in the chamber, but her presence was one of the largest.

"I know you're not him," she said.

Movement to his right caught my eye. The mad queen bowed her head and drifted silently into the shadows, cloaking the edges of the chamber.

"But he's in there," Gem continued. "He is a part of you."

The mad queen's footsteps were so light I could barely feel the shift in the air as she edged around the chamber, approaching me and Baal or, more likely, the window behind us.

Kar'ak jerked his chin, black horns catching the flickering light.

"He has the right to decide his future," Gem said.

"The pretend man inside has no rights," Kar'ak replied, adopting the haughtiness of all self-important princes.

The mad queen lifted her dark eyes and caught my gaze. Nobody saw her moving through the shadows. Nobody but me. She and I had a deal. I freed her, and in exchange, she would help us destroy Mother. That deal was complete. Her eyes turned shrewd. She had been imprisoned much of her adult demon life and all her human one. She would not quietly go back inside her prison.

The king's attention was locked on Gem, but it wouldn't last.

The mad queen shook her head. Just a tiny shake, a plea. Her voice eased inside my thoughts. *"Do not tell them, friend."*

She had done nothing to deserve a lifetime prison sentence. Yet she was chaos. Nothing good ever came from allowing chaos to go free.

I shifted and eased my wings open, appearing to merely relax, but their ragged expanse offered her cover.

"Stop her!" Mammon lunged.

I blocked his charge, wings splayed and teeth bared. "Back off, Mammon!"

"Get out of my way, fool!" Mammon moved to swipe me aside. I blocked his forearm with mine, hissing at the burn the block cost me. Crimson fire rimmed his black eyes.

"Let her go. She has earned it."

"You have no idea of what you speak. She—"

"And what if she's changed?" I challenged.

Mammon snorted. *Hypocrite.*

I pulled my wings in, revealing the empty shadow where the queen had been. "It seems she does not want to be imprisoned again."

I allowed a smirk to play on my lips. But where I expected to find fury in his glare, I found what looked like... humor? How could that be? Unless he had wanted her to escape? Wait, had I played into his plans? Oh, no, no, no... I narrowed my eyes at the Prince of Greed.

His responding grin was for me only.

Slippery beast.

Stone rumbled, and a doorway opened in the chamber wall.

"Go," Baal ordered. "Bring back my queen before she creates another crisis."

Mammon turned, deliberately dusting me with embers,

and marched from the room. It was an act, all of it. He had no intention of bringing her back.

The glower Baal cast my way was not kind. "Some things never change." He headed for the doorway. "You have until sunbirth. For your sake, I hope you choose the human world, Pride. I do not believe the netherworld is large enough for both your ego and Mammon's."

Baal paused and produced my feather. A lick of air stole it from his claws and delivered it into my hand. He snorted and slid his crocodilian gaze to Kar'ak and Gem.

The king considered his next words carefully. "Kar'ak, a new Court rises, and I suspect you will not enjoy its reign. The old ways are dead. Find a way to live with yourself. It doesn't have to be here. You should consider the half-blood's proposal before the veil closes for good."

"I haven't proposed anything," Gem denied.

Baal's grumbling laugh shook the floor.

Gem looked to me. If she wanted answers, I wouldn't give her any. That had never been part of our agreement. The answers were hers to find.

"Sunbirth," I told her. "I hope to see you in the City of Angels." Staying here or returning to LA was her choice. I would never take her choices from her.

Her little smile grew. She'd be there.

Kar'ak eyed me, his demon glare calculating.

I sauntered up to him. "Don't let my civilized manner fool you. Hurt her and I'll rip your wings off and yank your insides out through your throat. You don't want to know what I'll do with your horns. Let's just agree that I have the imagination you lack." I bopped him on the nose and he snarled in response.

Gem could handle Kar'ak. And she had my help.

"I am air and everywhere," I purred. I'd be watching him, but I also had a score to settle, and judging by the light bleeding across the horizon, I didn't have long left in the netherworld.

~

Soon, I'd be home. Soon, I'd rebuild my city. But revenge called, and I had been a long time answering.

I found the mad queen sitting atop a rocky outcrop, legs pulled up to her chest, her gaze fixed on the fortress across the barren plain below. She hadn't gone far, perhaps because the fortress was all she knew. A prison might become a home if there was no better option.

I approached from behind, deliberately disturbing dried twigs to avoid startling her.

"I want to unmake them all." She lifted her face to the breeze. "But there is one I want to unmake the most. I trusted him once, and he betrayed me. I want to unmake him, but when he is gone, I know I can't bring him back, and... I don't want him gone forever. Forever is such a long time."

She spoke of Mammon, and I knew those feelings well.

I stopped at the edge of the outcropping, letting the breeze filter through my naked wings. The veil twitched in the sky, and below us, lessers scurried in the grasses, cawing and sniping at one another for scraps. There was a terrible beauty in the netherworld, like the queen herself.

"I know revenge." I slid my gaze to the fortress. "It's a road that leads only one way."

She joined me at the edge and looked down. "I thought I would go home, but I am not human. Not anymore. This is my home now."

No, she wasn't human. She was gloriously demon. This world would need her chaos. "I find it's far better to get even than to get revenge."

Cocking her head, a curl of hair fell over her purplish eyes. "What does that mean?"

"Play him at his own game. He seeks to use you. Allow him to think he is, but make sure you're using him in return. It's the demon way."

Understanding flickered in her eyes. "You are not like the others."

I smiled into the netherworld wind. "There are no other demons like me."

"Am I interrupting?" a demon voice snarled from behind.

Mammon.

Not so long ago, I would have flung everything I had at him. Now, after everything we had seen, my decades of thirsting for revenge seemed trivial.

"The road only leads one way," the mad queen said. She turned and studied Mammon from head to toe. Wing tip to wing tip. He stood, unfazed by her visual exploration. If anything, the low-slung nature of his wings made him appear almost regretful.

His gaze settled past me on the colors of the veil. Mammon's veins pulsed softer. His wings bowed, and for a moment, the humanity in his eyes yearned for more, yearned for freedom beyond the veil. Akil was in there. The man. He had ties to the human world, perhaps even a life, should he want it.

To my surprise, I realized if he chose to return, I wouldn't stop him.

But when he looked at the mad queen, the regret on his face hardened into determination. He wouldn't leave the queen. Perhaps he felt responsible for her, or perhaps he had other plans for her. The latter was likely. Had he truly changed, or had I?

I offered my enemy my hand.

Mammon glowered at it, searching for the trick.

I thought I'd known these demons. They had changed, all for the better, and none could deny it.

Mammon clapped his hand in mine and shook. He took one last look at the veil, released my hand, bowed his head to the mad queen, and stalked away, out of sight beyond the trees.

"Will I see you again, Pride?" the queen asked.

I regaled her with a dazzling smile and bowed my head. "I never say never."

~

GEM STOOD on the scorched plains like the first star of the night. She tapped her foot and arched a razor-edged brow. "Fashionably late?"

"Worried I wouldn't show?"

"Not one bit."

Sunbirth crested the horizon, spilling its red light across the land and throwing the fortress in silhouette.

Time to go.

Gem scanned the nearby tree line and plains beyond.

"We must go."

She nodded. Her expression betrayed all the human emotions I sometimes wished I hadn't taught her to embrace. Kar'ak wasn't coming. Torrent was lost to her a second time. Some demons didn't change for the better.

She swiped open a hole in the veil, stepped through, and offered me her hand.

I hesitated, turning to imprint the world I loved to hate in my mind. If I left the netherworld, I would be leaving the Court behind. Like before, I'd be weak. A prince of nothing. Just a demon masquerading as a man. Without the Court, my strength would fade.

"Don't leave me hanging!" Gem reached closer, her icy hand offering another chance at another life.

I had people who needed me. I had a life and something like family. I was Li'el, restaurateur, Hollywood socialite, and guardian angel of the City of Angels. I couldn't leave that behind, no matter the lure of the Court. This wasn't my world.

The queen stood atop her jutting rocks. Shadows gathered behind her. She lifted a pale hand. I would see her again, some time, some place. Demons like her had a way of circumventing the rules.

I clasped Gem's arm and stepped through.

The veil fizzled and vanished behind us, leaving nothing but the burnt rubber odor of the netherworld and an echo of regrets in my head. All around, trees towered, blocking out the sky. The air smelled of wet pine and turned leaves.

Gem shook off her icy armor and shivered in her torn, wet clothes. In her human form, her pale skin took on a milky pallor. "I kinda liked Baal. Will he be okay?"

I curled my wing around her and hugged her close. "They have more hope in that world now than they've ever had before. They'll be just fine."

"And us?"

I looked up, catching glimpses of stars through spindly branches, and when I looked back at the girl tucked under my wing, those stars sparkled in her eyes. "Do you doubt it?"

"No." She smiled sadly. But the smile soon grew. "We're gonna be just fine." We trudged forward a few steps. "Do you know where we are?"

"Somewhere on the Eastern seaboard?"

She frowned. "You have no idea, do you?"

"I'm not perfect."

She scoffed, teeth chattering from the cold. "Oh, Pride

says he's not perfect. I died, didn't I? Because you would *never* say that."

"Hush." I shook my bare wings, disturbed by the memory of her lying dissected on the table. "Didn't you know? I've changed. *Evolved.* I am beyond perfection and critically flawed in all the best ways."

Her little laugh warmed some part of me that reminded me why I'd returned and why I wanted to stay.

CHAPTER 32

*M*arianna Ramírez's grave was one of several thousand new graves lining the cemetery hills. I had visited a few times over the past week, this time bringing flowers. Human women liked flowers, or so I had learned over the years. I wasn't sure which flowers Ramírez had liked, so I brought her a dramatic bouquet of lilies and set them over the mound of dirt, wondering if she would believe I had tried to make it right. I wasn't perfect, that was clear, but I had tried. Was that enough?

The sounds of construction work traveled on the breeze, and behind me, a city grew out of the rubble, like it had hundreds of years ago. A little thing like a god bent on recreating the world wasn't about to keep LA from its glitzy parties.

In the weeks since Mother had tried to remake LA, the city had begun to take shape again. Cranes jutted into the pale blue sky. Returning people milled around pop-up stores.

The ingenuity of humans never ceased to amaze.

The *Reely Nauti* was moored at the marina—sans rotting demon carcasses. Noah tossed me a wave from inside, but any warmth from the greeting was quickly doused by the sight of Christian lounging on the deck, soaking up the rays.

I turned the cell phone over in my pocket, the same cell I'd had Noah keep safe for me.

The boat rocked as I boarded. Gem drew the gangplank in, storing it safely away, and with a roar of the engines, Noah steered the yacht out of the marina. We navigated up the coast to where sand had been shipped in to reshape the beaches. Mother's island had been breaking up more and more each day. The Pacific wouldn't stand for a chunk of artificial land blocking its approach to LA. A few more storms and it would be swallowed beneath the waves. I watched those waves beat at the foreign land, knowing Torrent would have helped it along had he been here.

The growl of the engines died, and the boat bobbed gently on the surface. Out on the ocean, with just the breeze on my face, I could imagine nothing had changed. But everything had changed.

"Is here okay?" Noah approached. When I didn't reply, he touched my shoulder. "We've got your back."

Did he? He hadn't seen me attack Anna. Did he truly know what it was he believed he loved?

He was about to find out.

Gem was sprawled on one of the cabin couches, deceptively at ease, toes tapping as her earphones buzzed music into her ears. As I passed, the air chilled.

There was no such chill outside. Familiar heat beat down from a cloudless sky. I shrugged off my jacket and tossed it onto the deck chair next to Christian. Diamonds winked on the water's surface between us and the coastline, two miles out. After rolling up my sleeves, I crouched at the edge of the deck, draped an arm over my knee, and dangled my fingers in the warm water.

"You know," I began, tone light, "There's one thing I still don't understand."

Christian's brow arched over his shades. He'd unbuttoned his shirt, leaving it wide open to soak up the rays. His military-issue dog tags hung on a chain around his neck. I reached for Anna's little cross, hidden beneath my collar, and brushed my fingers over the bump in my shirt. He and I both had faith, albeit in different things.

He sat up and planted his bare feet on the deck. So casual. So comfortable. And why wouldn't he be? "What's that?"

"The lesser attacks around my restaurant. You remember those?"

He shrugged. "I thought we figured it was the mother demon driving the lessers crazy?"

I straightened. "Yeah, that was probably it." Water lapped and clunked against the sides of the yacht. "Still, it's strange, don't you think? Mother targeted other predators, and the lessers swarmed out of fear, but the lessers killing people around my restaurant? That doesn't seem to fit."

"Who knows?" He stood, rolled his shoulders, and tucked his thumbs into his jeans pockets. "It's over. They're gone." He squinted into the sun and nodded toward the shore. "We got our happy ending."

Did we?

"Not all of us." I watched him closely.

He scratched the back of his neck and sauntered to the edge of the deck beside me. "Not all of us," he agreed. A twitch fluttered in his cheek.

"I'm sorry."

He gave a dismissive grunt. "*I met a demon once. I didn't kill him. Now he may save the world.* Anna told me that. She thought she saw the good in you." He pulled in a deep breath and offered me his hand. "Truce?" Christian prompted.

Over his shoulder and through the cabin windows, I caught Gem's stark expression.

Trust had to start somewhere.

Christian smiled a bright, hopeful smile.

Gem's eyes widened.

Christian's hand plunged forward, striking lightning fast. I caught his wrist, twisted, and snapped his arm back. The sickening sound of bone cracking accompanied his howl. He dropped the injector. It rolled to a stop on the deck, sunlight glinting against the liquid inside the vial. PC-Eighty.

A snarl bubbled across my lips. "It occurred to me." Christian bucked. I pulled him close. "Just because some of us can change, doesn't mean we do. And you haven't changed, hunter." I bowed my head, hissing the next words against the curve of his neck. "You were always a killer."

Gem emerged from inside the cabin. I shook my head, keeping her back.

"You b-broke my fucking arm!" Christian barked.

"Be grateful it's not your neck." I shoved him away before the urge to kill could overcome me. I could end him and dump his body into the sea. Nobody would care. But where was the art in that?

The hunter stumbled, caught between Gem and me. She smiled, flashing sharp teeth. He looked toward the coastline, hopeful he could swim that far.

"It's a long way," Gem mused. "Especially with a broken arm."

"You gonna kill me?" He spun back toward me, cradling his broken arm against his chest. "Huh? Murder me like you murdered Anna!"

I plucked the cell from my pocket and tossed it onto the deck at his feet. "You probably don't remember, but I asked Noah to download the security feed from the night a lesser attacked and killed one of my staff. The night you attacked and caught me. Rosa, that was her name—the woman who died. Did you know that?"

His mouth twisted in disgust. "No, should I?"

"A killer like you, I would have thought you'd take the time to get to know your victims' names."

"I didn't kill this Rosa. I don't even know who she was."

"Hmm... then I suppose she was in the wrong place at the wrong time when you unleashed the lesser at the back door of my restaurant."

"I don't know what the fuck you're talking about!" His spittle flew.

"It's all on the security footage, but in the chaos, nobody thought to check for anything suspicious earlier in the evening. Anything like your familiar face driving a panel van to the back door. Why would they look? Being demon, I was always the guilty one."

He spun again, seeking help from Gem, but he wouldn't find any sympathy there. Noah peered down from the cabin above, eyes cold.

"Not much work for a demon hunter without demons. Only, you had an unusually high kill rate even after the demon population dwindled. Almost as though you knew where the lessers would attack. A cynic might assume you set those scenes and if you could do that, it wouldn't be much of a stretch to set me up and mail a few pictures to the local police department. A demon like me, worshipped by the masses? I was your ultimate prize, right?"

He quit panting, looked again at Gem as though assessing his odds of escaping, and straightened his back, shrugging off the innocent act. "You always wanted to kill me." He toed the cell back toward me. "Whatever is on there, it doesn't matter. You'd make up any shit to fit your story. This isn't about facts. It's about revenge. I beat you. I won. I put you in that cage! I own you!"

I clicked my tongue. "Bitch, you got our relationship dynamics all wrong." I flicked out my hand, releasing claws, and let him see the sharp teeth behind my A-list smile. "When you ran out of demons to kill, you set me up as your trophy prize. Only you didn't wager on me being different."

He swallowed, Adam's apple bobbing. "You're good now? Right." That smile was all over the place. Nervous, cocky, incredulous. "You said it, like you're some kind of angel?"

I stalked forward.

"You won't kill me!" He lifted his good hand, palm out, placating. "You've changed. That's what everyone's saying. The City of Angels, your city. They all fucking worship you even more now. That's what you've always wanted!" He backed up too far. Gem's icy grip clamped around his upper arms. He bucked, but Gem held firm. "You can't hurt me! You're good now!"

"Oh, I'm *good*, all right," I purred. "But I'm not the angel of redemption or mercy…" Six steps brought me nose to nose with the cold-blooded hunter. "I made you a promise." I freed the feather from my sleeve—the same the king had returned to me—and teased it between my fingers. "Take a guess which one of us deserves to live."

"I have a daughter…" he whispered, lips wobbling. "Don't kill me. For her sake. Please…"

Fear gave the air a coppery taste. I wet my lips and trailed the feather down his sweaty cheek. "Angel of Vengeance, how does that sound?" His mouth opened and closed, gasping for air I held back. Leaning in, filling his wide-eyed gaze with my glorious self, I whispered, "I met your daughter. Her mother brought her to me while I was trapped in your cage. She asked why I was sad. She asked me for a feather. I think I might give her this feather. You can make this feather a promise, Christian, or a threat. It's your choice."

I released my hold on his air and backed up. Gem let him

go and he fell to his knees. She looked up, the snarl on her lips making it clear she would have preferred to yank his heart out of his chest. I winked at her and circled my finger in the air.

Noah revved the boat's engines and banked back toward shore. Damn, it felt good to be righteous. One might even say it felt *divine*.

Christian clung to the deck, gasping against fear and pain. "You're not going to... kill me?" He said it quietly, reverently, because he knew damn well he would have killed me and would likely try again. And again. But only because I allowed the game to continue. He had caught me because I had allowed it. He lived and breathed because I allowed it. And by the look in the hunter's eyes, he finally understood exactly who he had crossed.

"Not today, darling, but I never say never." I plucked his shades from the deck chair and slipped them on, diluting the dazzling light from the water. Los Angeles sparkled as we drew closer.

Li'el, restaurateur, Hollywood socialite, the epitome of male perfection. And the Angel of Vengeance. Yes, that would do nicely.

EPILOGUE

Kar'ak / Torrent

Waves thunder against bare rocks. The Pacific Ocean churns and snarls. Its water is my sanctuary and my kingdom. But this is not the netherworld. I left for reasons I do not fully understand. I left because I couldn't stay without the angel of ice. It is a man's foolish need, a mortal's love. And there is only one place I find solace from its madness— where the rocks meet the sand, where once a pier jutted from the shore but now only its struts remain, thrusting up through the boulders.

She sits on one such strut now, dangling her feet into the water, tantalizingly close yet maddeningly far away. The girl with ice in her eyes. I know her, and every time I am pulled back here, she is waiting.

She waits for the part of me who believes he is part human. I despised him, this figment of my imagination—

PIPPA DACOSTA

what my father did, twisting my mind—but now I find the hate I reserved for Torrent is gone. Instead, I *feel* other things. Human things. He chose to follow the ice angel. Every day, his voice gets louder. And I wonder, who am I, really?

The girl who sits on the rocks and waits has the answer.

～

A NOTE FROM LI'EL...

The author of this book has made it clear if she discovers any of my notes, she will delete them. She doesn't understand how a being of my startling magnificence cannot be silenced. She says many things, most of human nonsense. Such as these acknowledgment pages being about *her* friends and colleagues, people who helped *her* write this book. A book, by the way, that is all about me. I did all the work. She merely threw a few words onto the page and spun a tale. I saved not one, but two worlds. Therefore, these are *my* acknowledgments. She can go write a book about herself and pen her acknowledgments there (if only she were that interesting).

Whilst we're all here, let's agree to *acknowledge* that I am wonderful. It need not be said, but there it is, in black and white. So, it must be true. There are many facets to my sparkling personality that didn't make it onto these pages. I can paint masterpieces, carve art with my claws, and tell a love story through interpretive dance, and I know of thirty ways to kill a *scorsi* demon and ten more to kill a man. I save puppies from burning buildings too. Really, there are many reasons to love me. I could fill a book with my talents, but the author assured me after the first fifty or so pages, few would care. She's wrong, but I've allowed her to believe she's right.

Let's also acknowledge the editor of this fine work, Elizabeth from Arrowhead Editing. It's a difficult job polishing my magnificence, but she does it with grace and humor. Naturally, I do many, many things with grace and humor, but apparently, humans need to repeatedly hear these things before believing them. Any mistakes in this work are the author's responsibility. I don't make mistakes (anymore). And if anyone else would like to polish my generous magnificence, you may find me at the renovated *Decadent-I Taverna*. Form an orderly line.

Among this odd crew of misfits the author relies upon is the delightful cover artist, Ravven. Clearly, she knows exactly how to capture my good side (all sides are perfect, but some are too painfully stunning and exquisite to grace the constraints of a book cover). I asked that all of me be put on display. Why would anyone not want to witness all my substantial naked glory? But apparently, "advertising filters" do not appreciate the art of the male body (hence why Facebook deemed my beautiful self too hot to advertise). It's a crime, but I do make leather pants look like a sin. It's good to be bad.

In addition to these fine people, there is one very fine lady, Marianne Almâs, who would likely be first in line outside *Decadent-I*, hoarding all my secrets. She has marvelous taste in music (and books, naturally), and she helpfully supplied the name "Reely Nauti" for Torrent's stolen superyacht.

And last, but not least, let's take a moment to acknowledge you, my dear reader. Without your emails, your reviews, your tweets and Facebook posts, this book (did I mention it's all about me?) would not exist. The author sometimes takes some convincing (she foolishly believed the *Chaos Series* had ended at #2), but your messages of love and support for me won her over. Rest assured, the messages and emails demanding an Akil book have been deleted. Naturally, there are no other demons like me. You're welcome.

Now, if you enjoyed this book (only this one—any book not about me clearly isn't as good), please spread the word through reviews. For each star rating, I promise to rescue more kittens from trees. It still counts if I place the kittens in the trees to begin with.

Oh, and remember, I am air and everywhere. Make a wish, tempt me with a deal, and you just might wake to find a single black feather on your pillow.

Li'el,
   Angel of Vengeance

~

The 1000 Revolution

#1: Betrayal

#2: Escape

#3: Trapped

#4: Trust

~

New Adult Urban Fantasy

City Of Fae, London Fae #1

City of Shadows, London Fae #2

ABOUT THE AUTHOR

Born in Kent in 1979, Pippa's family moved to the South West of England where she grew up among the dramatic moorland and sweeping coastlands of Devon & Cornwall. With a family history brimming with intrigue, complete with Gypsy angst on one side and Jewish survivors on the other, she draws from a patchwork of ancestry and uses it as the inspiration for her writing. Happily married and the mother of two little girls, she resides on the Devon & Cornwall border.

Sign up to her mailing list here.

www.pippadacosta.com
pippa@pippadacosta.com

Made in the USA
Columbia, SC
10 January 2018